"Careful. You're standing close."

Grier gave a small shriek and jumped, her hand flying to her pounding heart.

The prince lounged on a chaise just behind her. Stretched out, booted feet crossed in a relaxed pose, he looked beguiling. Not at all his usual stiff self.

"I didn't see you there," she said breathlessly, her pulse racing against her neck.

He gripped a handful of papers loosely above his chest. Several others littered the small rosewood table to the right of the chaise. A few even littered the carpet. She'd obviously interrupted him reading.

She'd never seen him like *this* before. He'd removed his jacket and neck cloth. Her mouth dried at the sight of smooth flesh peeping out from his loosened shirt. He looked human—an absurdly handsome man who was suddenly much too approachable.

By Sophie Jordan

WICKED IN YOUR ARMS

Sophie Jordan

AVON
An Imprint of HarperCollinsPublishers

AVON BOOKS
An Imprint of HarperCollins*Publishers*
195 Broadway
New York, NY 10007

Copyright © 2011 by Sharie Kohler
Excerpt from *Silk Is for Seduction* copyright © 2011 by Loretta Chekani
ISBN 978-0-06-203299-7
www.avonromance.com

First Avon Books mass market printing: August 2011

Avon Trademark Reg. U.S. Pat. Off. and in Other Countries, Marca Registrada, Hecho en U.S.A.
HarperCollins® is a registered trademark of HarperCollins Publishers.

Printed in the U.S.A.

10 9 8 7 6 5 4

For my editor, May Chen.
Eight books and counting!
Thank you for being in my corner all these years.

WICKED
IN YOUR ARMS

Prologue

The Royal Palace of Maldania . . .

*H*e lived.

This was Sevastian's sole burning thought as he advanced down the wide sunlit corridor. Not the blood seeping from the gash in his forehead and dripping thickly into his eye. Not the fact that he hadn't slept in days, and even then that sleep had been fractured and restless with artillery fire ripping deep wounds into the earth outside his tent. He lived and was not rotting away on a battlefield like so many of his comrades.

He was alive and breathing and whole.

His booted heels clacked a cold, precise rhythm.

He'd ceased to leave a trail of mud and blood several yards back. Every inch of him was covered in filth, blood and matter he dared not consider. He would dream nightmares of it later. He was a wretched sight, his once fine uniform beyond recognition, but he felt invigorated, victorious.

His footsteps rang out sharply over the marble floor, the same floor his ancestors had trod generations before him. A ragged breath tripped from his lips. The same floor *his* progeny would walk. Now that the war was over, that much was all but guaranteed. Whether it happened depended upon him. The weight of this new responsibility settled over him, tightening his shoulders.

His shadow stretched long over the stained-glass windows lining the corridor. His breath still fell fast from his hard ride to reach here—to be the first one to tell the king that it was finally over.

He nodded to the master guards standing sentry on either side of the massive double doors of the king's bedchamber. Their heels snapped together sharply at his presence.

He knocked once before entering. The king sat in a high-backed chair before a floor to ceiling window that overlooked the valley Sevastian had just ridden hell-bent through to arrive here. In the distance, where the mountains rose beyond the snow-blanketed valley, dark smoke rose in great plumes, reaching to the heavens.

The old man looked Sevastian's way, the tight lines of his face easing immediately at the sight of him. "You're alive," he whispered, his voice cracking with emotion. Moisture filled his eyes.

Sevastian nodded. Dropping on a knee before his king, he dipped his head and bowed low. "The kingdom is yours, Your Highness. The enemy is vanquished. Marsan is dead and the rest of the rebels have surrendered."

The king's gnarled hand came down on his head in a fierce caress. "You've prevailed. I knew you would."

He grimaced, watching as his blood dripped onto the king's royal robes. Over the years he hadn't felt the same conviction. He'd only known that he must prevail—or die.

He rose to his feet. The king closed his eyes in a weary blink, clearly grappling with the fact that the bloody ten-year-long rebellion had come to an end at last. It was a struggle for Sevastian, too. He'd grown to manhood amid war and death. It was all he knew.

The king seized his hand, his grip surprisingly strong for one in such weak health. "You know what must be done now. And quickly. This country needs a bright light as we emerge from the dark. You must give them that. Feed them hope, the promise of better days to come."

Sevastian's throat thickened. "I shall not fail you, Grandfather."

"Of course you won't."

"I know my duty. It shall be done."

Chapter One

Two months later . . .

"Y ou mean Miss *Hadley*?"

At the sound of her name Grier stopped chewing, her mouth stuffed full of her third frosted biscuit. Or perhaps it was her fourth. The tasty treats were thus far the highlight of her evening, but hearing her name mentioned with such ridicule amid titters of laughter turned the food to dust on her tongue.

The voices continued, and she pressed farther back into a column, as if she could somehow disappear into the plaster. "Well, she *is* rather . . ." The rest of their words were lost in a burst of guffaws.

Grier sucked in a deep breath, knowing that whatever the biddies had said was far from complimentary. She knew this with the same certainty that she knew they were speaking about *her* and not her half-sister. Not that she and Cleo weren't *both* a favored subject for the sniggering busybodies of the *ton*, but somehow Grier had received the brunt of attention as they went about Town.

She glanced down at herself, quickly assessing. The burgundy gown was the height of fashion, the color rich and flattering against her dusky complexion. The modiste had assured her she would stand out against all the other watered-down milksop misses on the market for a husband.

She grimaced. At the time, she thought standing out an advantage. What better way to attract some blueblood, after all? A proper gentleman to give her the stamp of respectability she had long craved. Standing out amid the other females, she'd reasoned, could only be a good thing. Now she wasn't so sure.

She'd endured many colorful designations since her entrée into Society a fortnight past. None complimentary. And yet she'd braced herself for that. Her father's fortune might gain her admittance to the finest drawing rooms, but it did not mean everyone would don a kind smile for the likes of her.

Nothing she'd endured, however, was intolerable enough to send her fleeing London with her tail tucked between her skirts. She lifted her chin and took another bite from her biscuit. She'd be a proper lady yet. In time, she'd marry a gentleman and everyone would forget her low beginnings. She'd have respectability at last, the pains of her youth forgotten.

Stiffening her spine with this heartening reminder, she swallowed her bite and took a sip from her glass. Besides, nothing awaited her at home. Nothing save loneliness. Long, looming years where she would suffer everyone's pity. Or censure. She was hard-pressed to say which was worse.

Ready to rejoin the masses, she peered through the fronds of the large potted fern that hid her from view. The two busybodies still lingered, their turbaned heads angled close, as if that would somehow stop anyone from overhearing their indiscreet voices.

"You do mean Miss *Grier* Hadley, of course." The other woman tsked and Grier supposed the sound was meant to be sympathetic. "She's such an unfortunate female. So . . . *tall.*"

The way the word *tall* was uttered, Grier was certain she meant to say something else.

"Indeed." The other matron clucked. "And so very dark, too. Did she labor in the fields before Hadley unearthed her?"

They shared a look and burst out laughing.

Grier snorted. They weren't far from the truth. She rolled her eyes at their guffaws, understanding perfectly their nasty humor. And yet her sturdy form and sun-browned complexion were the least of her flaws in their eyes. She wondered what they would say if she told them how she came to be so sun-browned. That before coming to Town she spent her time riding across the countryside in men's trousers, shooting game, jumping fences, and then, to cool off, stripping her garments to swim in secluded ponds, nothing between her and God's eyes except the wind. A secret smile curved her lips as she imagined their horror.

Tall and dark. They could have described her much worse indeed. They could have called her a bastard. She'd heard that often enough growing up. They could have declared her unfit for their elite company. And yet they dared not. Her father was none other than Jack Hadley, a renowned gaming hell owner, better known as the king of

London's underworld for all his dabbling in vice and corruption.

Perhaps not the most sterling of recommendations, but here she stood, in the ballroom of one of the *ton*'s finest homes, the special *friend* of Her Grace, the Dowager Duchess of Bolingbroke.

The guests could titter all they liked behind their hands, but abide her they would. Her fat dowry guaranteed that. The dowager had made it widely known that Jack Hadley's daughters had her full-fledged stamp of approval, and if one wished for the dowager and her three grandsons to attend any fête, then the disreputable Hadleys were to be invited as well.

Grier harbored no misconceptions concerning the dowager's generosity. She knew she would never have gained the old dame's favor and entry past the doorman tonight if not for the dowry her father dangled like a carrot before every bride-seeking blueblood of the *ton*. The dowager possessed three grandsons, all as destitute as she was. The only thing left to the Bolingbroke title was . . . well . . . the title.

Just then the biddies discussing her flaws noticed her amid the fronds. Their eyes bulged in affront. It took every ounce of will she possessed not to stick her tongue out at them. They might not like rubbing elbows with her kind, but *their* kind clearly needed her. At least they needed her father's money.

With noses in the air, they marched away.

Grier pressed her fingers to her mouth, stifling a giggle. She moved from her hiding spot to refill her glass of lemon water. With replenished drink in hand, she moved back down the buffet table and tucked herself once again behind the fern. Once again out of sight.

Even better, two gentlemen chose to stand before the fern at that moment, making her even more inconspicuous. Especially as one of them was quite tall and successfully towered over the potted fern. Feeling safe again, she took a refreshing sip and munched on another biscuit. Perhaps she could hide here all night until her father collected her.

The mention of her name quickly quelled such daydreams.

Holy hellfire. Again? Need she endure further slurs against her person? Even though she knew she should simply turn and leave, she froze, her feet rooted to the parquet floor as she eyed the two figures before her. While one was exceedingly tall, the other man barely came to her chin.

"The Misses Hadley are quite the catch, Sevastian. We should not leave them off your list," the shorter man said.

Unease settled in the pit of her stomach at mention of a *list*. She failed to recognize either gentleman, but then she only had a view of their backs. Still, the shorter man's shock of red hair would be hard to forget.

"These are the two bastards you mentioned?" the tall man demanded in a flat, emotionless voice.

She bit back her gasp at this bald question, and glared at the back of his dark head, her skin prickling with indignation at his rudeness.

He continued, his speech rolling and rich, laced with an accent she could not place. "The daughters of some unsavory *criminal*? And only God knows what female? Truly, Malcolm, you must jest. They scarcely sound eligible. My country is in dire straits, but *not* that dire. Grandfather would have a seizure at the mere suggestion of tainting the Maksimi bloodline with bastard blood, and you should well know that, cousin."

A royal then? That explained the haughty attitude. She sniffed. Explained. Not pardoned.

She began chewing again, her teeth working with a vengeance as she glared between leafy fronds at this, this . . . *Sevastian*.

He was big. And not just tall. Broad shoulders

stretched the fine fabric of his evening attire. She could not detect an ounce of fat, or a stitch of padding. She sniffed indelicately. His waist was trim, his hips narrow and lean. Not the standard among *tonnish* gentlemen. He reminded her more of the men back home—men accustomed to hard work.

Odd, to be certain. This arrogant peacock probably spent all of his time practicing fencing or some such worthless activity that kept him in passable shape. She doubted he could do anything truly manly or strenuous. She yanked at her biscuit with a savage tear, sending crumbs tumbling to the floor as she assessed what she could see of his rigid form. Bloody prig.

He probably couldn't even sit a mount properly or shoot a rifle with enough skill to actually hit his target. Why should his opinion matter? Why should it sting so? A faceless man that she could probably trounce.

Because he only speaks what everyone here already thinks.

She shook her head slightly, frowning at the unwelcome notion. She'd known this wouldn't be easy. She was seen as an intruder and tolerated, not embraced. Much as at home.

"I've been here a fortnight, Malcolm." Sevastian's voice rumbled deeply over the air, his faint accent thickening his speech. A manly rumble, she allowed. She might even have found the accent attractive if he had not proven himself an arrogant boor with every word uttered. "You promised to present me with viable candidates and this is all you can suggest to me? A pair of bastards with an ignominious father? Are the chits even lettered?"

Her hand shook, the contents of her glass sloshing dangerously near the sides. She inhaled an indignant breath. She was not one to lose her temper, but he went too far, royal pedigree or not. She might not have had the finest education, but the man she considered to be her *true* father had taught her to read and write beside the evening fire in their small cottage.

What's more, he'd taught her about dignity.

About what it meant to possess true character.

Who was this jackanapes to make such aspersions against her? He might have been born royal, but he clearly lacked any true sense of nobility.

"Well, you said you wanted to wed one of the wealthiest heiresses in England, and posthaste. It's not even the Season yet, Sev. Half the *ton* is wintering in the country. The Hadley girls are perhaps the best to be had."

"Bloody hell." He ran a strong, capable-looking hand through hair that was longer than fashionable. Perhaps that was the style in his homeland. "I should have taken that ship for America. I require an heiress with an impeccable pedigree. I can't present some nobody with ignoble roots as the future queen of Maldania. Grandfather would perish on the spot."

She swallowed. He was a *king*? Or soon to be? She stood an arm's throw from a *prince*? Her stomach heaved.

Grier suddenly longed for home, for cool, rolling hills of green and woods so thick one could lose herself forever. That was home, that was familiar. This ballroom with its columns and glittering chandeliers and liveried servants with silent, watchful gazes was not.

In her world princes existed only in the safety of fairy tales, and there they were . . . well, princely. Honorable and charming and not above rescuing a simple maiden with *ignoble* roots. They didn't sneer at the mention of someone like her. No. They would look her in the eyes, see the beauty within, and sweep her off her feet.

He continued crisply, "Solomon's treasure wouldn't tempt me enough to wed someone so *common*. Heiress or not. Come, Malcolm, you dragged me here. Is there no one else to consider this night? If not, then let's waste no more of our time and take our leave. I have an audience with the queen on the morrow. Perhaps she will have a recommendation."

Grier seethed. *Indeed. Take your leave.*

"I'm certain you'll wish to linger. I spot the lovely Lady Kirkendale beckoning you. Apparently she did not get enough of your company at the dinner party she hosted last week."

"Evidently not." The prince's voice took on a decidedly lascivious tone and she could well guess at the lewd turn of his thoughts. "She served a welcome diversion."

Grier felt her lip curl at the prince's mild tones. Lady Kirkendale was a married woman. Apparently he wasn't too *noble* to dally with a married lady. *Wretch.*

"Perhaps we can linger," he continued lightly. "She might provide a diversion yet again and make this evening not a total loss."

"It needn't be a loss. Look, there's Lady Libbie. I did not realize she was in attendance this eve. Her father is an earl with deep pockets. He made a fortune in railway. You may recall she's on the list I gave you. You should most certainly make her acquaintance."

"An earl's daughter certainly exceeds the thoroughly ineligible Hadley chits you suggested."

Again, that cool, unfeeling tone chafed her nerves.

"The kind of chits you wed, not bed, eh? That it?" Malcolm chuckled.

"Precisely," the prince agreed.

That did it!

Before she could stop herself, Grier peeled back a handful of fronds and lifted her glass high, watching in rapt horror as her hand tilted the cup high over his dark-haired head, tilting, tilting . . .

She watched as if the hand were not her own. The glass someone else's.

The moment the lemon water struck his head, he burst out with an exclamation in another language—an expletive, she was certain from the fierce growl-like sound. She took immense satisfaction at the reaction.

Grier jumped back, letting the fronds settle back into place. She held her breath, every muscle freezing as if that would make her somehow invisible.

Whirling around, he swiped a large hand at the frothy green fronds, clearly determined to see just who had dared to give him a soaking.

His incensed gaze landed on her. The breath

she had been holding escaped her in a hiss at the sight of his glowering face. Not precisely what she had been expecting. Where was the weak-chinned dandy? The pale-faced aristocrat who couldn't even lift a dainty hand to blow his own nose?

She scowled, exceedingly discomfited as she stared into a pair of fiery gold eyes. *Gold.* She would not have thought such eyes were possible.

She finally found her breath again, recalling how to operate her lungs. A ragged breath broke from her lips as she faced a single glaring truth. His arrogance derived from more than his royal pedigree. He was gorgeous.

Those extraordinary eyes gleamed like fire down at her. His gaze drifted to the cup she clutched in her fingers. The now empty cup. She rapidly tucked it behind her skirts.

A sound that sounded suspiciously like a growl rumbled from him.

Blinking, she snapped herself from her shocked stupor. "I beg your pardon," she said in a sweetly false voice. "Did I spill my drink on you? How clumsy of me." Grier extended her crumpled napkin to him in offering. "It's such a mad crush in here. I must have been nudged."

She almost choked to hear herself suggest that she had spilled her drink *accidentally*—through a potted plant no less—onto him. Those gold eyes flicked around them, clearly taking measure and seeing that no one stood near her.

Malcolm, his cousin with the shock of red hair, stared wide-eyed at her. There was more than scandalized horror in his gaze. It was almost as though he recognized her. And, she realized, he very well could. Especially if she'd made it onto his blasted list. Her father had dragged them about Town a good deal during the last fortnight, parading his long-lost daughters to a bevy of fortune-hunting bluebloods.

"Um, Sev," Malcolm began, but was silenced with a swiping hand.

That gesture, that swift slice of his hand through the air, said everything about him. That he was a man accustomed to being obeyed. That he would expect nothing less than total deference. *All for the mere matter of his birth.*

A foul taste filled her mouth as he stared down the straight line of his nose at her. Sadly, Grier knew firsthand that the matter of one's birth was not a *mere nothing* in this world. It mattered. She'd learned at an early age just how much. Her lack of pedigree had marked her for ridicule.

Only marriage to a respectable gentleman

would show the world that she was more than a circumstance of birth, more than a *nothing*. She would become a proper, respectable lady, and no one would dare toss slurs upon her again.

"Clumsy?" He arched a dark eyebrow superciliously. He studied the proffered handkerchief a moment, as though fearing it tainted, before plucking it from her hand and wiping at the back of his hair and neck.

She held his accusing gaze, her eyes wide with feigned innocence even as anger simmered at a low burn in her veins. With only a few words the pompous jackass brought out the worst in her, flooding her with memories of all the times the village children had taunted her. "I do apologize," she lied sweetly.

"No need," he replied brusquely, staring at her with cold eyes. "I shall dry."

She bobbed her head. "Indeed. No lasting damage."

More the pity. He deserved more than a soaking.

He angled his head to the side, staring at her almost in bemusement. He'd clearly detected her lack of sincerity.

Indifferent to the fact—even glad that he caught it—a satisfied smile curved her lips. Lifting her skirts, she turned and marched away. Even if she regretted her rash actions later, in this moment it felt good. She felt vindicated.

That imperious voice of his rang in her ears as he demanded of his cousin, "Who in the hell was that?"

"I was trying to tell you. *That* is Miss Grier Hadley."

A heavy beat of silence fell. And then: "*Oh.*"

Her smile deepened. *Oh, indeed.* Let him feel embarrassed. Let him pursue her with an apology. Then she heard his next words, and all her smug humor vanished.

"She's entirely what one would expect from a woman of low breeding."

She hesitated for the barest moment, contemplating turning around and giving him a piece of her mind. Inhaling a deep, fortifying breath, she marched on, her steps quickening as she went, unable to hear any more. Unable to bear it.

Chapter Two

"What was she doing hiding behind a fern?" Sevastian patted his neck dry with a slight grimace. That damn lemon water was cold. He still had goose bumps.

Malcolm shrugged. "Apparently eavesdropping. Good thing you ruled her out as a potential bride. She did not appear too impressed with you."

"Nor I with her." He dropped the napkin on the table. "Accident my foot, the little liar."

Sev looked after her as she wended through the crowd. She stood taller than most females. He easily followed her upswept auburn hair. It was on the tip of his tongue to comment that she had not been what he expected, but then he realized he had not expected anything because he had not

given either of the Misses Hadley a thought—
other than to deem the pair as unacceptable bridal
candidates.

He shrugged. So she possessed fine eyes, even
when spitting with temper. It mattered naught
to him.

His gaze narrowed on her slim back and he
marveled aloud, quite unable to reconcile it, "The
little hoyden tossed her drink on me." Low-bred
or not, what female did such a thing? To *him*? Such
a thing had never come *close* to occurring before.

"Quite so," Malcolm said, sounding dangerously near laughter.

Sev sent his cousin a quick glare. "Deliberately," he stressed. "She deliberately doused me
with her drink."

"To be fair, can you blame her? You did make
the most unflattering remarks about her."

"You're assuming she overheard."

"Given her reaction to you—"

"Very well. Let's assume she overheard then."
Sev stared after the woman as if she possessed two
heads. "As I recollect, nothing said was untrue."

He recalled her face those brief moments they
gazed upon each other. Nothing about her indicated a lady gently reared. Not her bold stare. Not
her brown skin or the brown freckles upon her

nose. Certainly not her manner of speech. She spoke too directly, defiance bright in her eyes. Indeed, nothing like a demure lady.

He scratched his jaw. "No one has ever poured a drink upon me."

"You mean after ten years of war you've never suffered a drink in the face?"

"That was war, Malcolm. I suffered bayonets, cannons, and bullets. Dodging lemon water was not part of the routine."

"I wouldn't know of such things." Malcolm plucked at a piece of lint on his sleeve. "And I don't see how you came to know, either. You're the crown prince. You should have been sequestered away and not fighting on a battlefield."

If his cousin couldn't understand Sev's need to rally his people and lead an army against insurgents determined to overthrow the royal house of Maldania, then he wasn't going to explain it.

"You do what you have to do," he muttered. "Come, introduce me to this Lady Libbie." Clasping his hands together behind his back, he strode across the room, all the while keeping an eye trained on the intrepid Miss Hadley.

"Very well. I think she may be just the thing you're looking for. Quite pretty, too—"

"Pretty is not a requisite, Malcolm."

"Very well." His cousin shook his head in wonder. "All business then."

Sev's roaming gaze caught sight of Lady Kirkendale standing to the far side of the ballroom near one of many shadowed alcoves. She beckoned him again with her fan. Not a requisite in a *wife*, but he found it most desirable in a bedmate of a less permanent nature.

A slow smile curved his mouth as he feasted his gaze on the buxom matron.

With the war behind him, it was time he performed the next duty required of him. His grandfather had tasked him with such, and Sev would not disappoint him. Not after everything he'd already lost. They'd *both* lost. Sev's father, his brother, his uncles, and various cousins . . . All gone. Either to assassins or on a battlefield.

His gaze trailed Lady Kirkendale as she drifted past one of the alcoves, looking over her bare shoulder several times, the invitation in her eyes unmistakable as she moved toward the threshold that would take her deeper into the house.

The memory of his grandfather, ailing and anticipating his return with a bride in tow—a *proper* bride—made his chest tighten uncomfortably. It was the only thing keeping the old man alive.

Now was not the time for dalliance, and yet the

prospect of matrimony, of taking that next step to secure his throne—to claiming *what should have been his brother's*—filled him with a helpless rage.

He'd do it. Of course. It was right. Necessary. He always did the right and necessary thing. Nothing could distract him from his course . . . However, he'd take what diversions he could.

From the corner of his eye, he glimpsed a flash of auburn hair and burgundy gown that had left such an unpleasant impression upon him moments ago. He forced his gaze straight ahead, training his eyes on Lady Kirkendale—a means for him to release his frustrations, his helpless rage over the fact that his life was not his own. His grandfather had ingrained that in him. A crown prince never served himself.

The thought settled like a heavy stone sinking into his gut. "Let us have this introduction with Lady Libbie in a little while. I've something to do. I won't be long."

Malcolm followed his gaze to Lady Kirkendale's departing back with a smirk. "Of course. Hopefully Lady Libbie doesn't take an early departure."

Sevastian slid his gaze back to his cousin. "See to it that she doesn't." He tugged on his cuffs. "I won't be long. I'll have that introduction . . . and perhaps even a private word with Lady Libbie's father if she proves to be all that you claim. Mind you, I'd like to be back home before the snows melt. This whole business has already taken entirely too long."

Something flashed over Malcolm's face, and Sev felt a stab of guilt knowing that the palace—Maldania—was somewhere Malcolm would never visit again. No matter how he might wish to.

Sev shook off the sentiment. He couldn't allow himself to feel responsible for Malcolm, too. He had enough to worry about—an entire country of people. Besides, he'd already done more than his grandfather would condone in striking up a relationship with his ostracized cousin.

Guests parted before him as he cut through the crush. Sev spared no one a glance as he left the ballroom. Just the same, he was well aware that *they* all looked after him. Such was usual. He was the Crown Prince of Maldania and handsome, if the tittering females who fawned over him were to be believed.

His boots strode a straight line, his steps muffled on the runner. Hopefully a quick tryst with Lady Kirkendale would aid him in feeling not so . . . *afflicted*. Perhaps a brief assignation would let him *feel* again and find release from the numbness encasing him.

He shook his head at his unrealistic ponderings. They were useless dreams. Funny that he would still allow himself to dream. That was another thing his grandfather taught him. A prince had no right to dream anything for himself. Even if he took ease in a soft, willing body, his world would remain the same. As Crown Prince of Maldania, his life could never be his own. The choices he made were not for him. Country came first. Duty and responsibilities faced him at every turn. He couldn't escape it.

After working her way through the ballroom, Grier ensconced herself safely at another of the many buffet tables—this one tucked well away from the brute prince upon whom she'd poured her drink.

She didn't care what royal blood flowed through his veins, the man was a boor. She didn't regret dousing him with her lemon water. It wasn't as though she'd ruined her chances to snare herself a prince. Recalling his severe expression, she knew entertaining such a notion was laughable.

He obviously didn't consider her eligible . . .

nor did she wish him to. She need only remember his wretched voice as he spoke to his cousin, his accented tones so scathing at the mere suggestion of her as his bride, and her hands curled into fists, her nails digging into her palms. She almost wished he stood before her again. She might toss something more tangible than a glass of punch at him. He deserved no less.

She inhaled through her nose, immediately missing the open space of home as she drew in the aroma of overperfumed bodies. She longed for crisp, woodsy air. Verdant green hills and mountains undulating around her.

She quickly reminded herself she couldn't return to Wales. Nothing was left for her there except more of the usual disdain. Papa was dead three years now. And Trevis . . .

Well, she simply couldn't go back.

"Grier, how many biscuits are you going to eat?"

At the exasperated voice, Grier shook off her troubling thoughts, vowing yet again to forget the past and focus on her future. "I lost count at twelve."

Her half sister Cleo shot her a beleaguered look as she slid up beside her. "Very amusing." She plucked the frosted delicacy from Grier's fingers as she was just about to take another bite. "Permit me to spare you that one."

Grier moaned and tried to snatch it back.

"Weren't you just at the table over there?" Cleo gestured across the room. "Will you do nothing but eat tonight?"

"The other table ran out of biscuits," she lied, trying to reclaim her food.

Cleo stuffed the biscuit into her own mouth and swatted Grier's hand when she reached toward the table to select a new one. "We've an agenda, if you don't recall. We need to mingle," Cleo chided around her mouthful. Candlelight struck her brown curls and made them appear as lustrous as freshly tilled soil.

Grier sighed. "The only thing I have to look forward to at these events is the food. Don't deny me that."

One thing she didn't miss about living alone and fending for herself was preparing all her own meals. It was nice having delicious fare on hand whenever she wished for it. She didn't have to step outdoors and shoot a grouse, then pluck and clean it and cook it. *That* she did not miss.

"We agreed to do this together and so far I'm the only one participating in this husband hunt. I don't want Jack scolding you again for being unsociable."

An image of the two gossiping biddies flashed through Grier's mind, followed quickly by that cad—*Sevastian.* Her stomach knotted. Even his name seemed to elevate him so very far from her. As if his bloodlines, manner, and appearance did not do that already.

If mingling at these affairs thrust her into the company of people like that, she'd rather hide—but Cleo was correct. She'd snare no husband by hiding. She knew that. How was she to find the security and respectability she long craved if she didn't marry a proper gentleman?

Cleo cocked her head, a glossy ringlet sliding over her shoulder. "Were you not the one lecturing me earlier about donning a good face and finding ourselves a husband posthaste?"

Grier twisted one shoulder in a reluctant shrug. "Yes, that was me . . . but then I arrive at these horrid affairs and endure all the stares and whispering." She sighed, her mind drifting to that dreadful prince again. "We're scarcely tolerated here, Cleo—"

Cleo waved a hand. "That's to be expected. Have you met our father, perchance? The man with the horrid accent wearing a cravat a miserable shade of plum and making a fool of himself in the card room?"

Grier winced at the sadly accurate description.

Cleo gently gripped her arm, her touch warm through her velvet gloves. "I suggest you do as you advised me. Find some grateful lord with a fondness for his country estate and get him down on bended knee. Once that is accomplished, we can say good-bye to all of this that we so dislike." She motioned about them with a flutter of her hand.

"You're right, of course." Grier nodded and straightened her spine, sweeping an appraising eye over the ballroom. Several gentlemen surveyed both her and her sister. *Like prime horseflesh at the market.* She shook off the unwelcome sensation. Was she not judging them with the same assessing eye?

"Come then. Let's take a turn about the room," Cleo suggested.

Cleo took her arm. Together they strolled. This time Grier paid no mind when a group of debutantes in flouncy pastel gowns presented them with their backs, giving them the cut direct. Grier forced her gaze from them and lifted her chin a notch. Who cared if a bunch of silly girls snubbed her? She wasn't here for them, after all. Once she was married to a respectable gentleman, all that would come to an end anyway.

"Ah, there's the dowager's youngest grandson, Lord Tolliver." Cleo dipped her head close to whisper, "Jack said we should show him particular attention. Let us go make ourselves amenable."

Grier pasted a smile on her face for her sister's benefit, if nothing else. They had been acquainted for only a short while, but as the bastard daughters of Jack Hadley they had much in common. In their brief time together they'd made up for lost years.

Raised an only child, Grier was thrilled to learn she was not alone in the world. It was the same for Cleo, but for different reasons. The oldest of fourteen half brothers and sisters, Cleo was a glorified nanny and servant all rolled into one. An ironic existence given she bore the name Cleopatra.

Grier eyed the dowager's grandson surrounded by other gentlemen. She looked him up and down, wondering if it was too early to inquire about his living preferences. She hoped to snare a husband who preferred country living to life in Town. She knew it would narrow her selection, but she wasn't accustomed to the crowds, to the constant fog, to the lack of fresh air. If she wanted to see trees, she had to venture to the park.

"Come, Grier. This isn't the time to be reticent." Cleo tugged her along.

Grier and Cleo idled alongside them, waiting to be noticed without appearing to be *waiting*.

They did not have long to wait. The viscount's gaze fell on them both. His eyes lit up with recognition. They had been introduced several evenings ago at the opera. His grandmother, the dowager, had seen to that. He'd doubtless been apprised of his *duty* as sacrificial lamb.

According to Jack, the dowager was quite ready for her youngest grandson to wed either Grier or Cleo. The oldest grandson, the duke himself, was hands-off. The duchess might have been agreeable enough to lend them her stamp of approval and support either one of them marrying her youngest grandson, but she clearly saw Grier or Cleo for what they were: bastards with fat purses, neither of whom would be good enough for the Duke of Bolingbroke. They were, however, suitable for the Viscount Tolliver.

Lord Tolliver eagerly stepped outside his circle of friends and performed a brief bow, settling his bright eyes on each of them in turn. "Ah, the lovely Misses Hadley. Are you enjoying yourselves?"

"We're having a splendid time," Cleo lied charmingly.

Grier assessed her younger half sister in her sparkling blue gown. She was really quite pretty, resembling their other half sister, Marguerite, whom they had only just met. Fortunately for Marguerite, she was happily married and needn't secure herself a husband through their father's machinations.

"I hope you both have not overly tired yourselves." He wagged a finger teasingly. "I recall you each promised me a waltz."

Considering only three waltzes were to be danced this evening, this was a clear mark of his favor. Cleo smiled and nodded, uttering something appropriately clever.

Grier, however, couldn't even summon a smile. Staring at him, she could see nothing behind his falsely bright gaze. No true excitement, no anticipation. She could not help thinking this was all at his grandmother's behest, that he was not truly agreeable to the notion of courting her or Cleo. Did he even have a choice? Was he simply the grand sacrifice to save his family from financial ruin? The notion gnawed at her and soured the prospect of marrying him. Viscount or not. Social acceptance or not. She didn't want to wed the chap and then endure his lifelong enmity.

"I have not forgotten, Lord Tolliver," Cleo promised.

"And you, Miss Hadley?" He looked expectantly at Grier, his expression bland and unassuming. Kind, she supposed. For now. But years from now . . . "You've saved me a waltz, I hope?"

Grier gave a small nod, shaking off her grim imaginings while trying to ignore the way his friends studied her from just beyond their little circle.

They stared openly, as if she were not a lady at all but a creature to be mocked and held to ridicule. And not just her. Cleo, too.

"Indeed," she heard herself replying, fighting down those familiar feelings. She wasn't that girl anymore. And this wasn't Wales. Lifting her chin, she reminded herself that she was on her way to becoming a genuine lady now. "I have not forgotten, either."

"Brilliant." He nodded cheerily.

Just then one of his friends leaned his head close to the others in the group. Covering his mouth with one hand, he muttered something low. The group burst into laughter.

Grier didn't hear what brought forth such merriment, but several of the popinjays glanced her way. Familiar heat crept up her cheeks. This really was unendurable. Lord Tolliver frowned and sent his friends a castigating look, which only seemed to prove that they were laughing at her, that the viscount himself *knew* she was a subject of scorn, but he would grit his teeth and bear courting her anyway. *Holy hellfire.* It was really too much. Was there no way she could find an acceptable husband without suffering these indignities?

"If you'll pardon me, I need some air." She quickly turned away before Cleo or Lord Tolliver might object, or worse, insist on joining her.

She squeezed her way through the crush of bodies, heat flaming her face. Reaching a pair of French balcony doors, she saw that it was raining outside. An incessant, sleeting winter drizzle that did not appear to be on the verge of letting up. *Blast.*

Whirling around, she scanned the hopelessly crowded room. Lifting her skirts, she pushed her way back through the thick press, careful to keep her head down lest she see anyone pointing or staring at her. She'd had enough of the stares. What she needed right now was a respite, a moment alone, a place to hide for the rest of the evening until her father decided he'd had enough of cards.

Tomorrow. Tomorrow she would renew her hunt for a husband. In earnest. But not now. Not tonight. Not after that bloody prince. Not after the viscount's leering friends.

Grier shook her head, almost laughing aloud as she wondered: Was there no nobleman who preferred a simple country existence? One who was in the market for a rich bride of low birth? Could he not take out an advertisement in the *Times* so that she might find him?

Chapter Three

Grier passed the ladies' retiring room and dove down a corridor rife with flickering shadows. Sconces lined the walls every few feet, plunging her in and out of darkness as she moved forward.

Likely one of these rooms deep within the house wouldn't be occupied. She selected one, pressing her ear to its length before turning the latch. Stepping inside, she saw it was a bedchamber. A fire burned low within the hearth. Closing the door, she drew closer to that delicious warmth, thinking she might curl up on the chaise and enjoy the sanctuary she'd found.

Only upon drawing closer did she see that the chaise was already occupied with two figures gilded in the firelight. She jerked still, her heart lurching to her throat. She must have made a sound. A small gasp of horror.

The couple flew up on the chaise, tearing apart as if split asunder by lightning.

The female squeaked, her hands fumbling to heft her gown back up over her exposed breasts. Grier recognized her at once. Few women possessed a bosom of such immense proportions.

"Lady Kirkendale," she murmured.

Before her gaze even drifted to the room's other occupant, the man responsible for Lady Kirkendale's state of dishabille, she knew whom she would see.

He stared back at her, a dark brow arched drolly. Nothing in his countenance reflected embarrassment. "You again?"

Her embarrassment fled as her indignation surged. She crossed her arms. "Yes. Me again."

"This isn't what it looks like," Lady Kirkendale choked as she shoved her very large breasts back into her bodice. "Sevastian, say something," she hissed to her companion.

The prince said nothing, merely maintained his cold stare.

"Oh, I'm certain I've interrupted nothing . . . unseemly," Grier lied, uncaring of the sordid business she'd interrupted, only wishing to escape the awkward situation. Backing away from the pair, she waved a hand reassuringly. "I didn't see anything. Please. Go about whatever it is . . . you're doing."

"Of course, you didn't see anything. We weren't *doing* anything," Lady Kirkendale replied shrilly. "There's nothing to see. Nothing untoward has occurred." She jabbed a finger threateningly at Grier. "And if you dare spread word that—"

"I assure you nothing will be said." Grier nodded, still backing away.

The prince chuckled, the sound low and deep. He shook his head almost as if he couldn't believe he was in such a state of circumstances. Or perhaps it was Grier. He couldn't believe that she was here. That someone like her should even be in the same room with him.

"Really, Sevastian." Lady Kirkendale patted her hair feverishly. "I don't see what is so amusing about any of this."

Inwardly Grier echoed that sentiment, but she wasn't inclined to linger to hear the prince's response.

"If you'll pardon me, I'll leave you to . . ." she floundered, and the bloody man cocked that black slash of an eyebrow at her, his gold eyes gleaming wickedly. "Pardon me, I'll leave you to that thing it is you're *not* doing."

Lady Kirkendale puffed herself up and made a shrill, unattractive sound that rather resembled the squeal of a pig.

Grier opened the door and hastily stepped out into the hall, eager to escape. Hand still on the latch, she froze. Advancing down the corridor toward her was none other than Lord Kirkendale. His expression was thunderous.

He hadn't seen her yet, too focused on slamming open doors and peering inside every room he passed.

Grier dove back inside the room and shut the door as silently as possible. The pair had scarcely moved since she'd slipped from the room. Startled at her sudden return, they stared at her with blinking eyes. Grier flattened her palms to the door, her heart hammering a furious beat in her chest.

"It's your husband," she hissed. "He's coming."

Lady Kirkendale slapped a hand over her mouth to stifle her screech. Grier winced, watching in fascination as the woman started hopping in place like a child caught in the throes of a tantrum. Despite the dire situation, Grier fought a smile at the ridiculous spectacle.

She lifted her hand. "Maksimi! Don't just sit there! What shall we do?"

The prince glanced around the well-appointed bedchamber, still maintaining his perpetual manner of ennui. For all the world, he looked icy cool and not at all perturbed that an irate husband was bearing down on them.

His gaze stopped on a large mahogany armoire, and a thoughtful look came over his carved features.

Rising from the chaise in one liquid-smooth motion, he grasped Grier's arm. She started at the touch, heat sparking along her veins from the contact.

"Come," he commanded, his voice that infernal tone again—the voice of one accustomed to being obeyed.

She dug in her heels, shaking her head fiercely. "Where are we going?"

"To place ourselves out of sight."

She sneered at his overly formal speech. "You mean hide?"

A muscle flickered along the taut flesh of his jaw. "I never hide. I merely know when to retreat until it is time to reappear."

Grier rolled her eyes. "Call it whatever you like. Why do *I* need to . . . *retreat*? I haven't done any—"

"You think your reputation shall remain unscathed when you're found here? When Kirkendale raises all hell and the entire household pours into this room, do you think you shall remain unsullied? The *ton* loves a sordid tale. Your presence here shall be made into a colorful account. You'll be tossed into the fray, too."

Her stomach dipped, her face flashing hot and cold. She didn't need another strike against her as she navigated the waters of the *ton*. She was here to achieve a modicum of status and respectability, not to earn further disdain.

Seeing no alternative, she stopped resisting and let him drag her the rest of the way.

"Hurry," Lady Kirkendale urged, shooing them with her hands.

The prince opened the door and shoved aside the few garments before folding his tall length inside. He extended a hand for her. She stared hard at the long, blunt-tipped fingers and broad palm for one heart-stopping moment in which she quite clearly heard the rush of blood in her ears. It seemed like forever but could only have been a moment before she placed her hand in his. He pulled her inside before him, his long arm brushing hers as he closed the door, sinking them into darkness.

Her breath caught in her throat. Shrouded in darkness, forced into such close confines with a veritable stranger—a prince, no less—her senses skipped into hyper-awareness. Too late, she realized she should have turned around. Her back to his chest would have been a vast improvement to this. Chest to chest. Heart to beating heart.

She couldn't see the hand before her face, but she was keenly aware that not an inch separated her from the *most* wretched, arrogant man to ever cross her path . . . and that he was all male. Solid, firm, warm *male*.

His breath fanned her forehead. She was tall, but he was taller. She pressed her lips shut to make sure not a sound escaped. She need only withstand a few moments of proximity and then she'd be free of him.

They'd hidden just in time, apparently, for a mere moment passed before she heard Lord Kirkendale's booming voice.

"Lucinda, what are you doing in here?"

Grier listened closely, straining to hear what possible explanation the lady would offer.

"Why, awaiting you, husband."

"Me? We made no arrangements to meet—"

"Precisely, but I knew you'd know I was miss-

ing and take pursuit . . . Did you not find the hunt
. . . titillating?"

Heavy silence ensued. Grier held her breath
and listened, wondering what was happening on
the other side of the door. Did Lord Kirkendale actually believe his wife? Or was he strangling her?

She had her answer when a long, pleasure-filled
male moan scored air. Heat fired her cheeks. *Holy
hellfire.* The idiot cuckold truly believed his wife
had planned a tryst for the two of them.

"Come here, you little minx. Ride me hard."

Mortified, Grier squeezed her eyes in a blink
even though there was nothing to see. Closing her
eyes did nothing to shield her ears.

Lord Kirkendale's groans floated on the air.
His wife's squeals came in fast succession. At that
point Grier was convinced she spent a great deal
of her time on a farm, for the noises she made resembled the sounds a piglet makes when being
chased. A great deal of banging came next and
Grier suspected they were on the bed, their actions rattling the headboard.

"That's it, my fine filly!" A loud slap echoed on
the air.

"Yes!" Lady Kirkendale shouted. "Spank me!"

Grier pressed her fingers to her mouth. She

wasn't certain what sound she was trying to suppress—a groan of mortification or outright laughter.

The broad chest in front of her shifted, lifting on an inhalation, and she stilled, biting the edge of her thumb. While she might feel a modicum of humor, that wasn't the only sensation affecting her. Body heat emanated from the man in front of her. His nearness overwhelmed her, scraping her nerves.

She hugged herself with both arms, hoping to make herself smaller, unnoticeable—and only succeeded in brushing against him. She squeezed herself tightly, careful not to move again, determined to merely wait out Lord and Lady Kirkendale's trysting.

The prince moved. Just the barest inch, but his chest brushed her crossed arms. As though burned, she arched away to escape the contact. Her balance wobbled and she had to take a step to brace herself. The clomp of her foot rang out in the tight space of the armoire. She cringed, her skin tightening in fear that they'd been heard.

He caught her up in his arms, holding her to his chest as though fearing she would move again and make further noise.

She gasped, gripping his arms to shove him

away. Only he wouldn't budge. She was a prisoner in his arms. Unless she wanted to struggle and alert Kirkendale of their presence . . . she was stuck.

Her fingers flexed against the superfine of his jacket, marveling at the hardness of his biceps beneath her fingers.

Trevis had not felt nearly so firm and muscled, and he was a physical man. She shook her head once as if to shake it free of such senseless thoughts. What was she doing making comparisons between the two? Neither was a viable option for her. In fact, both men had made it clear she was *unacceptable*.

Heat stung her cheeks, and she renewed her attempts to disengage herself with care, wiggling against him with constraint, still determined to break free of the unwanted intimacy.

He pulled her closer, his arms steel bands around her. One of his hands crept to the back of her head, pressing their faces horrifyingly close. His cheek rasped against hers. Her skin tingled where their skin touched. Her belly dipped, twisted. A ragged breath escaped between her lips.

She wanted to demand he move away, but fear of being discovered held her voice in check.

His lips brushed the sensitive whorls of her ear

as he whispered, "Cease your movements lest you wish to be caught and explain what we are doing in this wardrobe together."

Shaking from head to foot, she gave a hard nod, not trusting herself to speak in a voice that wasn't a shrill squeak.

"Good girl," he murmured in that low voice that pulled at her belly.

With one hand at her head, his other spanned her back. She felt the hot imprint of each finger through the silk of her gown. All else faded but this. But him. The hard length of him painted onto her.

She no longer registered any sounds outside the wardrobe. The world was gone. There was only this—them—captives in this tiny space.

His mouth remained at her ear, not moving, but still touching. *Still driving her mad.*

She tried to pull back once again. Surely he would see that she would be careful, that she dared not make another sound. But he fastened a hand in her hair while his broad palm at her back deepened its pressure, keeping her pinned against him.

Strength radiated from him. Unusual for a dandified prince. Unusual for any of the dandified lords she'd met about Town.

Upon arriving in London she quickly realized

she could overpower most of the lily-handed prigs. As a former game master for a vast estate, she was accustomed to working and pushing her body to the limits every day. And yet the hard male body against hers did not belong to any idle blueblood.

At least he wasn't *moving* against her, actively touching her. She could withstand this. She could tolerate mere closeness to him. As long as he kept still. He was only holding her to help keep her motionless, after all—

Then he moved.

Chapter Four

$\mathcal{A}$ir hissed between her clenched teeth.

His warm breath teased her ear as his head lowered, and lowered. Parted lips touched the flesh of her neck, skimming lightly. Another sharp breath pushed past her lips.

What are you doing?

The words formed in her mind, but she couldn't speak them. She could not risk speech.

She wished his mouth still pressed hotly to her ear. Better that than *this*. Sensation zipped along her nerves, reminding her that she wasn't immune to a handsome man. A handsome man who happened to be everything that was wrong for her. He was a prince with only disdain for her. But here she was, reacting, reveling in his sensual assault as if he hadn't said any of those horrible things about her. Which begged the next question: Why was he even taunting her with seductive caresses?

His mouth did not move into an actual kiss. Nothing so bold as that. Yet that didn't lessen the absolute shock of his soft lips grazing the side of her throat. Nor did it stop the shivers from racing along her skin.

When she felt the light, erotic scrape of his teeth on her neck she yanked her head away and stared up at his shadowed face. His eyes gleamed in the dark, the only thing she could discern in the gloom, and yet she couldn't read beyond their inscrutable depths. She couldn't determine what they said, *what he thought*.

She trembled in his arms like a leaf clinging to the last vine amid a storm. If he wasn't holding her up, she would collapse. Was this what she had become? Was this what loneliness did to a female? Shattered her? Broke her? Made her cave at the first man who— *No.*

She gave herself a mental shake. The Crown Prince of Maldania was no ordinary man. He didn't *look* ordinary. He didn't *talk* ordinary with that hypnotic voice of his. Unfortunately, she couldn't stop herself from reacting to him. Sad but true. She simply couldn't allow herself to forget that he was an arrogant snob who considered himself her better.

She felt a new touch then. His fingers brushed the side of her face. A caressing graze that sent a ripple of shock through her.

His warm, brandy-laced breath fanned her lips, alerting her that his face had changed position. She swallowed a suddenly dry throat and held herself as still as stone. Not about to move and accidentally brush against the warm press of his body. He might begin to think she deliberately wanted to touch him. That she liked *this*. Liked *him*.

Intolerable! She possessed more pride than that!

After the way he talked about her that would just be . . . pathetic. Not to mention vastly inappropriate. Not that anything about this situation was appropriate, but she wouldn't have him think she was a breeding cat so desperate for his attentions.

She was no stranger to a man's kisses. Indeed not. And she was not about to initiate such intimacy with such a cad as he—prince or not. No matter how he affected her, how she quivered at his touch in the small dark space they shared, no matter how he made her remember things best left forgotten. She was made of sterner stuff. She could resist the likes of him.

Still . . . if he should kiss her at this moment, she

questioned her ability to resist. In their dark sanctuary, she too well recalled the longing, the exhilaration, the belief that she was valuable enough that a man could look beyond the circumstances of her birth.

She missed such feelings, even false as they had been. Desire and longing only brought pain and allowed one to believe in fairy tales. She'd find her retiring gentleman with his home in the country and she'd have safety. Peace and contentment and respectability. That would be enough. Everything she ever needed. No one would ever hurt her again.

She held herself perfectly still, a seeming statue, cold and unfeeling. A ruse, of course. She was burning up on the inside as he touched her face, a blind man feeling her every feature. The slope of her cheek, the curve of the jaw she always thought a little too square. The mouth too full, especially the bottom lip.

He moved, leaned in yet again. The barest graze at the corner of her lips told her he was there, touching her, toying with her, exploring her face. Imprisoned in the dark, it was almost hard to imagine that this prince did this. That the austere, cold-eyed boor was moved to even touch her.

Unable to resist any longer, her face lifted. A

treacherous yearning filled her, betraying her. This was it. She would permit a kiss.

Only no kiss came.

"They've gone." His voice fluttered over her skin, quiet and even. Unaffected. As though he were commenting on the weather.

As his words sank in, she listened. Silence carried from the other side of the door. They both held still. Moments stretched as she verified what he said was true. She took measure of herself and the wholly unsuitable embrace she shared with a man who deemed her one step above the gutter.

His voice rustled the tiny hairs that had spilled free from her chignon to frame her face. "Of course if you would prefer to stay here, I'm quite sure we could occupy ourselves."

He spoke so calmly. As if he did not care one way or another if she accepted his offer, and perhaps that stung the most. Not the offer itself, but that he would proposition her and not care whether she agreed.

"Get away from me, you wretch!" Grier flung herself back. Twisting around, she fumbled with the door and burst from the armoire. Breath sawing from her lips, she whirled around, her burgundy skirts sweeping wide as she glared at the man emerging from the armoire.

Taking in his immense size, she marveled that the two of them had fit inside at all. She blew at a strand of auburn hair swinging before her eyes. It still dangled in the most annoying fashion, so she swiped at the offending strand furiously, never breaking her glare.

His cat-gold eyes followed her movements with mild interest, a notable change. He'd looked bored before. "Is this far enough away? I confess a woman has never asked me to remove myself from her side before."

The arrogant jackass!

His eyes were molten, fire burning as bright as sunlight. How did one possess gold eyes? She'd never seen the like. Perhaps he was the devil?

Suddenly he looked awake. Not even when she had doused her lemon water over him had he looked quite so . . . alert. Not as he did now, circling her like some sort of jungle cat. A predator.

A tiny frisson of alarm coursed through her to realize she was the cause for that. She was the reason his eyes burned brightly.

She sucked in a breath, marveling that her stays had not felt this tight at the beginning of the night. Right now her clothing felt constrictive, her body sensitive, swollen and chafing against her garments.

Her cheeks burned with mortification. She pulled back her shoulders and regretted the move when his gaze dropped to her décolletage. The modest cut was no more daring than that of any other lady in attendance tonight, but the sweetheart neckline felt very risqué beneath his regard.

She angled her chin and clasped her hands in front of her. "Was it necessary to accost me while we were hiding?"

An indolent smile curved his sinful lips. "Forgive me," he said without a hint of apology. "When I have a woman pressed against me, it's only human nature to react."

Heat fired her cheeks. "Human nature," she bit out, "does not give you leave to *touch* me. I don't care if you're a prince or not. No one touches me," she growled. At least not again. Not without the protection of marriage. Never again would she lose control when a handsome man put his hands on her or whispered promises in her ear.

Not that the man before her had whispered such words. Nor would he ever. On the contrary, he'd said only the most insulting things to her— *about* her—since they'd met.

He shrugged one broad shoulder, clearly unbothered by her outrage. And that only outraged her further. Did he think himself so above the conventions that governed the rest of Society?

"You did not seem . . . opposed." He drew closer, staring at her in the most perplexing manner. "I thought perhaps you wanted to become friends."

"Friends?" Her eyes narrowed.

"You're not unattractive," he drawled.

She blinked. "So therefore I'm worthy of dalliance?" She shook her head, marveling at his arrogance. "This may come as a shock, but I don't care for your opinion of me."

He continued as though she hadn't spoken, "Your hair isn't the most modest shade, but it is appealing." He cocked his head as he surveyed her. "Your skin has seen too much of the sun," he announced. "Have you never heard of a bonnet?"

She pulled back her shoulders in affront. "Have you never heard of *manners*? Does being a prince exclude you from basic courtesy? I don't recall asking your opinion regarding my appearance."

He folded his hands behind his back, ignoring her words as he began circling her, ever again the stiff and judgmental prince. Even with his burning eyes, she faced the fact that he would always be that—a man far removed from her. He knew it. She knew it, too.

She turned with sideways steps, following him as he moved, not about to have him at her back.

He stopped before her, still considering her with those gold eyes of his. "How old are you?" There was a fair amount of suspicion in his voice as he asked this . . . as though whatever she said would be wrong.

She eyed him, answering slowly. "Not that it's any of your concern, but I'm eight and twenty."

He blinked. "You're a bit long in the tooth, aren't you?"

She gasped. "For what? Being alive?"

"For being yet unclaimed."

"Unclaimed? As in unclaimed by a man?"

He nodded once.

"A little archaic, aren't you? I've been busy . . . haven't gotten around to a man . . . claiming me yet."

"I see," he murmured, either missing her sarcasm or deliberately ignoring it.

Propping her hands on her hips, she demanded, "And how old are you?"

"It doesn't matter how old *I* am. I'm a man."

"No, you're a jackass!" she retorted.

His expression didn't crack at this accusation; if anything, he looked only grimmer.

Her hands clenched at her sides, opening and

closing into fists. She couldn't recall a man ever exasperating her more. Even when she was a child, when the village boys would torment her with lizards and various other creepy crawly creatures, they'd never infuriated her like this.

He shrugged as if it were of no account to him. "I'm eight and twenty, as well."

She blinked. He must be jesting. "You mean to say we're the same age?"

"Yes, but as I pointed out, I'm a man." He held up a broad palm when she began to protest. "Albeit a jackass, as you've said." His mouth twisted into what almost resembled a smile. "The question that begs answering is who is older? When were you born?"

Shaking her head, she replied coldly, emphatically, "I'm not telling you my birthday."

"I can find out," he said with maddening confidence.

"Why should you wish to?"

"You've put yourself on the market for a husband, have you not? I've a right to consider your assets."

She snorted and dropped her arms. "Do you mean to say you're considering me as a prospective wife? Heavens! Have the stars truly shined down on me? Could I be so blessed?" She flattened a hand to her chest and cocked her head at a jaunty angle, enjoying herself and almost laughing as she played out her mockery. Sobering, she looked him squarely in the eye. "I overheard you earlier. I know what you think of me."

"So the drink on my head was no accident. I thought as much."

Too late, she realized she'd been trapped. She propped a hand on her hip. "No, it was no accident. I believe you called me a nobody with ignoble roots. You deserved my drink on your head. That and more."

He nodded sagely, assessing her again, not appearing the least remorseful at the reminder of his insulting words. "I said that. Quite so. It was the truth. You'd do well enough in my bed. You smell like vanilla and you tremble sweetly when I touch you, but—"

"Stop!" she cried, lifting her hands to her ears as if she could block out his outrageous words. All her humor vanished as scorching heat swept over her face. That he spoke matter-of-factly, almost dispassionately, over the issue of her beddableness galled her.

"But as a wife?" he continued as if she had not spoken. "Indeed not. Your age alone would offend my grandfather."

"So long as you're picking a wife to please your granddaddy." She smirked.

That earned her a glare, for which she felt immense satisfaction. She needn't be the only one discomfited.

"I've more than *my* wishes to consider when choosing a wife." His voice fell hard and flat. "I've a duty to my country." He waved a hand in her direction. "It would be foolish and irresponsible to consider you. I should be lucky to beget a single child, much less the half score I require."

Her hands flew back to her hips. "Holy hellfire! Is there no end to your conceit and arrogance? This isn't the Middle Ages. Wives are more than broodmares, you know."

"I'm not merely looking for a wife. I'm looking for a princess. A future queen."

That silenced her. What did she know about such matters, after all?

"Aside from your age, your speech and manner hardly befit a princess—"

"I quite understand you. I'm not wife material for you. I don't recall ever vying for the position." Hot indignation swarmed over her in tiny hot prick points. "It's a good thing that you have no interest in me," she said, deliberately forgetting that he said she would do well in his bed. "And I most assuredly have none in you." She swallowed, hating the way her voice sounded tight and out of breath.

He continued as if she hadn't spoken. "Indeed, you won't do at all as the future queen of Maldania, despite having a certain . . . raw appeal." He angled his head again and a liquid-dark lock of hair fell across his forehead, making him look rakish. She could almost excuse the simmer in her blood. For all that he said, all that he was a cad, he was darkly, irresistibly handsome. And yet that changed nothing. As much as her blood simmered, so did her temper. He was an insulting boor and she would not abide him another moment. "So let us discuss how firm you are on the matter of marriage. Are you opposed to another type of arrangement?"

She glanced around, searching wildly for anything she might use as a weapon. "You're abominable! Is there no end to your—"

"Honesty?" he supplied with a bold lift of an eyebrow.

"No," she shot back. "Wretchedness. You can't make an indecent proposition and pride yourself on honesty." She shook her head. "It simply does not work that way."

"I merely pointed out you were appealing and I would perhaps care for more of your company."

With her face still flaming, she lifted her skirts and moved for the door, ready to put His Bloody *Highness* behind her for good. She felt sorry for whatever female married him. She could well imagine listening to him pontificate over her failings all the days of their union. Grier would jump off a cliff first.

"I wouldn't leave just yet."

She paused, looking over her shoulder at the much too handsome wretch. She couldn't help thinking that it was vastly unfair that such a wicked man should be wrapped in such packaging. It hid all that was twisted inside him. "And why not?"

"Rather soon on the heels of Lord and Lady Kirkendale, is it not? You don't want them to spot you leaving." He lowered himself to the bed, stretching out long legs before him as he observed her with his keen lion's eyes.

He smiled then. The suddenness of that grin stole her breath. Austere and unsmiling, he was a sight to behold. Smiling like this . . . She was in trouble.

She scowled at him. His smile deepened, flashing blinding white teeth. Apparently her scowl did not affect him. She was not sure much of anything would.

She cleared her throat and lifted her chin. "It's unlikely they're lingering—"

"They're properly wedded," he reminded in his rolling accents, her skin tingling in the most bothersome way. "They have no cause to hurry back. And knowing Lady Kirkendale, she's probably distracting him along the way."

She loathed his logic. The couple had sounded quite amorous moments ago, after all. She should put nothing past their salacious natures.

She crossed her arms and gazed at the . . . *prince.* Her thoughts still stumbled over the fact that he was royalty, that he was here. With her. That he had propositioned her and seemed unmoved by that fact. Her chest tightened. He probably did it all the time to lowly females such as her.

Who would have imagined that Grier, more comfortable in trousers and astride a mount, would ever find herself in such a scenario? The Grier of old had spent several evenings a week at the local tavern, drinking ale with lads who viewed her as one of them. Simply another low-born lad. As a game master, she'd spent little time in dresses and even less time in ball gowns.

She swallowed. The blasted prince was right. She would make a poor queen. And that wasn't something she regretted. She didn't aspire to be a queen. She only sought a marriage to a gentleman. She knew how hard life could be. She wanted to make sure she was shielded from the worst of its storms. Nothing more.

Leaning back on his elbows, the prince continued to stare at her as she made no move to leave. "Thought you might see my point."

"Concerned with being caught with a lowly serf such as me, are you?" She could not stop the biting question. He, a prince. She, a bastard who'd fallen into some money. The two did not mesh.

He tilted his head, firelight gilding the dark strands. She swallowed again, vowing to stop letting his looks addle her head.

"Not especially," he answered. "*My* reputation shall not suffer if we're caught together, after all." A corner of his mouth pulled seductively. "Sorry. That man thing again."

He mocked her. Her fingers dug into her palms, the nails cutting into the tender flesh. She stared at him for a moment, cocking her head. "You mean I alone would bear the shame of being caught alone with you in a bedchamber?"

"Naturally."

"Such an occurrence shall not affect you in the least."

"You needn't sound so indignant." He nodded a single time. " 'Tis the way of things. In your country and mine."

Yes, she thought grimly. It was the way of things. She'd suffer scandal, and he would merely become more desirable in the eyes of the *ton*. Men would admire him and women would only think him more the dashing rake.

If she thought the whispers about her were bad now, they would be nothing if she was caught alone in such intimate quarters with the bloody Crown Prince of Maldania. She bit her lip, looking anxiously to the door again.

He certainly wouldn't salvage her honor by offering to marry her. A bitter taste filled her mouth. Make no mistake, he did not deem her worth saving from ruin. She was merely a bastard. Too old. Too freckled and sun-browned.

"Then I best not linger here," she retorted at last. "Since every moment with you places me at risk."

She turned for the door, determined that this time, he would not stop her.

And he didn't. He didn't utter a word as she fled the room.

And why should he? As she hurried down the corridor, she grasped her skirts in two clenched hands, chasing her repeating shadow and reminding herself that she was nothing to him. Nothing. Just as he was nothing to her.

Chapter Five

Sev stared at the closed door that Miss Grier Hadley had departed through as if the hounds of hell chased her heels. He scratched his jaw in bemusement.

Grier, Grier. *Grier.*

He let the name roll around his head. What kind of name was that anyway? He could visualize his grandfather grimacing at the sound of it. So very . . . *common*. Not like Elizabeth. Or Catherine. Those were queenly names. Names all of former Maldanian queens.

He caught his blurry reflection in a mirror and grimaced. Why was he even thinking about her name?

He stared at the door again, imagining the

swish of her skirts as she fled the room. And why wouldn't she flee him? He'd been his most boorish toward her. But there was no help for it. She was an exceedingly unsuitable female, no matter how interesting he found her. The best thing to do was send her running.

He rose from the bed and strolled aimlessly about the chamber to give her several more moments to find her way back to the ballroom before following. It would not do to be spotted too closely in her wake.

What he'd said was true. Wagging tongues wouldn't harm him, but what he hadn't said was that he did not wish for her to become fodder for the gossip mill. He imagined with her shady pedigree she already endured a fair share of censure.

Contrary to what he'd shown of himself, he did possess a heart. Even if only a small, charred bit of one. That was the only thing left to him after the last ten years of war . . . years of watching his family and comrades die all around him, his country dwindle and wither like something rotting on the vine.

He needed to make a good match. Simple as that. It wasn't a matter of *want* . . . this *needed* to be done.

Unbidden, the image of Miss Hadley rose in his

mind once again. He saw her flushed cheeks when she'd stumbled from the armoire, and a smile pulled at the corners of his mouth. She was quite correct in her accusations. He had not needed to touch her so intimately. He hadn't needed to, but he had. He'd been unable to stop himself.

She smelled of brisk, wild winds and verdant hills. She'd reminded him of home. The hills and mountains of Maldania. And her skin had been as soft as silk. His fingers twitched at his side in memory.

The smile slipped from his mouth as he carried that memory further. She'd rebuffed him. True, he'd not been his most charming, but his crown alone usually had women throwing themselves at him.

He shook his head as if to clear it of thoughts of her. This was frustrated desire, nothing more. She must plague him because his tryst with Lady Kirkendale had been interrupted. He simply suffered from unfulfilled lust. Nothing more.

There was nothing about her that would normally attract him. She was not at all his sort of woman. Not her sun-browned skin, not her waspish tongue, especially not the unfortunate circumstances of her birth. All combined to make her a female beneath his notice. At least she *should* be far from his consideration. Some English noble-man in need of funds might deem her acceptable, but not a future king of Maldania.

And yet she had his full notice.

She was precisely the sort he'd put up as his mistress and keep in one of the family's seaside estates, a safe distance from court. *If* he were here to find a mistress. *If* she would entertain such an offer.

He knew his duty. He would not fail. He'd find the perfect bride. One to fill his coffers and the nursery. A female who would breathe life back into his country. The needs of his heart or body did not bear consideration.

"Well, let's hear it. How was your evening? Any-thing interesting to report?"

Grier covered her yawn with her hand and stared bleary-eyed at her father, a man she had only recently come to know.

The faint tinge of dawn painted the air that crept in through the carriage curtains. Now she understood why the echelons of Society slept the day away. They didn't fall into bed until sunrise.

Jack didn't look the least tired as he gazed at her with bright, expectant eyes. No, in fact he looked invigorated after a night spent with the aristocrats among whose ranks he so badly wanted to be counted. She grimaced. Enough so that he suddenly decided his illegitimate offspring were worth acknowledging.

Grier glanced at her half sister. If either of them could gain him access to that glittering world through marriage, then they were suddenly worth something in his eyes.

Grier was no fool. She didn't look to the older man seated across from her and anticipate he would harbor a soft spot for her. Essentially he bought her presence in his life. He hadn't been struck with sudden tender feelings for the daughters he never knew. She accepted that. She, in turn, would never hold a warm place for him in her heart, either. His love was not something she had spent her life missing. She'd had a father. The man her mother married after Jack Hadley tossed her aside. The man she had called Papa. He'd comforted her and shielded her as best he could from the cruel world that would punish a child for being illegitimate.

Her mother's husband had taught her to ride and fish and shoot. He'd never treated her like another man's daughter. He'd treated her like his own.

She rubbed fiercely at the center of her chest, feeling a pang there at the memory of Papa. He'd been gone almost three years, but she still missed him. If he was still alive, she was certain she would not find herself here, sitting in a carriage with Jack Hadley, complicit in his scheme to see her wedded to some blueblood and convinced that was the answer to all her troubles.

"Well?" Jack prompted. "Tell me. Who did you charm this night?" He rubbed his thick hands together as if she had already succeeded in snaring an aristocrat.

Grier turned at the sound of Cleo's sigh. She managed a wan smile for Grier as she slumped against the side of the carriage, waiting for Grier to take the lead, as she usually did with their father.

In the month they'd resided with Jack it had been a constant whirlwind of routs, balls, fittings with the modiste, and nights at the opera. They'd scarcely had time to breathe between each event.

Jack, too, was apparently waiting on her. He said her name with heavy emphasis, "Grier? Have you nothing to report about tonight?"

He'd made his expectations clearly felt. As the oldest, she should wed first.

"The evening went well," she lied.

"Well?" Jack's lips puckered around the word as if it were something distasteful.

"Yes. Very . . . fine," she amended.

"Fine?" Jack frowned, spitting the word out. "Merely . . . fine? That doesn't sound very heartening. Did you win no hearts tonight? I thought you wanted to snare a husband, my girl. A *fine* evening doesn't sound like you were working toward gaining a proposal."

Grier looked helplessly at her sister. Cleo arched an eyebrow as if to say, *You did spend a good portion of the night hiding behind a fern.*

Moistening her lips, Grier finally said, "It's not as easy as you think. Most members of the *ton* find our lineage less than impressive."

Jack waved a thick, meaty paw. "Nonsense. I've made it clear the extent of the dowry placed on each of your heads." *Your heads.* Like they were scurrilous outlaws.

"Since your sister Marguerite married that partner of mine, I've withheld her share, so there's more for the two of you. I've made that known as well. Trust me. There's plenty of interest out there. Just make yourself obliging and you'll have a proposal within the fortnight." His eyes narrowed ruthlessly and she was reminded of what her father was. He'd made his wealth through crime and upon the misery of others. "Unless you aren't obliging. Unless you don't want to be here—"

"I'll be obliging," she replied, feeling oddly hollow inside at the bitter realization that she had to do very little to attract a husband. If Jack was to be believed, she need merely be *obliging* and she'd soon have a proposal. Her father did it all, *everything*, by offering a king's ransom to the man who married her. It was humiliating when considered in that light.

She lifted her gaze back to her sister and read some of the same disillusionment in Cleo's gaze. They were sacrificing any hope, any dream of a man marrying them . . . for *them*. For affection . . . for love.

Unwanted, the image of Prince Sevastian rose in her mind. At least he'd been attracted to her. Even if his manner had been wholly offensive, he'd made no attempt to hide that he'd found her desirable. Could she even expect that from her future husband?

She sighed and closed her eyes, pressing at the backs of her eyelids with her fingertips where they ached.

Yet the reward was great—respectability, security, comfort in home and hearth, in knowing a roof would forever be over her head. Having lived on the brink of poverty and hunger, Grier and Cleo both knew that these things were essential in life. They did not take such things for granted.

"I'll be more obliging next time," she promised, meaning it. She'd agreed to this venture. She might as well go about it in earnest. No more dragging her feet.

"Very good. I expect to see an improvement." He nodded. "We leave tomorrow."

"Tomorrow?" Cleo sat up straighter, suddenly alert. "For where?"

Jack puffed up his chest a bit. "The Dowager Duchess of Bolingbroke has graciously invited us to her country seat for a week. Along with a few other feted guests. It's a great honor. Not many among the *ton* are gifted with an invitation to a house party at Pemberton Manor."

A house party. There would be no escape this time. Grier swallowed. She could not hide behind potted plants or in her rooms for the week.

A small shudder racked her before she summoned her resolve once again. This was for the best. She was no coward. She'd set herself on this course, and she'd see it through.

Jack pointed a finger at each of them. "I expect one of you to snare the youngest grandson, the viscount. And while we're there it wouldn't hurt to focus some attention on the duke as well."

"You said the dowager told you he was not

for us," Cleo reminded as their carriage slowed before their father's Mayfair home, an obscenely large monstrosity that perfectly summed up the ambitions of Jack Hadley.

He shrugged. "So use your wiles. He's a red-blooded man." He waved at each of them. "He can just as easily fall for one of you as any other chit. You're more comely than some of those horse-faced hags the *ton* boasts."

A groom opened the door just then and her father clambered down from the carriage. He strode up the steps and into the house, leaving them to descend the carriage with the help of a groom.

Arms linked, Grier and her sister advanced up the steps side-by-side.

"It will be a small group," Cleo voiced, and Grier wasn't certain who she was trying to reassure—herself or Grier. "No mad crush of another holiday ball or soiree."

"There *is* that," Grier agreed.

"And we'll be away from Town for an entire week."

A smile curled her lips all the way up to her bedchamber. The thought of fresh air and trees and unfettered winds lifted her spirits. She wouldn't have to visit Hyde Park for a ride on one of her father's placid mares. The next time she climbed atop a horse she would race the wind. The breeze would tear at her eyes. She'd feel the pins tug loose in her hair.

A sleepy-looking maid arrived and helped her from her gown into her night rail. When the girl offered to help her with her hair, Grier waved her away, unaccustomed to being waited on hand and foot.

Sitting at her dressing table, she removed each pin, one by one, until the mass of auburn hair fell past her shoulders. Several curling wisps that refused to grow as long as the rest of her hair framed her face. She ran her fingers through the thick strands, massaging her tired scalp.

Picking up her brush, she tackled her hair until it crackled and gleamed in the low glow of firelight. She paused, staring at her reflection. Even in the dim light, the brown freckles spattering her nose stood out clear as day.

"I'm not *that* brown," she muttered to her reflection, her tone defensive, as if she addressed one of the gossiping biddies from tonight who'd called her dusky. It was simply that all the ladies in the *ton* preferred a paleness usually reserved for the dead. Grier liked color in her skin.

"And I'm not *old*." She set her brush down with a clack and climbed into bed, sinking deep in the center of the soft mattress and wondering why thoughts of a certain prince still plagued her. Her cheeks washed hot and cold at the memory of him. The stolen moments in the wardrobe played so vividly in her head.

It was almost as if he were there, beside her, whispering his taunts, touching her with hands that were far too bold, too calloused to belong to a blueblooded prince.

She'd never reacted to Trevis this way. Rolling onto her side, she allowed herself to think about her former employer, careful that she did not collide into any of the humiliation that usually accompanied thoughts of him.

He'd been her best friend since childhood, comfortable and constant—he even stood up to those who would bully her. She thought they would spend the rest of their lives together. His kisses had been nice . . . but apparently that hadn't been desire. Not true desire. She recognized that now. She knew.

After what she felt tonight in that armoire, she knew she'd been wrong. Rather appalling when she considered the prince had not even truly kissed her. Her belly had never filled with butterflies before tonight, her lungs had never felt so tight she couldn't draw breath.

Her cheeks warmed as she imagined what an actual kiss from Prince Sevastian would feel like. She curled into a small ball, drawing her legs tightly to her chest, and let her imagination take over.

She closed her eyes, visualizing his face as close as it had been earlier. Only in her mind his mouth closed over hers, his lips moved, caressed . . . .

Her eyes flew open with a gasp. She had no business entertaining such fantasies. Certainly not for a wicked man who thought her beneath his regard—save for a quick tryst. Eyes wide, she stared out at her bedchamber. Suddenly the night loomed endlessly.

Snow started to fall in fat wet flakes, licking at the windowpanes. She rearranged the pillows behind her head and settled back. Slipping a hand beneath her cheek, she watched the flurries of white outside her window, letting the sight block out everything, everyone, especially her fleeting glimpse of Prince Sevastian's smile.

Chapter Six

The dowager duchess's country seat sat nestled amid manicured lawns. A great lake stretched before the massive gray-stone edifice like an inviting carpet of velvet blue. She could almost imagine the geese floating across the lake's glassy surface in the spring.

Grier held her breath as they were ushered up several steps into a cathedrallike foyer and tried not to feel like a total impostor. The butler led them to the drawing room. Discordant music erupted from a pianoforte within, escaping through the tall, cracked double doors. The butler pushed the doors open and guided them to the gathered group.

Apparently they were the last to arrive. Several

other guests took their tea, the dowager included. She sat in a great throne of a chair before the fire, reigning like a pasha over the assembly. Following the butler's stiffly delivered introductions, the grande dame waved them to chairs with plump, beringed fingers.

Jack forged ahead like a blustery wind, greeting the dowager in jarring tones, heedless of the soft tones everyone else used as a young lady painfully banged her way on the pianoforte.

Grier and Cleo exchanged glances at the smirks her father earned from the half-dozen guests lounging in chaises and sofas about the room. Wealthy or not, invited or not, they were objects of disdain for the dowager's guests.

Grier pasted a polite smile on her face and tried not to feel like a mongrel who snuck inside to escape the storm. She belonged here just as much as anybody else. She was an invited guest.

For some reason the image of Prince Sevastian's face swam in her mind just then. He, of course, would disagree. He thought she was common and beneath such elevated company. The realization stung as it shouldn't. She bit back a groan of frustration that he'd found a way into her head again.

Shaking memories of him away, she lifted her

chin a notch and inquired after the dowager's health.

The dowager offered a reply and smiled. Grier tried to detect artifice in the brittle curve of her ashen lips—the same artifice she met at every turn within the *ton*—but then she called a stop to such wonderings. Such thoughts were pointless. Of course the smile was a sham. The dowager didn't *want* Grier or Cleo to wed her grandson. She merely wanted Jack's fortune to save her family.

It didn't take much to assess the direness of the dowager's situation. The evidence was there, all around Grier. The faded wallpaper wouldn't be so obvious but for the few squares of brighter, cleaner paper where paintings had once hung. Sold to fetch much-needed funds, she surmised. Grier's gaze darted to the maids standing in attendance. Likely to pay for the servants required to run this mausoleum.

And there were other signs. The drawing room furniture, once of the finest quality, was worn and faded. Something she easily noted after residing with her father for the last month and being surrounded with the finest furnishings and most lavish decor.

The dowager snapped her wrist and the viscount appeared, lifting up from a chaise across the room, where he had been in close conversation with a pretty brunette. The girl's eyes followed him longingly as he moved to his grandmother's side and bowed over Grier and Cleo. On the other side of the girl, her plump friend patted her arm consolingly and stared sourly at Grier.

Grier frowned. Was the girl in love with him? Was he in love with her? Perfect. Another reason to feel uncomfortable.

The viscount did his part admirably though. He smiled and bowed over their hands with perfect grace. His boyish good looks betrayed nothing. He showed no sign that his heart was otherwise engaged. A gentleman to the core. Unlike a certain prince whose memory she could not seem to dismiss.

Grier angled her head and took a bracing breath, reprimanding herself for thinking of that brash scoundrel again. Would he never be far from her thoughts? Over the course of their journey to reach the dowager's estate, his face and taunting words filled her head more often than not. Strange, really.

Holy hellfire. She almost imagined that one of the two gentlemen stepping inside the drawing room even now resembled him.

She blinked and looked again as he approached. The gentleman didn't *resemble* him. It *was* he.

He was here. Her prince was here. No! Not *her* prince. She swallowed tightly, cursing herself for that slip. He wasn't *her* anything.

Panic swelled up in her chest, tightening her throat. How was she to forget him when he attended the same house party with her? He would be here, underfoot the entire time. For well over a week. She would see him down the length of the dinner table, constantly hear his voice everywhere she turned.

His gaze found her, those gold eyes widening with recognition. Something akin to amusement flickered in his eyes before it was gone, banked. His well-formed mouth flattened into an unsmiling line.

She sniffed and held up her chin, struggling to appear unaffected. She stared coolly at him, *through* him, behaving like him—the austere, unfeeling royal. She behaved as though she didn't know him at all. And she didn't. Not really. Their one evening together scarcely constituted an acquaintance.

Her sister lightly touched her elbow, and she dragged her attention back to the viscount, focusing on what he was saying.

". . . delighted you are here. When you did not arrive yesterday with everyone else, we feared the elements would keep you from joining us. Such wretched weather. I profess all the gentlemen present are heaving a sigh of relief at the arrival of two more such lovely ladies."

"That's kind of you to say, my lord," Grier murmured.

The viscount pressed a hand to his heart. "I only speak the truth."

"Quite so, quite so," an elderly man exclaimed, banging his walking stick upon the floor as he swept both Grier and Cleo a lecherous look.

Lord Tolliver nodded. "The marquis was quite displeased at the lack of females present."

"Now it shall be a true country party." The old man's leer deepened, revealing missing teeth and a wet, roiling tongue that seemed to have difficulty staying inside his mouth.

Cleo managed to get out a polite response, but Grier could only cringe at the old man. Surely she was not to consider him? The viscount was vastly more appealing.

"Eh, lovely." The marquis crooked a finger at Grier. "Come sit beside me."

Grier gave him a wobbly smile, eyeing the small settee upon which he sat with great reluctance. Never had she felt so out of place, wondering what the proper thing to do was.

She felt the prince's gaze on her back, burning through her clothing, branding her, seeming to call her out for the impostor she was. At that moment, she had never felt the truth of that more keenly. She was an impostor, fighting for position in a world that didn't want her. Resolve firmed her lips. A world that didn't want her *yet*.

"Cease your flirting, Quibbly," the dowager called. "Can't you see you're frightening the girl?"

Frightening wouldn't be precisely accurate. *Repulsing* would be closer to the truth.

Grier smiled, but her lips felt brittle and tight on her face. Thankfully Jack provided a distraction just then, diving into a diatribe on their perilous journey across snow-laden roads.

Her father did not exaggerate. Cleo had come down with an ague, delaying their departure a day. A day in which a winter storm arrived. The roads had been nearly impassable, but that hadn't deterred Jack. Not from a house party at the dowager's estate.

Grier and Cleo settled back onto the comfortable sofa as a silent maid placed a teacup in her hands. Grier took a warming sip, listening as her father described the two hours they spent mired in a snowdrift while the driver, the groom, and her father labored to pull them free.

"Quite the adventure," a voice murmured beside her.

She sent a sharp glance to her left.

Stealthily as a jungle cat, the prince had positioned himself just above her, standing with soldierlike rigidity, his hands clasped behind him. She straightened her spine and looked away. His voice, however, was still there, puckering her skin to gooseflesh. "How fortunate we are to have you here safely with us."

She slid him another look, trying to decipher if he mocked her and unable to hide her shock that he even deigned to speak to her where it might be witnessed. Lifting her cup to her lips, she murmured softly, "Are you certain you wish to be seen speaking to me, Your Highness?"

His gold eyes glinted down at her. "I see no harm."

"How magnanimous of you."

"Ah, Your Highness, have you met the Misses Hadley?" The viscount had apparently noted their exchange. He looked back and forth between them.

She opened her mouth to deny having met the prince, but he spoke first. "Yes. In Town."

"Ah, of course." The viscount nodded cheerfully. He really was a nice sort. Quite willing to be the sacrificial lamb. Or was he? His stare drifted, floating somewhere beyond her shoulder as he sipped from his teacup.

She followed his gaze to the lovely girl she'd spied him talking with earlier. At Grier's stare she quickly looked away, a pretty pink stain coloring her cheeks. But not before Grier saw that she, too, had been looking at the viscount.

Shifting uncomfortably, she faced forward again, feigning interest as her father regaled the room with their adventures. Only she couldn't focus on him for long. Not when she felt the stare of the prince mere feet away. A hot itchiness spread across her face until she had to look up at him again.

He stared at her with what was becoming familiar aloofness. Why did he bother to look at her at all?

With a snap of her head, she faced forward again.

After some moments, the dowager interrupted her father's narrative. "My, how harrowing. Perhaps your daughters would care to see their rooms and refresh themselves before dinner?"

Grier tried not to nod too earnestly at the suggestion. Cleo rose beside her. A maid appeared as if by magic from a remote corner of the room to escort them.

As they left, Grier felt one intent stare drilling into her back. It did not require much imagination to conclude who watched her so intently. The very same man who stared at her so coldly and deemed her fit only for a tryst—not for mingling among the echelons of Society.

This time she managed not to look back.

Dinner was a tiresome affair, with too many courses to count. Even after a rest in her bedchamber, concentrating so hard on how she sat, ate, and conducted herself throughout the elaborate meal made Grier's shoulders knot with tension.

The duke was present. Apparently he'd spent the day hunting game in the woods with his dogs. Grier envied him that. It sounded decidedly more enjoyable than her choices: taking a nap or suffering the company of ladies who preferred to discuss the latest fashion plates and gossip from Town. Still, she could endure it. She *would*. The end goal would make it all worthwhile.

As the highest rank present, the prince held the seat of honor at the head of the table. The duke sat beside him. The snatches of conversation drifting her way proved far more interesting than the conversation at her far end of the table.

She was seated beside Miss Persia Thrumgoodie, the young lady she'd caught staring so hungrily after the viscount. All Grier's attempts at conversation with her were met with stilted responses. It was like talking to a wall. She couldn't decide if this derived from shyness or simple disdain.

Grier again glanced with longing down the length of table. Not, she assured herself, because the prince himself sat there, looking handsome and formidable as ever in his all-black attire, but only because, at that particular moment, they were discussing the merits of bow hunting.

One of her slippers tapped a fierce staccato beneath the table. It was difficult sitting still in her chair and remaining silent when a subject she was actually interested in was being discussed several feet away. But what could she do? Shout down the length of the table?

She bit her lip and swirled her spoon in her leek soup, reminding herself that no one here would care to hear her thoughts on matters of hunting. In fact, they would be appalled to know she possessed knowledge on such an unladylike subject.

Her father slurped loudly beside her. Several

distasteful looks were sent his way. Grier felt the gulf between herself and all these lily-handed aristocrats widening.

You need only find and marry your country gentleman and you'll endure no more of this. With a title attached to your name, you'll be free to be yourself. No one will dare ridicule you again.

She turned her attention to the viscount sitting several seats away. The candlelight cast shadows on his boyishly rounded features. Was he younger than she? The notion sent a frisson of discomfort through her. The uncomfortable feeling settled in the pit of her belly. Again she thought of the prince and his comments. He'd called her *old*—made her feel like a veritable hag.

She shook off such musings and blinked her attention back to the viscount—where it should be—resisting the temptation to look even farther down the table where the prince sat. The length separating them served as reminder enough of the distance between them. He had no business in her thoughts.

Focusing on the viscount, she wondered if he enjoyed the hunt and what he would think of a wife who did. What would he think of a wife who eschewed parties and shopping on Bond Street and would rather flush out grouse?

It was worth finding out. What else was she here for except to explore her options?

"And do you, Lord Tolliver, enjoy the hunt as well?" Grier lifted her voice to carry to the viscount, sending a slight nod in the direction of the duke and prince, who talked without once looking down the table length, even though the subject of his conversation could be heard.

Tonight it was as though she did not exist for the prince. He never looked her way. Unlike before, his aloof stare did not so much as stray in her direction.

Lord Tolliver cast a glance toward his brother, his smile rueful. "I'm a passable shot and spent a fair amount of time chasing the hounds in my youth. Growing up alongside my brother, how could I not?" He took a sip from his soup spoon. "However, I confess I can hardly claim to be the expert huntsman my brother is. I spend a good amount of time in my library, nose buried in a book. I'm not much for the outdoors." He chuckled then. "That must make me sound a dreadful bore."

She smiled and lied, "Of course not." Not that she didn't enjoy a good book then and again. But to claim no liking for the outdoors? That was not at all what she had been seeking, but then must her future husband have to hunt and ride as much as she to tolerate *her* love of hunting and riding?

Persia cooed. "I love to read as well. Novels, mostly."

The viscount smiled. "Perhaps it's unmanly of me to say, but I'm quite the fan of Mrs. Radcliffe."

Persia clapped her hands merrily, her chestnut curls bouncing on each side of her head. "Oh! But I adore her work!"

Grier stifled a wince. Her reading preferences were mostly histories and biographies.

She swept another spoonful of savory broth into her mouth. Unable to stop herself, she let her gaze drift to the table's far end—and it collided with the prince. Heat flooded her face. Was he aware how many times she had been looking his way tonight?

His inscrutable stare gave nothing away. He studied her over the rim of his glass of claret. Her fingers tightened around her spoon and she resisted the urge to toss it down the length of table at his head. It was unaccountable really, this effect he had on her.

Looking away, she returned her attention to those around her and reminded herself that her purpose this week was to become better ac-

quainted with the dowager's youngest grandson
. . . and any other gentleman worthy of consideration.

With that thought firmly in place, she pasted
a smile on her face and did not glance down the
table again for the rest of the night.

Chapter Seven

*A*fter dinner that evening, they all moved into the drawing room. Grier took a spot on the sofa beside Cleo. Lady Libbie quickly followed the dowager's directive and took up playing on the pianoforte. She played well, and the music soon became an airy background to the conversations in the room.

No one paid Grier and Cleo much heed where they sat together on the sofa. With the exception of the viscount, who dutifully paid them his polite attentions, everyone seemed oblivious to them. Cleo sent Grier a smile and lifted one shoulder in a small shrug.

"Are you riding in the morning?" Cleo asked

when the viscount drifted away to converse with the marquis, Lord Quibbly.

"Perhaps. Or I might just take your example and sleep in," she teased.

Cleo blinked wide eyes. "You? Never. Surely the world would end first."

Grier smiled. She always rose early and rarely missed an opportunity for a ride. Even in this weather, she enjoyed escaping outdoors.

Understandably, Cleo enjoyed sleeping late since it was a luxury she never experienced before. Before, she had children to dress and feed and countless chores to perform.

"You should do so, of course," Cleo said in all seriousness. "It feels marvelous waking up to sunlight streaming through your room. Much better than waking when it's still dark and then stumbling around beneath the eaves for your shoes, in your too small room you must share with five others.

"It does sound like something I should experience." She grinned. "At least once."

"Quite." Cleo nodded. "I heartily recommend it." Her expression grew rather intent. "I vow to never go back to my old life where I'm forced to complete a day's work before the sun even rises."

Grier nodded and hoped that Cleo demanded more than that for herself. A life of luxury and indolence wouldn't guarantee her happiness. Cleo deserved more than that. She deserved love.

And don't you, as well?

Grier pushed the small voice aside. She knew it wasn't a question of what she deserved but more a question of what she could expect. Aside of her fortune, she possessed nothing to recommend her to these bluebloods. A fact made glaringly clear by how little notice they paid her.

She was no beauty. She lacked grace and youth and breeding. Cleo was young and pretty and charming. She could expect a love match. It was within her reach, and Grier wanted that for her. For herself, she was more practical.

Grier observed Prince Sevastian from the corner of her eye. He stood ramrod straight, one arm tucked behind him in a very military pose that appeared somehow natural to him, and she wondered at that. Did he never relax? Never let himself *go* in the slightest? In the privacy of his rooms, did he carry himself with the same stiffness?

Her fingers twitched against her silk skirts, tempted with the impulse to muss his hair and loosen his cravat, to make him look more . . . *human.*

He stood at the mantel beside the duke. Naturally, the two men of highest rank in the room would gravitate toward each other. The fire in the great hearth crackled behind them, casting a red glow on their dark trouser-clad legs.

The Duke of Bolingbroke swept a bored glance over the room. His gaze passed over Grier and Cleo as if they were not even present. Grier followed his gaze where it did rest, stopping with interest on Lady Libbie. Apparently the prince wasn't the only one interested in her. She was lovely and elegant as she played, the perfect wife for the likes of a duke. Or a prince.

Lady Libbie finished and Cleo was called upon next. Grier listened with pride, impressed that her sister played so well. Even with a household overcrowded with children, Cleo's mother had installed a pianoforte in their small cottage to ensure that her daughters all knew how to play. Not such a surprise, she supposed, from a woman who named her eldest daughter Cleopatra. She had high hopes for her daughters . . . hopes that might come to fruition, after all, with Cleo.

The duke's eyes followed Lady Libbie's lithe figure as she reclaimed her seat between Persia and Lord Quibbly's granddaughter, the plump, apple-cheeked Marielle. The contrast between the two girls was marked. Swathed in a gown of peach chiffon, Libbie was a vision. Grier couldn't help taking a peek to see if the prince gawked in the same manner as the duke.

Indeed, he did not. He was not looking at anyone really. Angling her head to the side, she studied him curiously, wondering what went on inside his head. He gazed down into the great hearth. The fire's red-gold flames appeared to mesmerize him. In that moment he didn't look arrogant, he simply looked intense, troubled. She wondered what could possibly plague him. His country was war-free after many years. He was the toast of every gala, the most coveted guest on any list. He had his pick of brides. He should be carefree, not this darkly pensive man.

Cleo finished and Miss Persia Thrumgoodie rose to take a turn. She played liked a goddess. As much as Grier disliked the girl—or rather as much as the girl appeared to dislike her—she enraptured everyone in the room, Grier included.

The men were especially spellbound. She risked another glance from the corner of her eye, satisfied to see that not every man had fallen beneath her spell. The prince still gazed into the fire as if he was above everything else taking place around him. Even a beautiful woman like Persia Thrumgoodie was beneath his notice.

Deciding she'd spent enough time contemplating a man who certainly did not waste a moment's thought on her, Grier snapped her gaze away from him, telling herself not to look in his direction again. The last thing she wanted was to be caught ogling him. He might think she wished to accept his indecent proposition from the other night.

Watching Persia, however, was a rather lowering experience. The female knew how to win over an audience.

She played with her whole body. It was quite the sensuous display. Everyone watched, riveted as she rolled her shoulders and dipped her cleavage toward the keys. Lord Tolliver watched with his lips parted. Grier thought she even detected a small amount of drool gathering at the corners. If he wasn't smitten before, he was well enamored of her now.

Despite her avowal of moments ago, Grier feigned interest in the cuff of her sleeve and slid a look at Prince Sevastian beneath her lashes to see if he showed any similar effects.

She breathed easier. Although he no longer

stared down into the fire, he looked out at the room dispassionately, not at all agog over the stunning Persia. Her performance made no impact on him. He wore his usual impassive expression, not even the hint of a smile cracking his face. For once his stoicism didn't annoy her.

Dipping her head, Grier smiled, slow and satisfied, as she recalled the only time she had seen him smile had been in her presence. She'd brought out his smile, and the realization gave her a surge of feminine power.

Then her smile fled with sudden memory. Her brow furrowed as she recalled that he had been smiling in the course of propositioning her—as if she were the lowest female and not a lady given due accord.

"Miss Hadley, can you hear me? It's your turn now."

Grier winced as Cleo elbowed her ungently in the side.

"Perhaps she is deaf." Marielle giggled inanely.

The dowager stared at Grier expectantly from her overstuffed chair. With a imperious cock of her eyebrow, she motioned to the pianoforte.

As the hum of Persia's final chords faded on the air, Grier felt like cornered prey.

"Yes, Miss Hadley. I should love to hear you." Persia rose with a soft swish of her skirts.

Grier blinked and looked around. She suddenly found herself the center of attention. A most unwelcome sensation, to be certain. She stopped breathing, watching with a sick twisting in her stomach as Persia moved smoothly through the room to reclaim her seat. How did she sway her hips like that?

With all eyes fixed on her, there was only one stare she felt as keenly as the prick of a knife. She knew it was he, knew the prince was watching her.

"M-me?" Despising the quiver in her voice, she spoke again, her voice firmer. "You wish to hear me play?" She flattened a hand against the bodice of her gown.

"Yes, Miss Hadley. Do take a turn." The dowager motioned to the pianoforte with a sweep of her heavily beringed hand. "Such a lovely evening we're having. Our own impromptu musicale. Let us continue with it. "

"Indeed. Most entertaining, however . . ." She moistened her suddenly dry lips.

Cleo sent her a sympathetic smile, well aware that Grier did not know *how* to play. In fact, she'd never even seen a pianoforte until arriving in London.

Grier cleared her throat to finish. "Oh, I'm not very good, you see—"

Persia clapped her hands together. "Oh, I'm certain you're most accomplished. Please, don't deny us."

"I can play!" Marielle volunteered, half rising.

"That's quite all right, Marielle, we've heard you play before. We'd like to hear Miss Hadley."

The marquis's granddaughter dropped down with a pout.

The viscount smiled at Grier kindly. "Shall I turn the pages for you, Miss Hadley? I'd be most happy to oblige."

Miserable heat washed up her face. Even Jack looked sorry for her, no doubt aware that she couldn't play. Playing the pianoforte was a lady-like occupation, and Grier was no lady.

She moistened her lips again and admitted, "Truth be told, I can't actually play."

"Oh." Persia blinked with mock surprise, a slender hand drifting to cover her mouth as if Grier had just confessed to murder.

Grier glared at her, not fooled for a moment. Persia wasn't the least surprised. She'd guessed that Grier wouldn't know how to play an instrument that was commonplace in all elegant households of the *ton*. Heat crept up Grier's neck. Was it that obvious she was an impostor among them? A simple, *common* girl playing at being a lady?

Persia lowered her hand. "I-I didn't realize. I assumed you . . . well—" There was a beat of silence as her words faded. A moment of silence in which Grier felt that infernal yawning gulf again . . . between her and everyone else in the room.

The one person she both wanted and didn't want to glance at—to see how this evidence of her lack of breeding registered upon him—stood silent. She could not bring herself to look at him again, to see in his eyes the conviction that he had been right. She didn't belong here. The dowager's kitchen maids were better suited to the role of lady than she.

"She can sing," Jack abruptly volunteered. "Like an angel!" His ruddy face looked anxiously at the dowager.

Grier glared at her father, shaking her head at him in mute appeal. His eyes stared earnest and hopeful back at her and she realized he thought he was helping.

He'd once walked in on her in the library sing-

ing an old Welsh ballad as she was browsing for a
book. She had a passable voice. He'd remarked on
the song, that it was one her mother used to sing,
which, at the time, had quickly silenced her. She
didn't want any comparisons made to the mother
who had been so weak-willed as to fall for Jack
Hadley. As far as Grier was concerned, marrying
Papa was the only good thing her mother ever did.

Grier wasn't like her. She was stronger. She
would marry. She *would* be a proper lady.

"Sing for us," the dowager commanded.

"Oh, I'm not really very—"

"Cease being so reticent, will you, Miss Hadley."
The dowager was beginning to look annoyed.

Grier sighed in defeat. "Very well."

Rising, she moved near the pianoforte, reminding herself that her voice was passable. She
wouldn't embarrass herself on that account . . .
and it wasn't as though anyone here would understand the lyrics. They were in Welsh, after all.

As she opened her mouth and began to sing,
she took secret delight in knowing that she sang
a tawdry tale of a buxom milkmaid to a room full
of nobles.

The prince watched her, his gold eyes inscrutable as her lungs expanded and the words rose

up from inside her to hang mournfully on the air. She tried to look away from him, or at least let her stare sweep over the room, but it was hard to do so when he stared at her as if he understood every word. As if he could see into the inner workings of her mind.

When she finished, the room was silent for a moment. Then the clapping began.

"What language was that? Gaelic?" Persia asked over the applause as Grier passed her on her way back to her seat.

"Welsh," she replied.

"My, how . . . rustic."

"It was simply haunting," Cleo exclaimed, still clapping. "I have chills."

"That was lovely, Miss Hadley, and sung with such feeling," said the viscount. "You must tell us what it means."

Several others in the room echoed the request. Except Persia. Her face flushed at the viscount's praise.

"Oh, a love ballad, I'm sure," Cleo insisted.

"Of course." Grier lowered her gaze at the lie. "A love song."

"How quaint," Persia inserted, her voice tight. "Peasant songs always have such charm. Thank you for treating us. It's not something we get to hear every day."

Grier's cheeks caught fire. Trust Persia to deliver a thinly veiled insult.

Perhaps not so thinly veiled. A heavy pause of silence filled the room as Persia's words sank in. No one save Persia could meet Grier's eyes. Lord Tolliver seemed suddenly fascinated with the carpet pattern. The implication was there—that Grier was a peasant.

"You were marvelous, Miss Hadley." The rich, rumbling voice broke the deep silence. Grier started at the sound of it, her gaze flying to the man near the fireplace.

All heads swiveled in the direction of the usually aloof prince. Everyone stared at him, clearly surprised that he had spoken such high praise on her behalf. Of course, no one was more surprised than Grier.

Did he mean his words? A glimpse of his face hardly indicated that she'd managed to impress him. And yet if she hadn't impressed him with her singing, then why had he spoken up? It was unfathomable that he should wish to spare her from Persia's ridicule. Why should he care how others treated her?

strike me as the type to praise someone for being merely *good*."

Cleo squeezed her arm. "Perhaps he fancies you."

"Unlikely." Grier snorted.

"Well, who cares? The evening was a success. Lord Tolliver certainly looked at you with approval."

"Yes," she murmured. All due to the prince. A fact that would greatly mystify her late into the night.

Chapter Eight

$\mathcal{G}$rier couldn't sleep. The wind howled a mournful tune outside her window, the perfect lulling song to help one fall asleep. Only she couldn't sleep. The only thing she could think about was the prince's rumbling voice. *You were marvelous, Miss Hadley.*

Her face flushed with warmth. Giving up on the notion of sleep, she tossed back the coverlet and donned her robe, tightening the sash about her waist. The corridors were empty as she made her way downstairs, the house silent as a graveyard.

She paused at the library doors, making certain the gentlemen had long since quit their cards and retired for their beds. Not a sound greeted her.

Intent on selecting a book, she entered the quiet room. The fire in the hearth still burned high. A log crumbled and sparks flew and popped. She must have just missed the others.

She edged closer to the fire, drawn by its heat. Holding out her hands, she sighed with pleasure, letting them get almost too warm.

"Careful. You're standing close."

Grier gave a small shriek and jumped, a hand flying to her pounding heart.

The prince lounged on a chaise just behind her. Stretched out, booted feet crossed in a relaxed pose, he looked beguiling. Not at all his usual stiff self.

"I didn't see you there," she said breathlessly, her pulse racing against her neck.

He gripped a handful of papers loosely above his chest. Several others littered the small rosewood table to the right of the chaise. A few even littered the carpet. She'd obviously interrupted him reading.

She'd never seen him like *this* before. He'd removed his jacket and neck cloth. Her mouth dried at the sight of smooth flesh peeping out from his loosened shirt. He looked human—an absurdly handsome man who was suddenly much too approachable.

"H-hello," she added, feeling silly but unsure what to say. Her breath shuddered past her lips.

"Hello," he returned, his deep voice a feather's stroke on the air.

He removed the papers from his chest and dropped them all on the table. "Have you come to sing for me, Miss Hadley? Perhaps you wish to honor me with a solo performance?"

For some reason his question made her feel shaky inside, driving home the reminder that they were all alone. "No. I thought I would pick a book to read. What are you doing?"

He motioned to the mass of papers. "Going over correspondence from home."

She stepped closer, fidgeting with the ruffled edge of her night rail. *"All* that?"

He ran a hand through his hair, sending the ink-dark strands into wild disarray. "I receive this much every week. I'll spend a good portion of my day tomorrow replying."

She arched a brow. "Indeed?"

"With my grandfather ailing, many matters need my attention. I've lingered here for much too long." For a brief moment, he looked frustrated, before the calm mask fell back into place.

She frowned, seeing him in a new light. Apparently his life wasn't all leisure and vain indulgences as she had assumed.

"I won't disturb you further." She crossed her arms, suddenly chilled. "Good night." She took only one step before his voice stopped her.

"Please. Stay. You came for a book, did you not? Pick one." He motioned to the many books lining the shelves.

"Thank you. I will." She turned and tried to focus on the titles, angling her head to read the spines. The letters swam before her eyes. She could only think that *he* sat a few feet behind her. That she wore only her night rail. That he looked delicious and relaxed and thoroughly accessible.

That they were all alone.

She snatched a book off a shelf and whirled around, prepared to flee to the sanctuary of her bedchamber.

"What did you find?"

She blinked, stopping. "What?"

"Your book. What did you select?"

"Um." She glanced down and turned the book around in her hands. Her stomach sank. *"A Comprehensive Study of Oxen Husbandry."*

He snorted.

Heat swamped her face.

"Sounds fascinating," he murmured. "A real page turner. I must read it after you've finished."

It took a moment for her to realize he jested. One side of his mouth curled faintly. He actually possessed humor?

She stifled a chuckle and patted the thick volume. "Nothing like a little reading on animal husbandry to help one sleep."

"Are you having trouble sleeping, Miss Hadley?"

That gave her pause. "The wind . . ." She motioned lamely to one of the windows. "It's so loud tonight." Better that excuse than the truth. She wasn't about to admit that thoughts of him kept her awake.

Then she heard herself asking before she could reconsider, "Did you really enjoy my singing?"

He cocked his head to the side. "Are you fishing for more compliments? I said as much."

"Yes, but did you say that because you felt sorry for me or because you truly thought I was good?"

At this question, the other side of his mouth curled upward. "Perhaps . . . both."

"Hmm." She murmured, unsure how she felt about that. "Well, good night then."

"Your song." His voice stopped her. "What was it about?"

She smiled. Before she could contemplate the

wisdom of such honesty, she admitted, "It was a tale of buxom milkmaid with . . . er, an insatiable appetite."

This time he laughed outright. *She made the Crown Prince of Maldania laugh.* Her chest swelled.

"Little hoyden. I suppose I shouldn't find it so amusing that you regaled us all with a tawdry song."

"No, you shouldn't," she countered. "It's not often I entertain members of the *ton* with naughty songs. Especially princes."

Immediately she regretted the reminder, however playful she had meant it to be. His laughter faded, and the stoic prince was back.

He looked back down at the mass of papers, as if that somehow reminded of who he was—and who she *wasn't*. "Good night, Miss Hadley. I've much still to attend to this night."

Feeling dismissed, she gave a curt nod and skirted past the chaise.

Minutes later, secure in her bed, she opened her book and started to read, doubtful that she would find any rest tonight.

Chapter Nine

The following evening, the ladies retired to the drawing room after dinner and the gentlemen departed for cigars and brandy in the library.

Persia made it a point to rebuff Grier and Cleo, gathering Lady Libbie and Marielle close and herding them to a chaise near the fire.

Cleo whispered near her ear. "Lady Libbie is purported to have a fortune nearly as large as our own."

Grier arched a brow and surveyed the lovely young woman. The firelight gilded her curls a lovely gold. She would meet no difficulty in securing an offer even without a fortune. Her title and beauty alone would see to that. "Indeed."

"No competition for us though. At least as I hear it. She's not here for the viscount."

"No? The duke then?"

"Well, perhaps. He should like to win her hand, I imagine." Cleo leaned in again, her voice dropping even lower. "She's baited her hook for a bigger fish than that. It's said the prince has already spoken with her father. They occupied the library at great length yesterday. Just the two of them."

Grier's heart plummeted to her stomach. She drew a ragged breath and rose to her feet, uncertain why such news should affect her. Did she think a few stares and stilted words from him meant he might actually be interested in her as a bridal candidate? He had already let her know she was acceptable for dalliance and nothing more. Lady Libbie would be an ideal match. Precisely the type of lady the prince had traveled to England to find. She possessed it all—wealth, breeding, youth, and gentility.

Grier approached the dowager and babbled an excuse. "I'm afraid I'm still wearied from travel, Your Grace."

"Of course," her hostess clucked. "According to your father the journey north was quite the trial. No wonder you're wearied."

"I shall stay on a bit longer." Cleo settled herself down on the sofa beside the dowager.

With a murmured good night for all, Grier lifted her skirts and departed the room. Her fingers caressed the deep green silk of her skirts as she moved up the stairs. The modiste insisted she wear deep, lush colors—that bold colors would complement her coloring. But tonight, beside the light and pastel colors of the other young ladies, she'd felt obtrusive.

It was as though she were proclaiming herself different. The *older* groom-hunting female with unfortunate dusky skin and unfortunate auburn hair that could hardly be contained in its pins. She despised this feeling of being somehow . . . *less*. She'd never thought anything was wrong with her before, contrary to the stinging remarks her neighbors made about her.

She genuinely liked who she was. She didn't want to change. Even after she married, she'd still be herself. She would find a gentleman who didn't mind that he'd married a woman who steered clear of needlepoint and watercolors. The prince would never be that man.

Her steps slowed as she approached the study. Male laughter rumbled from the parted doors.

She couldn't help peering within the male-only sanctuary.

She told herself it was simply curiosity. That she was not looking for anyone in particular. Her gaze swept over the half-dozen assembled gentlemen sitting in the smoke-fogged room. The prince stood near the hearth. Ever his stern, unsmiling self, he seemed at ease, if not a bit bored in his setting.

Her father's jarring voice was instantly recognizable. Her gaze sought and spotted him—the precise moment he caught sight of her. She jerked back into motion, hastening down the corridor. She didn't make it very far before she heard her name.

With a deep breath, she turned and faced Jack.

He approached, his expression stormy. "Grier? What are you doing? Where are you going? Why aren't you with the rest of the ladies?"

She released a heavy breath. "I'm tired."

His eyes flashed. "Tired? You can sleep later. You agreed—"

"Yes," she snapped. "You needn't remind me. I'm to court the dowager's grandson and any other gentleman of worthy rank." Her voice sounded as tired as she suddenly felt. "I can do that well enough tomorrow. I won't even see the gentlemen again until then. It's just the ladies in the drawing room."

He motioned wildly behind him. "You should be in there with Cleo cozying up to the dowager, winning her over so that she pushes her grandson into proposing!"

"Fear not," she bit out, feeling the heat creep up her face. "I'll get a proposal. Some fine lord desperate for funds won't pass up the fortune you're offering. Who I am, *what* I am, or how I behave won't overly signify. If it did, neither one of us would have been permitted past the gates."

He rubbed his hands together with excitement, not registering her bitter tone. "It is splendid. We're actually at a house party with the Crown Prince of Maldania! I never thought such a day would arrive." His gaze snapped back to her. "You need to put on your best performance. A fat dowry alone won't do the trick with these swells. Use your feminine wiles. You're your mother's daughter. You must have some skill in that arena."

The heat in her face was blistering now. His words shouldn't sting her—her skin was tougher than that—but they did. "Don't speak of my mother."

He shrugged. "I've a right to do so. After all, she and I were—"

"Another word on the subject and I'll leave." She knew next to nothing of her mother's relationship with Jack Hadley and she preferred to keep it that way. The knowledge that they conceived her was enough. She wanted to keep the stories Papa told her about her mother as her only facts. Not whatever sordid tale Jack would spin.

Jack puffed his chest and tugged at his waistcoat. "You need to make your mind up if you really want to do this."

"I do!"

"Then make yourself amenable and stop being such a contrary creature." He looked her up and down. "Aside of my fortune there's not much to recommend you to this lot."

"Nor you," she bit back. "You eat your soup like a pig at a trough."

For a moment it looked like he might explode at her, but then a grin split his weathered face. "Yes, I've my share of flaws. Perhaps that's what makes us family. As ourselves, we're thoroughly defective." Without another word he turned and left her standing in the corridor.

Defective. The word sat like a boulder in her

stomach. Yes, that's how the prince probably saw her. In that moment, she wished she'd never met her father. Never discovered just who he was. The mystery of him that she'd lived with for most of her life was better than this reality.

But then Trevis swam before her eyes and she recalled that she'd come because she had to. There had been nothing left for her in Wales. She couldn't have remained on as Trevis's game master after everything.

Her fate rested in her hands now.

Turning, she fled down the corridor, away from her father, away from the library and the deep voices of the men.

She would forge her destiny in her own way and time. Not because Jack Hadley demanded it of her.

Sev stepped from the shadows, watching thoughtfully as Miss Hadley fled the corridor. As far as he was concerned, her father was as foul and brutish as the lowest fishmonger. And yet Miss Hadley stood toe to toe with him. Dignified even. Regal as a queen.

He winced and shook his head, quickly banishing that thought. He'd seen queens. Known several, including his own mother and grandmother.

Miss Grier Hadley was nothing like them. Not at all refined and distinguished. She'd never be deferential to her husband. She'd never speak with slow gentle tones that charmed audiences.

He would keep searching until he found a woman like that. He'd promised his grandfather as much. He'd keep searching until he succeeded in finding a suitable female to be the future queen of Maldania. That was the foremost concern. Who would be the future queen. Not who would be the woman he'd bind his body and soul to before God. He doubted such a woman would ever exist for him. Nor did he have the luxury of finding her.

Even knowing this, believing it with every fiber of his being, he found himself walking away from his shadowed corner, away from the library full of men eager for his company.

With hard, firm steps he followed in the wake of Miss Hadley.

Shortly upon fleeing her father, Grier quickly realized she was lost in the labyrinth of hallways. With her head spinning and temper high, she hadn't paid much attention to which corridor led to her bedchamber.

Biting her lip, she studied each door. She seemed to recall that her bedchamber had been toward the end of a corridor and on the right. Yes, definitely the right. Selecting a door she imagined looked familiar, she closed her hand around the latch and eased it open to peer inside.

She was mistaken. The chamber was not hers.

In fact, it was not a bedchamber at all. Several instruments stared back at her, nestled among furnishings of faded and worn fabric.

Moonlight bathed the room, streaming through the parted draperies. She stepped more fully into the pearlescent light, her steps muffled on the carpet. A reverent hush lingered in the room, as if every instrument within waited in anticipation for her to attend them and create music. As if they'd been waiting years for someone to care about them again.

A wistful smile curved her lips. She drifted further inside the bereft room, letting her fingers stroke the strings of a beautiful harp. Papa had loved music. Almost every household in Wales possessed a harp. Many an hour he sat before the fire and played either the harp or his hornpipe for her.

Her smile wavered a bit as thoughts of him rushed over her. She missed him. Especially on an evening like this—when faced with Jack Hadley and the glaring reality that he would never be *that* kind of father to her. Never doting and affectionate. That was something she'd lost and could never reclaim.

A lump thickened her throat as she accepted that she may never know that kind of unconditional love again. She fought to swallow, but try as she might, she couldn't dislodge the thick lump.

Without lifting the instrument, she strummed a few chords of the harp, closing her eyes against the surge of emotion rising within her.

Papa, if you were still here none of this would be happening. I'd be safe with you at home. I wouldn't so desperately crave acceptance and respectability because the love you gave me always meant more than any of that. I could tolerate it all when I had you.

She couldn't help the pathetic thoughts from winding through her head. It was weak and useless thinking, but she allowed herself the feelings. For now. Tomorrow she would be her stalwart self again and forget that deep down she longed for something as ephemeral as love.

Footfalls sounded behind her. Grier whirled around, almost expecting to find Jack returning to castigate her further.

It wasn't Jack. No, worse than that.

She inhaled thinly through her nostrils and blinked burning eyes, determined that he not see the evidence of how close to tears she was.

"What are you doing?" she demanded. "Following me now? Haven't you someone else to bother?" She blinked free the lingering burn in her eyes. "Someone who might welcome your attentions? You're a bloody prince after all. You shouldn't be caught speaking with me."

He stared, saying nothing. Her chest tightened as she gazed upon his face, his features starkly handsome in the room's gloom, even tense and brooding as usual.

She gave a harsh laugh, shaking her head. "What do you want?"

He merely stared.

She stared at him in frustration, wondering why he did not speak . . . wondering why he was here at all. Had he come to insult her with another indecent proposition? An ever so helpful reminder of where he thought she belonged in the order of things? Or had he come to bewilder her further by treating her almost kindly—as when he complimented her singing.

The prince slid a hand inside his deep black waistcoat and pulled out a handkerchief, extending it to her with a steady hand. She stared at the pristine white square rather resentfully.

"What's that for?"

"There appears to be a . . . glimmer in your eyes," he explained, his words stoic, like he was uncomfortable pointing out the fact that she was on the verge of tears.

"There is not," she snapped.

Just the same, she snatched the fabric from his hands, careful not to brush those blunt-tipped fingers. She turned and dabbed at her eyes.

After a moment, she peered over her shoulder, tensing, waiting, dreading for him to ask why she was upset. The last thing she wanted to do was unburden herself to him. As if he would care.

She dropped her gaze to the soft patch of linen in her hands and looked back at him curiously. Well. Perhaps he cared a *little*. At least enough to extend her the courtesy of his handkerchief. A fact which did not mesh with the opinion she'd formed of him.

Frowning, she motioned back toward the doors. "Any number of individuals would gladly grovel at your feet. You are wasting your exalted company on me." She offered him back his handkerchief.

He shrugged, and accepted it, replying with an idleness that set her teeth on edge, "One can only abide so much groveling."

"So you seek someone who will not pander to your ego, is that it? Is that why you've followed me? You wish to consort with someone who will denounce you for what you are?"

"And what am I?" His gold cat eyes danced with something dangerously akin to merriment as he stopped before her. Close. Too bloody close. "Do enlighten me."

She could smell him. He smelled like no man she'd ever smelled. Not that she went about sniffing men, but she'd stood close to a few. He smelled clean and crisp and . . . and *manly*. Was that a scent? A faint whiff of brandy teased her nose. Was this what a prince smelled like, then?

She swallowed, suddenly unable to speak. His nearness rattled her. Her tongue struggled to form the words.

"Come now, you claim to possess the courage to denounce me." His gaze looked her up and down.

His seductive, rolling accents stroked like velvet against her skin. His voice was an aphrodisiac, impossible to resist. She took a hasty step back. She must. Otherwise she would be just what he judged her. Not a lady at all—no better than a light-skirt.

"*I do!*" she retorted. "You're a bounder—and a snob!" She lifted her chin a notch. Not such a simple task when he stood so much taller than she. "You'll not see me making a ninny of myself simply because you were born with a golden spoon in your mouth."

Wrong, perhaps, but he became the perfect target for her ire—for the despondency that had filled her the moment she stepped within this room. He never knew what it felt like to be lost or lonely . . . or rejected for the circumstances of his birth. Indeed not. The circumstances of his birth afforded him great advantages.

"And why is that, Miss Hadley? Why are you so opposed to showing me the due reverence everyone else does?" he prompted, his keen eyes fixed on her in that ever unnerving way.

"Aside from the boorish things I overheard you say about me upon our first encounter?" For some reason she couldn't make herself bring up the reminder of his proposition. Just the two of them, alone in a room no one would likely enter . . . it seemed a bad idea. As though she perhaps wanted him to remember. Wanted him to recall that he'd found her attractive and put his hands on her . . .

"Why should you take my words so personally?

You *are* illegitimate. Daughter to a man with a most unsavory reputation." Even as he spoke, his expression remained cool and impassive . . . as though he were not being the least insulting. "Fortune withstanding, you are exceedingly unsuitable."

"And what are you?" she shot back, her temper simmering at a dangerous degree. She inhaled a deep, angry breath that lifted her chest high. "You're nothing more than a penniless prince with a country drowning in debt!"

His mild expression dissolved. A steeliness entered his eyes, but still she pushed on. "Oh, indeed! I've heard the tales. Gossip flows both ways. Just as you've heard the rumors about me, I've heard the whispers about you. Your ego and arrogance are certainly without justification given your dire straits, and yet you still act the haughty prince—"

"I am a prince—with all the responsibilities and duties that accompany the title," he countered. "It's not an *act*, Miss Hadley."

The tightness of his formal address should have alerted her to his sudden turn of mood, but still she could not hold her tongue.

Abruptly, he became the cause of it all—everything that was wrong in her world.

"A prince of a lost kingdom," she shot back. She

knew she was being unkind, but he had not been particularly kind to her. "I heard you lost half the men in your country to your war."

His expression altered. The carved mask of stone cracked, and she knew she had pushed too far.

He grasped her arm and yanked her close, thrusting his face near hers. "It was never *my* war. I didn't start it. I was scarcely a man when it began, but I had to face the hard reality of it. I sure as hell didn't *want* it, but I ended it. Take heed, you know nothing of which you speak," he hissed.

She glared down at where he gripped her arm. "Perhaps ladies in your country find primeval manhandling charming, perhaps even the delightful Lady Libbie would enjoy such treatment. Why don't you seek her out and unhand me?"

He said nothing. Simply stared—clung to her arm with hard fingers.

Grier inhaled raggedly, her chest rising and falling with deep breaths. She couldn't remember ever feeling so angry. And truth be told, it wasn't all entirely at him. She found herself frustrated with this whole wretched scenario. Finding a husband . . . a man who only wanted to marry her for her sudden fortune . . . It was becoming quite the distasteful task, contrary to the hope she had felt when she started this whole endeavor.

She shook her head. This night had simply been too much. Her temper had gotten away with her.

She glared down at his hand on her arm. He followed her gaze before lifting his stare back to her face. "Perhaps Lady Libbie is a *lady* who doesn't go about casting aspersions on those whom she does not know."

"Perhaps," she returned, not about to argue that she was more ladylike than the elegant Lady Libbie. Garbed in her silks and satins, Grier felt about as out of place as an elephant in the dowager's drawing room.

The moment stretched interminably, so unbearably intense as they stared at each other that Grier thought she could hear the rush of blood in her ears.

She felt the clear shape of his hand, each press of his fingers on her arm. Awareness of their closeness, the shocking intimacy of the situation, came crashing down over her. Her gaze flicked around the empty music room with its lonely instruments.

Her skin snapped, awake and alive. In fact all of her felt alive.

More alive than she had felt in quite some time.

Her gaze drifted, settled on his perfectly carved lips. Temptation incarnate. A man's lips should not look so beautiful. He was as seductive as the princes of all her girlhood fairytales. For a moment she allowed herself to forget that this prince lacked the heroic qualities to accompany such looks, that he thought her unsuitable, a mere nobody rubbing elbows with her betters.

With a deep breath, she let herself forget all of that. She let herself step outside her numb self and dive into *life*.

Before she could regain her common sense and think to stop herself—before she could let *him* think enough to stop her, she stood on her tiptoes and slid a hand around his neck, delighting in the sensation of his silky hair against her fingers.

This. She'd have *this* before sentencing herself to a cold marriage of practicality, to a life of loneliness.

Chapter Ten

 $\mathcal{G}$ rier glimpsed the prince's widening eyes as she pressed her lips to his. Her heart beat so fiercely she feared it might burst from her chest. *Almost.* If she allowed herself to think about what she was doing and allowed such a thing as fear to enter her heart.

She saw nothing anymore as her eyes fluttered shut.

In closing her eyes, she only *felt*. She surrendered herself to sensation, to the waking of desire within her blood.

She was no stranger to kisses, but it had been a while. The moment she tasted the prince's lips, she knew he was the perfect cure for her numbness.

For several heartbeats he didn't move, held himself still as marble against her, and she feared his rejection. That he would set her away from him.

Then his arms slipped around her and he was kissing her back, his lips parting against hers. She opened her own mouth for him with a small gasp. He swallowed that sound, drank it deep into himself. She pressed herself closer, tighter against him, her muscles straining to get nearer.

A shudder racked him when she tentatively tasted him with her tongue. She buried her hands in his hair, pulling him down just as he urged her up against him. He tasted her back and she moaned at the sinuous stroking of his tongue along her own.

His large hands roamed over her back, holding her tightly, fiercely. One of those hands slid around to span her rib cage, his thumb grazing the underside of one aching breast, and her body burned from the inside out.

There was nothing delicate or dandified in the way he kissed. She felt consumed. By her own desire and by the magic of his expert mouth on hers. Her hands delved deeper into his hair. With a hard tug on the strands, she forced his head to a different angle, repositioning his head for her and slanting her mouth against his one way, and then another. She didn't know herself anymore, this woman, this stranger losing herself, taking, seizing what she craved as if it were hers. As if *he* were hers.

He groaned into her mouth, and the sound shuddered through her.

She relished the feverish movement of his lips on hers, the slide of his tongue deep in her mouth. He made her feel wanted, and that made her feel powerful. In that moment, she didn't feel as if any of it could ever be enough—as if she could ever have enough of him.

Impossible as it seemed, the kiss deepened. They staggered together, clutching one another, stopping only when they collided with a pianoforte.

He nipped at her bottom lip and then sucked the bruised flesh into his mouth, clutching her closer for his starving mouth.

And still she wasn't close enough. Her body hummed, alive and awake as she hadn't ever felt before. That's all that mattered. The extraordinary thrill of this moment.

She wanted to crawl into his drugging warmth, let it continue its waking heat through her. Nothing could ruin this moment.

Nothing except him.

As she dragged her lips to his jaw, kissing his bristly flesh, his voice rumbled in her ear. "My, my, Miss Hadley, I had no idea such a hellcat lurked beneath. Perhaps you've reconsidered my offer."

She stilled, his words sinking in, reminding her where she was, *who* she was . . . who *he* was.

The fire in her blood cooled. The humming life that had so thrilled her slipped away until she was naught but the cold, numb shell again.

However nothing had doused his ardor. His hand drifted up from her rib cage to brush over her breast. The touch jolted her, sparked her to move, to react as any female of proper breeding should. *As any unwed female who had not initiated a passionate kiss would do.*

The crack of her palm against his cheek rang through the cavernous room. His arms dropped from her.

She stumbled away, gaping at him as he lifted a hand to his cheek, fingering the afflicted flesh.

"What was that for?" he demanded.

"You—you—" Her hand waved between the two of them, words of outrage strangling in her throat.

"Kissed you *back*?" he finished.

"No!" she denied. "You touched my—" She swallowed, unable to say, unable to utter how close she had come to surrendering herself to the wretch. "You touched *me*. *Intimately*."

"The way you *attacked* me with your lips, is it any surprise? I thought that's where we were headed."

"So this is *my* fault?" she charged, even as a small voice inside her head whispered, *Yes. This is your fault. You attacked him with your lips like a man-starved harlot. Just as he said.*

Heat swept over her face. "You were hardly a victim of my attentions."

He shrugged in the shadowy room. "I reacted as any red-blooded man. I did not expect my *touch* would be unwelcome to someone so eager to kiss me in the first place."

Mortified, she closed her eyes in a slow blink. She could deny nothing he said. She'd behaved the wanton and then slapped him when he reciprocated.

She opened her mouth to apologize. For everything. The kiss. The slap. She loathed nothing as much as admitting she was wrong. A weakness, to be sure, for she knew she was far from perfect. Papa had accused her of being too headstrong on more than one occasion, and rightly so.

Only she didn't get the chance to utter those difficult words.

He stepped back from her, putting space between them as though she were something foul. And he likely thought she was. A tart or *worse*. The terrible notion seized her. What if he thought she was a desperate debutante hoping to get herself compromised so she could land herself a prince?

Hot gall rose up in her chest that he should think such a thing of her. The bitter taste coated her mouth at the thought of his suspecting she had set her cap for him. *Holy hellfire!* She fumbled with her hands, unsure where to put them and desperate to appear dignified now—to bury the wild, tempestuous female of moments ago and convince him she was a staid, respectable female with no designs on his person.

She watched him as he wiped a broad palm against his jacket, as if the feel of her was a regrettable sensation.

"Perhaps we should avoid each other during our stay here," he announced.

His words stung. Absurd, of course. She completely agreed with him. Nothing good ever came from their encounters. He didn't like her and she didn't like him—contrary to that brief lapse in judgment moments ago when she had thrown herself into his arms. He was an escape. A break from the numbness. That's all the kiss had been.

She had seized a chance to feel again, to let sensation flood her as she lost herself in the arms of an attractive man.

She nodded roughly. They simply couldn't get along. Every time they shared the same space sparks flew, and not sparks of the good variety. Well, any variety was really not to be desired with him.

She stopped nodding and finally found her voice. "I couldn't agree more. You're obviously here to pay court—"

"Not to you," he cut in, his voice angry.

"I know that," she gritted past clenched teeth. "And I wouldn't want you to court me, make no mistake of that."

He gave her a look that said he didn't believe her. And she admitted to herself that she probably wouldn't believe her, either. What girl wouldn't want to be a princess? Even tomboy that she was, she'd often fantasized about living in a castle with a hundred-horse stable. It had been her favorite fantasy as she fell asleep every night.

She perched a hand on her hip. "Just because I kissed you doesn't mean I *like* you. You were a welcome diversion from what's been a less than pleasant few days."

"Diversion?" He crossed his arms over his

chest, clearly not liking the sound of that. Satisfaction curled through her. It was nice to offend him for a change.

Her lips twitched as her gaze swept over him— every glorious masculine inch. She knew it was improbable that anyone had ever called him a diversion before. Women probably thought the sun rose and set upon his manly visage. She was glad to make a dent in his overinflated ego.

She lifted her chin. "Yes. It won't happen again, rest assured. The experience wasn't quite what I hoped for," she lied.

His cat-gold eyes swept over her as if he didn't quite know what to think. A smile threatened her lips again. She doubted she was like any female of his acquaintance.

He straightened. "Happy to hear that, then. I'd hate for you to think that our interlude meant anything."

"Oh, I wouldn't think that," she assured in her most offhand tone.

He stared at her for a long moment, his gaze penetrating through the shadows, searching her face. She held herself poised, as still as an arrow that moment before it flies from its bow. Finally he broke his gaze, turned from her, and strode out the door without a backward glance.

Grier waited several moments, gathering her breath and her composure before making her way from the room. Her steps fell silently as she moved down the corridor, her shadow stretching long into the night.

"Where've you been, ol' boy?" Malcolm asked.

Sev downed his brandy in one smooth move before motioning for the waiting footman to refill his glass. He cursed under his breath at the sight of his shaking hand.

"Nowhere."

"Well, you were *nowhere* for some time."

Sev shrugged. "Took a stroll. It clears my head."

"What do you need to clear your head about? The world lies sprawled before you, yours for the taking. You've won the war and you have the plumpest of heiresses baited on hooks for your choosing. Life, cousin, for you at any rate, is good."

Indeed, he should agree with that sentiment. For the first time in years, his country was at peace. He was alive and his kingdom was on the mend. He should be able to put the years of war and pain and loss and uncertainty behind him. He should.

Malcolm stared at him, still waiting for a response.

"I only needed a bit of air," he replied, once again vague.

"Ah." Malcolm smiled as if suddenly understanding. "Would that air happen to be in the company of a certain Lady Libbie?"

Sev grimaced. The lovely Lady Libbie had not even been in the vicinity of his thoughts, which was unfortunate because she was on the top of his list of prospective brides and the reason he found himself here at all. He'd already received her father's hearty approval for the match.

His cousin mistook his grimace for guilt, it seemed. "Ah, I see."

Malcolm winked in an exaggerated manner and Sev was quite certain he did not *see* anything at all. With a covert look for the other gentlemen in the room, he leaned in close. "Well, she is a fetching bit of skirt, I'll give you that. Couldn't blame you for stealing away with her for a spell. And her papa did encourage you to better acquaint yourselves, did he not?" A snort of laughter followed this.

Sev slammed down his drink. "I wasn't with *her.*" Too late he realized he overly emphasized *her.*

"Oh." Malcolm's eyebrows winged high. "Not her, eh? Who then?"

Sev merely grunted and flung back another

drink. He wasn't about to confess he'd been occupied with the elder Miss Hadley and have Malcolm think there was something afoot between the two of them. Because that most assuredly was *not* the case.

Certainly she had kissed him with all the fire and skill of a seasoned courtesan, but that meant nothing. His cheek still stung from the memory of what Grier Hadley thought of their kiss . . . thought of *him*. He was not the sort to chase any woman. If she was not interested in a dalliance, then so be it. He wasn't interested in her.

What desire could he feel for a female who insulted him and the country he'd spent half his life fighting for? She was not the sort of female he liked at all. Too impertinent. Too tall—sunbrowned and freckled as any field hand.

Suddenly her bright eyes, seductive and heavy-lidded as they had been in that shadowy music room, filled his memory, and his throat went dry. Naturally he'd responded to her. She was a warm, willing female, and he was merely a hot-blooded man. Certainly there was nothing he found appealing about the female. Nothing at all.

Still, the image of Miss Hadley swam through his mind and the taste of her burned on his lips.

He set his unfinished drink down. Malcolm

blinked up at him. "I believe I'll retire for the night. I should like to rise early for a morning ride."

"In this weather?"

Sev snorted, recalling spending many nights in tents with arctic winds raging outside and distant cannon fire lulling him to sleep. "An English winter is no match for Maldania in winter. You should remember that."

Malcolm's eyes clouded over. "Perhaps. I was just a boy when we were banished."

Sev nodded and squeezed his cousin's shoulder, regretting reminding Malcolm of the sore subject. "You know you are free to return home. Grandfather does not blame you for your father's transgressions."

"It fails to signify. Mother shall never set foot on Maldanian soil again, and I cannot leave her here. It's all water under the bridge at any rate. I'm an Englishman now. Thank God they love titles. I may be destitute, but I have no dearth of invitations to the finest homes and parties. I'll not starve."

Sev clapped his cousin on the back. "There is that."

"Maybe I'll wed an heiress myself. Mother says it's about time." Malcolm scanned the room with a judicious eye, his gaze stopping on Jack Hadley. "One of the Hadley chits could be ideal. That fiery one with the freckles who tossed her drink on you." He chuckled. "Bet she'd be a fine ride between the sheets. No boring romp there."

Sev's hands fisted at his sides. "Leave her be," he commanded.

Malcolm looked sharply at him. "What? She might be unsuitable for you, but not me. She'd probably be grateful for my regard. She hasn't had an easy time of it."

"She's mine." He didn't anticipate the words. Did not know he felt so possessive toward her until he uttered them.

Yet staring at his cousin's shocked face, he found he did not regret them.

"Yours?"

Now was the time to take back his words. To explain he meant something else. "You heard me." The notion of Malcolm—or any man—laying a finger on her filled him with a deadly rage.

He did not regret the words and yet he should not have said them. Should not feel them.

With a tight nod, he bade good night and left the room, before he said anything else he could not retract.

Chapter Eleven

$\mathscr{A}$ misty dawn peeked through the parted drapes as Grier hurriedly dressed in her riding habit, a fashionable burgundy velvet ensemble trimmed in violet fur. She paused long enough to roll her eyes at her reflection.

The sight of her attired thusly was ridiculous when she thought about herself a month ago in her small, thatched-roof cottage. A pang of longing for that simple abode and simple life consumed her. She quickly squashed the sentiment, reminding herself she had left because that life had suddenly ceased to be so simple.

No use longing for her trousers. She'd left them behind . . . along with everything else she used to be.

Lifting her chin at a determined angle, she

coiled her plaited hair atop her head and hastily pinned the unruly mass in place, not caring if the wind made short work of her efforts. From the way it howled against the mullioned panes of glass, likely nothing she did would keep her hair tidy. She wouldn't let a little thing like that stop her. The prospect of a solitary ride through the countryside was too great. Her efforts would have to suffice. She certainly wasn't going to call a maid to attend to her hair at this early hour.

Even as she hurried to slip from the house before anyone else woke, her lips twisted in a smile at the unlikelihood. She'd learned that the aristocracy didn't rouse before noon.

The prince flashed across her mind, an image of him wrapped in luxurious bedding, sheets tangled around his legs. Legs she had noticed appeared strikingly muscular in his trousers. Not what she would have imagined for a dandified prince.

She cringed and banished the too frequent image of him from her head. He would not cloud her thoughts this morning, casting a pall over her much-anticipated ride. He'd done that enough last night.

Rising from her dressing stool, she slipped quietly from the room.

* * *

Sev rode hard across the countryside. He lost track of time as the wind churned around him, tugging through his hair and chafing his cheeks. A soft predawn gray tinged the air, so he knew it was still early. The world breathed its quiet breath around him, and he reveled in it.

He felt alive, which was something unique considering that a little over a year ago he was on a battlefield soaked in his brother's blood, certain that he, too, would be the next one cut down.

He shook off the bleak memory of that day when his world spun forever off course, when he no longer became the "spare" but the heir to a kingdom.

He was here for Gregor, so that his death was not in vain. Even more than that, he was here for every single one of his countrymen who died on a battlefield. He owed it to them to stick it out and bring home a bride who would help inject life back into Maldania. His own personal preferences mattered not at all.

For some reason, the image of Miss Hadley floated before him. Scowling, he bent low and kicked the horse faster, until both he and the stallion were winded and panting hard. When his mount became lathered, he pulled back on the reins.

At the crest of a hill, he pulled the beast to a halt, rubbing his neck. "Good lad," he murmured. "Got you sweating even in this cold."

Sitting back, he stared down at the picturesque landscape. Snow draped the forest-thick valley. Winter-withered greens and browns peeked out at him from the veil of white.

After sleeping in tents for several past winters now, he was quite immune to the cold. This time of year, one could see nothing save a blinding white blanket surrounding the palace. Even the bark of the trees was difficult to detect.

His thoughts drifted to his grandfather. At his age, he was not so unaffected by the elements, even snug in his bed within the palace. The winters were always the hardest. Gave him aches and pains that only worsened with every passing year. The old man had hung on this long, lasting through the war, but Sev could not expect him to last much longer.

Leaving Maldania, he'd determined to give his grandfather peace. To reassure him that not only was the war over and the country on the mend, but that the Maksimi line was secure upon the throne for a generation more.

That being the case, he needed to get the matter of finding an acceptable bride over and done. He'd hoped to return home before spring with a wife already increasing with his future heir.

And yet he had not approached the matter of finding a bride with the haste needed for that to happen. He released a pent-up breath as he faced the bitter truth. He was dragging his feet. It was time to tackle matrimony with all due speed. With fresh resolve, he turned his mount around, hesitating when he caught a flash of movement in the distance. Pausing, he squinted into the distance. A horse and rider streaked across a snow-dappled rise.

For a moment he marveled that anyone else should be up this early, but then his breath seized in his chest.

The rider was female. Even from his vantage he recognized the wild mane of auburn hair flowing loose in the wind. As he stared down at the distant figure riding hell-bent across the landscape, he knew no other female would take it upon herself to ride so early for a solitary ride.

It took him a moment to realize she rode *too* fast. He sucked in a breath. Evidently she'd lost control of the beast she rode, a stallion she had no business riding in the first place. Senseless female!

He pushed aside his questions of her intelligence. Now wasn't the time to consider the ill-bred female's reckless ways.

With a deep cry, he dug in his heels and sent his mount soaring down the hillside, snow and mud kicking up around him in great wet clods.

Bloody hell, she was fast. And she had a lengthy lead on him. He lost sight of her as she dove into thick trees. He followed, cringing inwardly, imagining he was going to have to peel her off one of the ancient oaks and carry her corpse back to the house. The thought spurred him on to a dangerous, breakneck pace, and he soon caught sight of her again. She flashed in and out of the trees ahead, a rich burgundy blur.

Her hair whipped in the air like a wild banner.

He shouted for her, but the sound was swallowed in the wind. The fierce air tore at his face and eyes, blurring his vision.

Icy wind stung his eyes. He blinked rapidly and hunkered low over his mount's neck. The hooves of his stallion pounded the earth, and he felt the wet spray of snow and earth all the way up to his thighs as he careened down an incline, at last drawing abreast with her.

That's when she saw him.

Her eyes flared wide in her expressive face. In that split instant he noted that the freckles on her nose seemed darker against her pale skin. She opened her mouth and shouted something indecipherable over the screech of wind and thundering of hooves.

She clutched her reins in her gloved hands and he quickly surmised that he wouldn't be able to wrestle them from her grasp. She was undoubtedly too panicked to release that lifeline.

He could do only one thing, rash as it seemed. There was no other choice.

Releasing his own reins, he dove from his mount and across the air separating them. He snatched her up, mindful to wrap his arms around her. He managed to twist in the air, turning to take the brunt of the fall.

He hit the snow-covered earth with a jar. Stunned, he lay there for a moment, registering little beyond the thundering hooves vibrating the ground and fading away into the distance.

A sharp jab to the shoulder forced him to peel his head off the ground and look up—stare into the flushed face of a furious Miss Hadley.

"Holy hellfire!" She blew at several strands of auburn hair dangling riotously before her eyes. "What's wrong with you? Are you mad? Is it your custom to go about tackling women down from their mounts?"

He gawked at her as she pushed back the wild fall of hair from her face and glared down at him, abruptly, achingly aware that every soft inch of her was draped over him. His mouth suddenly grew dry.

"You're lucky you didn't break your neck—*my* neck!" she hotly corrected.

With a groan, he dropped his head back down on the earth, mindless of the icy-wet. The hat he wore was lost in his frenzied ride. "Is this the thanks I get for saving you?"

"Saving me? From what?"

Was she dim-witted? Had the fall knocked something loose in her head? "Your horse ran away with you."

"What on earth makes you think that?"

He lifted his head back up to stare at her. "I saw you racing out of control—"

She made a disgusted sound and scrambled off him as if he were somehow contagious. "Don't tell me you're so antiquated you've never seen a woman ride before?"

He propped himself up on his elbows. "Indeed, I've not seen a woman ride *sidesaddle* at such a foolish speed."

She smirked down at him, propped her hands

on her hips. "You should see me ride astride then. I daresay you would be quiet impressed."

Arrogant chit. He tried not to smile at her utter gall, reminding himself that he had nearly broken their necks while under a misapprehension, however reasonable a misapprehension it might have been.

Her smile slipped a bit when he unfolded himself to loom over her.

"You . . . ride astride?" No proper lady would do such a thing. It was too incredible.

At her nod, he blew out a deep breath. Was there no end to her astoundingly unseemly ways?

"I loathe the constraints of a riding habit," she returned blithely. "When I ride, it's usually astride. I only conceded this time having no wish to offend the duchess's sensibilities." She gestured at her figure to illustrate her very proper riding habit. He deliberately tried not to focus on how her riding habit hugged her curves. The mere notion of her in trousers sent a surge of heat in his blood. He scowled. As he couldn't bed her and he most certainly couldn't *wed* her, his attraction to such an unacceptable female was really becoming a nuisance.

"You're quite the hoyden."

Color flooded her already windburned cheeks. "Because I eschew the constraints imposed by men on ladies of *Society*?" She gave a small stamp of her booted foot, as if this were a sore subject with her. "Because I enjoy living and not being stuck indoors browsing fashion plates and working on needlepoint?" With a growl of what he assumed was frustration, she whirled in a circle, scanning the countryside. "Holy hellfire! Thanks to you our mounts are probably already back in the stables."

"Again, I'm struggling to see how this is my fault."

Without another word or glance for him, she started marching away with long, sure strides.

He stood still for some moments, amazed as he watched her retreat. She was without a doubt the most singular female he had ever encountered. She wasn't impressed by him or daunted. Most females tittered in his presence, in awe of either his title or his form. He towered over most gentlemen with their lily-white hands and soft, fleshy bodies. Years of combat had given him a muscled physique. He was accustomed to inspiring admiration or at the very least deference in the fairer sex.

With a sigh, he followed after the termagant. In moments he caught up with her. His boots crunched softly over the snow, alerting her to his presence.

She slid him a wary glance as they marched. "You really thought you were saving me?"

He grunted. "A wasted effort on you, it seems. I'm gathering you're not the type of female ever in need of rescuing."

A smile twitched her mouth. "No, I'm not. I've been on my own now for years."

He frowned. "And how is that? You are not without family. Your father—"

"He is scarcely a father to me," she quickly inserted. "We've only just recently reunited. My mother passed away when I was very young. I have no memory of her. My . . . stepfather raised me."

He sensed the sorrow in her as she uttered this, the difficulty she'd had in saying the word *step-father*, and knew that this man had been a true father to her.

"I'm sorry," he murmured. "I know the pain of losing someone you care about. I lost my brother in the war. He was everything to me. To our people." He swallowed against a rising tightness in his throat. "He would have made a much better king than I ever shall."

She slowed her pace and sent him a peculiar

look before continuing her strides. She shook her head.

"What?" he prompted, touching her arm and making her face him again.

She angled her head, tossing her tangle of auburn hair. She tried to capture the tendrils that blew across her wind-chapped face. "I did not expect humility from you." She tugged a strand from her lips.

"Oh." He squared his shoulders, the wind whipping his face not nearly as icy as the inexplicable surge of cold he felt at hearing she thought he was some unfeeling monster. "Well, you do not really know me."

"I suppose not." She nodded once. "Just as you know nothing of me."

He couldn't resist. He reached out and pulled several strands of hair free that clung to one wind-chafed cheek. "I think I'm beginning to know you."

She cocked an eyebrow. "Indeed? A few brief encounters where we spar words constitutes familiarity?" She crossed her arms in front of her. Trying to erect a barrier, he supposed. Her voice was withering as she asked, "You mean you didn't know me when you said I was *common*? When you said I was fit for a mistress but not a wife?"

He winced. "That was badly done of me."

She snorted. "But nothing you disagree with. And yet I suppose that's the closest I'll ever get to an apology." If possible her eyebrow winged higher. "You're sorry I overheard you, not that you actually said unpleasant things about me. *To* me. As far as you're concerned I'm still some lowly serf unfit for your *estimable* company."

With a huff, she stalked ahead of him, kicking snow up around her hem as she marched.

With several long strides, he caught up with her. Grabbing her by the arm, he whirled her around. "Why must you be so combative? I'm trying to make amends." The words astonished him the instant he said them. He was trying to make amends? With a woman who should be beneath his notice.

"Why?" She tried to twist her arm free from him, but still he clung. "Why should you care—"

"Because—" He stopped at the sound of his voice, loud and jarring. "Because," he repeated, his voice level, "I suspect you are one of the most singular women I'll ever know." His face heated at the declaration. It was as if the words spilled forth with no volition.

She eyed him suspiciously as if unsure whether he complimented her or not. "Singular?"

Truth be told, he wasn't certain whether he complimented her or not either. He only knew he spoke the truth. "Singular," he repeated. "And I should hate for you to . . ." He hesitated, searching for the word. "Dislike me because of the way I conducted myself on our first encounter."

She moistened her lips. His gut tightened as he followed the movement of her pink tongue. "You care whether I like you or not?"

He gave a single nod, wondering how he'd gotten into such dangerous territory. He was actually trying to convince the female that he liked her. Why? To what end? Did he expect for them to be friends? That did not seem realistic. He'd never been friends with a woman before.

"Why?" Her eyes narrowed on him. "Why should you care whether I like you?"

The only thing he could think about just then was his ominous warning to his cousin. When he'd staked a claim on Miss Hadley and called her *his*.

With that single thought burning through him, he inched his head toward hers, moving in slow degrees, as a hunter might close in on his prey. "I fear if you did not like me, I would never be able to do this."

Chapter Twelve

Grier watched with wide eyes as the prince's head descended toward her, certain she was dreaming. He slanted his lips over hers. She didn't draw breath as the cool dryness of his mouth pressed to hers.

This was no dream.

She didn't move, not even a stir. Much too shocked, too afraid that should she move it would be to toss her arms around his neck and drag him tighter against her. It had been too long since she had *this*. Since anyone felt inclined to reach out and touch her. She didn't trust herself. Last night proved she shouldn't.

He pulled back to look at her and her chest tightened at the sight of his handsome face. This close she could see that the tips of his lashes were far lighter than the rest of his hair.

His lips curved in a slow, seductive smile that pulled at her belly. "And I'm so glad that I can."

"Can . . . *what*?" Her head felt like it was stuffed full of cotton.

"Kiss you."

The words rolled over her, thick as syrup. And just as decadent.

"Oh." She blinked, murmuring rather dreamily, "Yes. Kissing. You can do that . . . some more."

"Excellent. Although you should know that this sort of thing generally works better when you move your mouth." His head inched back toward her, his breath fanning her lips. "When you part your lips. Just a little. Remember?"

Her eyes drifted shut, lulled by that deep velvet voice, by the brush of his lips on hers. His breath was warm and sweet and she sighed.

She moved her lips tentatively at first, her thoughts racing, jumbled, trying to remember why this was wrong . . . why she shouldn't be doing this. She'd known why last night.

All thoughts fled as he deepened the kiss, parting her lips wider for him. She shuddered at the first stroke of his tongue against hers and lifted her hands to his shoulders. She curled her fingers

into the hard shape of him beneath his great cape
and surrendered to his mouth, kissing him back.
Their lips fused hotly, the perfect fit, like two long-
lost pieces of a puzzle.

She wrapped her arms around him, clinging,
pressing herself close with abandon. He moaned
with satisfaction and slipped his hands beneath
her cloak. Palming her back, he hauled her
against him.

Splayed against the hard breadth of him, she
was instantly enveloped in his heat. The wintry
world around them disappeared. There was nothing but him. His hard pulsing body. His warm
hands. His mouth. Those delicious lips with the
faint taste of chicory coffee.

He slanted his mouth over hers one way and
then another, exploring her, tasting, gliding his
tongue sinuously against hers until a low throbbing twisted in her belly.

The kiss deepened until they clung to each
other. Her hands moved, roved, reveling in the
impossible strength she felt radiating from every
inch of him.

Small starved whimpers rose from her throat.
He slid one hand down her back and grasped her
bottom, pulling her against him. She felt the definite bulge of him through his trousers. She was

no green girl that she didn't know what that signified. He wanted her.

It should have horrified her to know that she was all alone with a virile man, engaging in intimacies that could lead to only one thing. That should be reserved for her husband.

And yet she was not. In that moment, Grier did not care.

All her life she'd tried so hard to do what she thought was *right*, the good and proper thing. She'd tried so desperately to earn everyone's acceptance and approval. Even when no one expected it of her. Even when all they saw when they looked at her was the game master's mannish bastard daughter. But then it occurred to her that *that* voice had never served her well before. It had never won her acceptance. Why should she listen to it now?

He tasted delicious. And his kiss was deep and smooth, nothing messy or slavering like the way Trevis had kissed. This was bliss and she had no wish for it to end.

This man would know how to make your first time exquisite.

The shocking thought rushed through her head unbidden, making her cheeks flame hotter, her body ache and burn in places she never knew could even feel. She would be clay in his hands.

Suddenly the prince stiffened, and she wondered rather insensibly if he had gleaned some knowledge of her outrageous thoughts. Just because he kissed her did not mean he wished to take it that far after all.

He broke their kiss and lifted his head, looking beyond her shoulder. She tried to pull from his embrace, but he held fast, tugging her close.

She cleared her throat softly, distrustful that her voice would rise a mere squeak from between her kissed-numb lips. "Unhand me, please."

His arm tensed around her and his brow furrowed as he continued to study the horizon. "Do you hear that?"

She listened, at first hearing nothing but the wind, but then she caught sound of it. Voices. Very faint. As whispery as the wind itself. "Yes."

He released her then. Grasping her arm, he guided her forward. Together they climbed the small rise. She risked a glance at his face, but he stared ahead, his features impassive. Did he regret their lapse of restraint? Of course he did. He was here to find a bride, presumably the very worthy and estimable Lady Libbie. A rich earl's daughter. She fit his needs perfectly. He certainly didn't wish to become entangled with her.

Topping the rise, Grier spotted the several figures on horseback. "Stable lads?"

"The horses must have returned and they've come to find us," he murmured.

She nodded. "They shall be quite relieved to know we've sustained no injuries." She lifted an arm and waved to gain their attention, quite eager to take her leave of his company and reflect on her improper response to his advances—so that she did not repeat such a mistake again. Because, truly, this needed to stop.

"You are quite the surprise, Miss Hadley."

She turned to find him gazing upon her. "I thought you claimed you were coming to know me. Am I not predictable anymore?"

"Ah, knowing someone and being able to predict someone are two very different things. I'm coming to know you in that I know you're not someone who can be predicted."

With a cool voice she was much proud of, she suggested, "It would behoove us not to waste too much time contemplating each other, do you not agree, *Your Highness*?" She placed emphasis on his title, letting it stand between them as a reminder of the gulf that forever separated them.

He stared at her for some time before answering. "Indeed so, Miss Hadley."

The grooms were upon them now. And not a moment too soon as far as she was concerned.

"We're quite well," Prince Sevastian assured the concerned faces staring down at them. "Thank you for your hasty rescue. Just a slight mishap. Nothing to fret over. Miss Hadley here is quite chilled, however. Would one of you see her to the house at once? I'm quite well enough to walk the rest of the way."

A groom hastily dismounted and gave up his mount for her.

"That's not necessary," she objected.

Her arguments were silenced with a wave of the prince's hand. She glanced at each of the grooms' faces. They looked only at the prince, eager for his next command. Nothing she said would sway them.

Sighing, she held her tongue. Best to let people think she was the missish type of female who gets chilled and cannot walk out of doors. Besides, she didn't want the staff gossiping that she was some hot-blooded virago. She already had a strike against her with her father in tow.

She narrowed her gaze at the prince standing so stalwart in the morning wind. As if nothing untoward had occurred. He didn't spare her a glance even as she couldn't stop devouring the sight of him. Her cheeks blazed afire.

Perhaps he only wished to be rid of her and that's why he wished to send her ahead. A groom assisted her as if she were some delicate lady who could not manage. In moments, she was riding at a ridiculously slow dawdle, led by the groom who gave up his seat for her. She sent a glance over her shoulder at the prince, speculating that his strides might very well overtake her.

He gazed straight ahead, his eyes unreadable beneath his slash of dark brows. Sucking in a deep breath, she faced forward again and plodded ahead, letting him fall behind as she waited for the house to appear.

By the time Sev reached the house, he had done nothing to exorcise Miss Hadley from his thoughts. He spent the half-hour walk attempting to persuade himself that he merely craved a woman and not her specifically. One of the comely housemaids whose eyes followed him about hungrily should satisfy his needs.

There was no glimpse of Miss Hadley upon entering the high vaulted-ceiling foyer and his heart sank with a disappointment he couldn't deny.

There was something about her—a fire, a passion he had not seen since before the war. She was no simpering, naïve, spoiled miss. She possessed an air, a certain knowledge of life and, perhaps most astounding of all, she wasn't jaded for it.

His steps echoed a lonely sound across the aged marble as he moved toward the grand staircase.

It already seemed long ago that he had held her with winter winds buffeting them on all sides. If the sweet taste of her didn't linger on his mouth, he might have convinced himself the entire encounter had not occurred. Surely only in a dream would he have disregarded logic and acted so rashly.

What on earth motivated him to kiss a marriage-minded female he had no intention of wooing for the purpose of matrimony? His goal was clear. He'd traveled to England for one reason only and he needn't waste his time chasing after an ineligible female.

And yet somehow, in the course of their brief acquaintance, she had transformed in his mind. He no longer saw the unfortunate sun-browned, freckled female with the unfashionable hair and miserable pedigree. No. He saw a strong, enticing female who would do quite well in his bed. Too bad she was not angling for the position of mistress.

Shaking his head as if that might free him of such a pointless wish, he entered his chamber, startling his valet from where he dozed in the chair by the window.

"Your Highness? Back already?" The elderly man had been his father's valet and closest friend. His brother had inherited him first, then Sev next. There was no question that he should find a younger, spry valet. As long as Ilian was willing, he would serve as valet to the Crown Prince of Maldania. Tradition was not something to be tossed aside lightly, especially one involving Ilian.

For some reason the thought of tradition only further drove home how wholly inappropriate his feelings for Miss Hadley happened to be. She was an heiress hunting for a husband, and he best not dally with such a female.

"I'll ring a bath for you." Ilian's joints cracked as he passed Sev.

He spared the man who was like family to him a tender smile. "Thank you, Ilian."

His valet nodded. "Can't have you looking mussed if we're to woo the future queen."

Sev's smile slipped further. His mind drifted to the lovely Lady Libbie, feeling strangely empty as he imagined her as his bride. "No. We can't have that."

A short time later he was the first to arrive in the dining room, but he was not to be alone for long.

His cousin entered the room as he was cutting into a fat kipper. Sevastian greeted him with a nod, studying Malcolm's back as he moved to the sideboard and made himself a generous plate of food.

Malcolm tugged down his jacket as he seated himself, and Sev couldn't help noticing it had already grown snug in the fortnight they'd spent together. A definite paunch had grown there since Sev located him in his rented rooms in Seven Dials—a far cry from the fashionable lodgings Sev had expected to find him occupying.

When Grandfather banished his uncle twenty years ago for daring to ravish a visiting Italian dignitary's daughter, Malcolm and his mother accompanied him to England, despite Grandfather's offer for them to remain behind. Aunt Nesha refused to believe the Italian girl's accusations and wouldn't let her husband depart without her, so the entire family fled to England. When they left they were by no means penniless. His uncle, Sev learned, had lost everything at the gaming hells and then only inconvenienced his family further by dying in a duel and leaving them to endure poverty without him.

Sev felt only pity for Malcolm when he learned that they had been living in genteel squalor, pride preventing them from returning to Maldania.

"Even if I wanted to, Mama refuses," his cousin had explained when Sev offered to send them home now. "She feels shame over Papa's banishment . . . and she's still angry. She'll take nothing from Grandfather."

Sev had seen his aunt only a moment, a wan figure reclining on a faded chaise, her smelling salts in one hand and a much-read novel in the other—which she had thrown at his head. The genteel aunt of memory was nowhere in evidence. That woman would not have known the curses to heap upon his head for Grandfather's lies and cruelty—as she phrased it.

Sev did not blame his grandfather for banishing his uncle—by all accounts his uncle had badly damaged the girl. But none of that was Malcolm's fault, so he had taken his cousin under his wing, supporting him with his own dwindling funds since he arrived.

Malcolm wasn't to blame for his father's sins. And besides that, his cousin might be penniless, but his rank still gave him access to the *ton*. Malcolm knew everyone. There wasn't a hostess who did not dote on him. With Malcolm as his guide, Sev saved precious time. Malcolm knew instantly what debutantes Sev should consider.

"Pleasant ride this morning?" Malcolm asked, lowering down to the table and digging vigorously into his breakfast. "I don't know how you rise at such an ungodly hour."

Sev took a lingering sip of his coffee. "Cousin . . ."

"Hmm," Malcolm murmured as he sawed into a kipper.

"I would like to know more about Miss Hadley." Malcolm stilled his sawing. "The one you staked a claim on already?" He snorted. "Sounded like you knew enough about her."

Sev stifled his wince, determined to suppress the emotion of the previous night when he'd reacted so possessively to Malcolm's interest in Grier.

Malcolm continued, "I should think you could make better use of your time than inquiring into an ineligible bastard. She's hardly suitable as the future queen."

Sev shrugged, pretending his cousin's words

did not annoy him. He loathed revealing more of his interest in her, but Malcolm was the only one he could ask and expect discretion.

Rising from the table, he stared down at his young cousin. "Just learn everything you can about her. Will you do that?"

Something flickered in Malcolm's face that Sev had never seen before, and for a brief moment he was reminded that he really did not know him, cousin or no. Before he could identify the sentiment, the expression was gone, replaced with Malcolm's usual affable smile. "Of course, Sev. It's the least I can do for you after all you've done for me. What do you wish to know?"

"Everything."

As he departed the room, Sev didn't want to think about why it had become so important to learn everything he could about a woman whose company he would not keep for much longer.

Chapter Thirteen

It never ceased to impress Grier how many well-bodied ferns could occupy one room, and then she told herself to simply be grateful for that fact. Garbed in an emerald green gown, the great, green leafy fronds camouflaged her form perfectly. A smile lifted her lips. She should only ever dress in green.

Presently she cowered behind one of the plants, happily munching on a tart from her small plate of candied pineapple and iced tarts and sugared fruits—delicacies she'd never tasted before departing Wales. She had to give the aristocracy due credit, they ate like royalty.

As if the mere thought of royalty summoned him, a deep rolling voice asked, "Where do you put it?"

Grier nearly dropped her plate. Whirling around with her hand pressed to her pounding heart, she blinked up at the prince.

"You startled me."

Her heart pounded harder at his nearness. The memory of the last time she'd seen him surged inside her. Not that the recollection ever lurked far. She'd only kissed two men in her life and he was one of them. And of course his kisses had branded an imprint onto her very soul. Standing near him, she couldn't recall her own name.

"I see that. I've watched you for the last quarter hour. I believe that's your fourth tart."

She opened her mouth to respond, but her voice failed her. He'd been watching her? Her fingers grew lax. Her plate tipped ever so slightly. A scone escaped.

His gaze shifted from her face, lingering a long moment on the hand she pressed to her bosom before lowering to stare at the floor where a scone had tripped off her plate and rolled in a gradually slowing circle. "Do they not have food in Wales? In Carynwedd?"

Her attention snapped back to him. "How did you know that I'm from Carynwedd?"

He cocked his dark head. "I know a great many things about you, Miss Hadley."

"Oh." Her skin prickled with alarm.

Did he know everything? Did he know that she'd been a game master? A vocation typically reserved for men? Heat flooded her face as his gaze drifted to her mouth, fixing there long enough to make her knees tremble beneath her skirts.

She forced a laugh. "Then you know I am quite the dull creature." Hardly as exciting as the sophisticated and elegant ladies of his acquaintance, she was sure.

"On the contrary. Is it true you acted as game master after your stepfather's passing?"

He knew. She winced, unsure how to respond to that. Her father had taken pains to suppress that information. Could Cleo have mentioned it? Or perhaps the dowager had nosed about and learned the details of Grier's background. She wouldn't put it past the old lady.

He stared at her intently, waiting.

She tugged the cuff of her sleeve. The fabric suddenly felt constrictive.

"Unusual occupation for a female."

"One does what they must to survive."

She held her breath, waiting, expecting his censure—at the very least a display of the same arrogance he'd treated her to before.

Instead he merely nodded, his gold eyes glowing softly in the room's muted light. Almost as though he understood. And agreed. *Absurd.* Of course the rude boor she'd first met wouldn't understand anything about her. Nor would he look at her with compassion. "I know a bit about doing what one must to survive."

She blinked, wondering—and then understanding. The war. He would have a sense of what she meant.

Feeling out of sorts, and not knowing what to make of him, but realizing there was more to him than she had first judged, she glanced from the fern to her plate. She forced a lightness into her voice. "You always seem to find me like this."

He crossed his arms and studied her with seeming amusement, his gold eyes sparking in a way that made her breath catch. "You mean hiding? Indeed I do. And why is that?"

She shrugged. "Sometimes I tire of making polite conversation at these affairs."

"Would you rather make *impolite* conversation?"

Her lips twitched. "No. But that would be decidedly easier. Or rather speaking freely would be, without having to weigh each and every word."

"It would be amusing, I wager."

She laughed. "Only for you, I fear. Others would take offense." A day ago she would have thought *he* would have taken offense.

"I daresay others would enjoy an interruption to the monotony, too. I'm convinced you would be vastly entertaining if you gave your tongue free rein."

Her laughter faded. She motioned to the gaudily attired group assembled in the drawing room. "It always feels like a strategically orchestrated arrangement with them . . . and I'm forever clueless as to how to navigate it."

He considered her for a long moment, and then she realized he was one of them, too. The bluebloods she referred to. *Idiot.* He didn't understand what she was talking about at all. And why should he? The heat in her face only burned hotter.

Instead of holding her tongue, she cleared her throat and forged ahead. "Should *you* not be in their midst hunting for your bride?" *Lady Libbie.*

"It's not much of a hunt," he replied distractedly.

She pulled a face. "No, not for you. I suppose not. For others of us it's not so simple a task."

Were they actually talking? She and this prince?

It almost felt natural. It almost felt like they were . . . *friends*.

He angled his head, studying her as he uttered, "Don't be so hard on yourself. I'm sure you will have no difficulty winning yourself a proposal."

Heat climbed her face at his words, at the rather intense look in his eyes. Her chest suddenly became too tight, air a struggle to draw in.

Just not from you.

She looked away, lest he read some of the disappointment that thought fed into her heart. The totally misplaced disappointment. She had no business longing for a prince. It was wishing for the moon.

"When is your birthday?" he asked, the question smoothly inserted into the lag of conversation.

Her gaze shot back to him. The wretch. She should have known it was too good to be true.

"Not that again," she snapped, suddenly turning cold when confronted all over again with the cad who'd declared her *old*. "Why must you insist on pressing me for that information? You already know my age—"

"Not your exact age."

"What difference can my *exact* age make to you? You already know I'm eight and twenty. The same age as you."

"You're right. It's a trivial matter. So why won't you tell me?"

"Perhaps because it's not trivial to *you*," she retorted. "You only want to know if I'm older than you."

He stepped closer—until it was just the potted fern at her back and the breadth of his chest at her front. She was instantly assailed with the sheer masculine presence of him. "Are you ashamed?"

"Why would I be ashamed of my age?" She sniffed, angling her chin. "That's ridiculous."

"Precisely. So tell me." He smiled an infuriating grin down at her and she wanted to smack it off his handsome face—only the sight of it weakened her knees and made her stomach flip wildly. With that smile directed at her, it was easy to forget other people lurked near, only feet away.

"Why do you care one whit how old I am?" she breathed.

"Simply . . . curious."

She moistened her lips. "Curious to know if you dallied with a woman older than yourself?"

At his slow, deepening smile, she knew she'd made a fatal mistake bringing that up. Instant awareness sparked between them. "Been thinking about that, have you?"

Only every waking moment.

"No," she denied. "Not at all."

"I have," he countered, encroaching even closer. "Every moment of the day."

He didn't mean that! Her heart pounded violently against her rib cage.

"Well—well—stop. You shouldn't!" She looked wildly from him to the drawing room at large. No one seemed aware of them behind the fern. They were shrouded. Lost in their own private world. A very dangerous situation indeed.

He shook his dark head. "I'm afraid I can't stop. You see, every time I close my eyes, I see these dark eyes." He gently stroked her cheek. "These freckles." He brushed a finger over the bridge of her nose—against the brown freckles she'd done her best to ignore for most of her life. His finger drifted down and stroked her bottom lip. "This mouth."

"Stop," she repeated, but her voice lacked conviction. It was little more than a puff of breath, released from her trembling mouth.

His dark gaze slid up, locked on her eyes. "Really, Grier. Is that what you want me to do? You want me to stop? Be honest with yourself. I've decided to stop lying. Why don't you? Can you really leave this house party knowing you and I will never see each other again?"

It was the first time he'd uttered her name. And the way he said it . . . she trembled.

He continued, his voice a purr, "Can we part knowing we will never satisfy this . . . *thing* that we feel between us?"

"Ah, Sev, there you are. And Miss Hadley, didn't see you there."

Grier jumped at the sudden arrival of another into their midst. Sev stepped back easily, as if his cousin were not interrupting an intimate moment. Only his eyes showed a flicker of regret.

Her heart racing, face flaming, Grier quickly darted past him, convinced that anyone who took one look at her face would know she was a woman lost. She had to get away. Quickly. She needed to find someplace to regain her breath, to still her racing heart and remind herself just why she loathed the Crown Prince of Maldania and why she should detest his flirtations.

He was merely toying with her, attempting to make another conquest.

He thought her less than himself—a female of no worth. *Common.* She mustn't forget that.

No one called out to her as she slipped from the drawing room, further evidence that she was of no importance and would not be missed.

* * *

"Your timing leaves a lot to be desired, cousin."

"Thought you might need rescuing."

Annoyance flared sharply inside him, a pinch in his chest. With great effort, he tore his gaze from Grier's fleeing back. The light gilded her auburn hair in certain spots, and his palms tingled, longing to touch the strands, to feel for himself if they felt as silky and warm as they looked.

"And why would you think that?" he asked with a mildness that he did not feel.

"You're inordinately fascinated with her. I confess it concerns me. You can't possibly be considering her for a potential bride—"

"Of course not," he said with far more lightness than he felt. He'd been trained early to school his face into a perfect mask of impassivity. No one should ever know what he was thinking. "I've said as much."

"And yet you wanted me to find out as much information on her as I could."

He shrugged and admitted, "She's of minor interest to me."

"As what? A mistress? Her father will not countenance that. He'll only take a husband for her. Sorry, cousin. You'll not be easing yourself between those thighs."

His hand knotted at his sides. Jaw clenched, he

slid his cousin a dangerous look. "Malcolm, your assistance has been useful thus far. If I require advice I shall ask it of you. Tread carefully."

Malcolm flushed, doubtlessly thinking he did not wish to return to his rented rooms in the stews any sooner than he must. "Of course. Forgive me. Anyone can see she's struck your fancy."

He looked sharply at Malcolm. "What do you mean, *anyone*?"

"Well, not *everyone* here, I suppose, only the most perceptive. As a prince you're a point of fascination. You can count yourself fortunate that Lady Libbie appears unaware of the many stares you're sending Miss Hadley's way." His eyes grew cunning. "Nor do I think her father is aware."

Sev swiped a hand through the air at the reminder of the rich earl's daughter. He was definitely taking things too far with Grier if he was risking such a promising match. One that would get him home where he belonged. "I'll press my suit with Lady Libbie." And forget about a pair of deep brown eyes and bewitching freckles. "No more dragging my feet." He swept a glance across the room, searching for the golden-headed girl with fresh determination. "Grandfather should be quite satisfied with her."

"Yes. Yes, he would," Malcolm agreed.

Feeling the need to ease any tension between them, he offered, "Thank you for advising me in this, Malcolm. I wouldn't have gotten far without you."

"What are cousins for?"

With a decisive nod, Sev murmured, "I'd best locate the lady and begin to woo her properly."

Ignoring the heaviness tightening his chest, he strolled out into the room, scanning for golden curls, even though he only saw rich auburn hair in his mind.

Grier knew Jack would reprimand her severely for taking her leave so early in the night, but she could not abide another moment in the same room as the confounding Prince Sevastian. What did he want from her? Did he think she would toss convention aside and embrace an illicit affair the duration of this house party?

She could tolerate no more of his teasing, no more of his gold-eyed stare, no more of his proximity. Not if she wished to keep her sanity. One look at his handsome visage and she was overwhelmed by the memory of his body pressed against hers those times she'd been so foolish to forget herself with him.

Her shadow stretched long before her as she

walked briskly down the corridor—as if she could escape her vexing thoughts the faster she walked.

Her tread fell silent on the runner. She was close to her bedchamber now. The tension ebbed from her shoulders as she contemplated the warm bed waiting her.

A sound disrupted the tomblike hush. Soft as smoke curling on the air, hushed whispers reached her ears, penetrating the silence. She paused, listening. They were the type of whispers that actually succeeded in achieving the opposite of their intent, which was clearly discretion.

With a glance over her shoulder to make certain no one else lurked about, Grier moved to the door of the room where the voices originated. Pressing her ear close, she listened.

"Listen carefully to me, Hannah, you'll delay as long as possible. Do you understand?"

"But Lady Libbie, your papa will beat me when he discovers I've been lying to him. Please take me with you."

Lady Libbie? Where was the earl's daughter going?

"I need you to stall anyone from finding out I've snuck away. Allow no one into my room. Tell them I'm exhausted."

At this, someone started sobbing—Hannah

presumably. Lady Libbie sounded resolute and calculating, quite above tears.

"Oh, come now, Hannah. Cease your weeping."

"Oh, my lady, I'm sorry. I'm a selfish, wretched creature, I am! I should be thinking of you—so happy that you've found your prince at last! Ever since you were a girl you dreamed of this . . ." The rest of the maid's words faded away.

Your prince. A prickly sensation washed over her skin. Lady Libbie and Sevastian . . .

Grier felt ill. She pressed a hand to her suddenly roiling stomach. She shook her head, told herself to walk away. Everyone knew he was here to court Lady Libbie. This shouldn't come as a shock. It shouldn't matter that he'd kissed her. It *didn't* matter.

"Oh, very well." A sigh of exasperation drifted through the door. "You may come with us. I suppose you might serve some use. Your presence may help to still the wagging tongues when they learn of the elopement. At least I can claim to have had you as a chaperone, although I must confess I was looking forward to being alone with my love on the journey. Now I must contend with you. I do hope you won't complain the entire time."

My love. Grier rolled her eyes. She hardly knew

the prince. Did anyone truly know the man? He held himself as aloof as a Grecian statute.

Of course, Grier had thought she might have had a glimpse of him, of the real man beneath the façade. Evidently she was just as foolish as Lady Libbie. The girl actually thought the presence of a maid would lessen the gossip surrounding an elopement? Fool girl. Did she think that would matter? One need only look at the virile prince to be assured that Lady Libbie did not reach the altar with her virtue intact.

As she stood there, with her ear pressed to the door and her palms flat against the polished wood, the utter awfulness of the moment sank deep. Lady Libbie was running away. To marry Prince Sevastian.

The man was a cad! Grier had begun to read something more into their exchanges. Something beyond a prince trifling with a woman of lower rank. She'd begun to think he felt something genuine for her. Clearly she'd been naught but a distraction until he and Lady Libbie made their escape.

She stepped back from the door, her hands knotting at her sides as cold fury swept over her. He was quite the seducer. When had he even wooed

Lady Libbie? She scarcely saw them together. She hadn't imagined he spoke to any female at the house party as much as he spoke to her.

She was filled with a sudden vision of him sneaking into the young lady's bedchamber, kissing away her qualms and charming her from her night rail as he lowered her to the great bed.

Feeling like a total and utter dupe, she strode from the door as quickly as her feet would carry her. How dare he flirt with her—*kiss* her—while planning to elope with another woman?

Somehow this was different—worse—than *knowing* he was here to court Lady Libbie. She knew that he'd eventually wed the lovely girl or some other such acceptable female. He did not hide the fact that he was on the hunt for a bride. Just as she did not hide the fact that she was here to find a husband.

But learning that he was strategizing an elopement in the same hour that he flirted with her— it was abominable. Were all men so duplicitous? Were they all as wretched as Trevis?

It only made her feel all the smarter for choosing to wed for practicality. Security, respectability. She required nothing more than that.

And yet her indignation burned hot to know that while he toyed with her he already had a secret understanding with Lady Libbie. *The wretch.*

And why was he so anxious that he must elope with the lady? Did he lack all patience? Or was there another reason? Did he fear the earl would refuse his proposal?

Well, whatever the scenario, she wouldn't let him get away with it. She was not the spoiled and naïve Lady Libbie, believing him to be a romantic hero—the prince of her girlhood fantasies.

No, Grier knew him for what he was. An arrogant brute whose kisses singed one's soul, whose kisses could trick a young girl with less experience into believing he was the stuff of girlish fantasies.

For a moment she had forgotten who she was. She had permitted him to tempt her, even letting his whispered words weave a seductive fog inside her head to such a degree that she had begun to ask herself what would be so very wrong with engaging in a brief liaison.

She'd created quite a convincing argument. She was no green girl. Sentiment would not be involved. She would receive carnal satisfaction. Perhaps that was right, justified, given that she was preparing to enter a union that promised none of that.

Her stride increased, every step quick and agitated. It only took secret whispers in a corridor to jerk her back to reality.

Hardening her heart, she slipped inside her bedchamber to plan exactly how she might thwart the prince from stealing away into the night. She rationalized that a man so arrogant, so deceptive, so amoral, should not get what he wanted. At the very least, she intended to give His Bloody Highness a piece of her mind.

He may very well abscond into the night with his wealthy and *eligible* bride, but not before she let him know what she thought of him, and that she was not someone he could toy with and then so easily forget.

Chapter Fourteen

Sev retired early. He'd never located Lady Libbie as he'd set out to do, so he felt little desire to indulge in cards and drink with the gentlemen in the library. He would start fresh on the morrow and begin wooing Lady Libbie in earnest—and stay as far as possible from a certain female whose every breath, every look, managed to entice him.

As he passed the library, he took heed of the viscount with his jacket removed and sleeves rolled up to his elbows at the card table.

Sev had noticed the dowager's grandson had a particular affinity for faro and was quite willing to lay down a considerable wager. His horse, his curricle in Town . . . even his ruby cuff links. Fleetingly, he wondered if Miss Hadley knew of his proclivity and then he told himself it was none of his concern. Grier Hadley's future was none of his concern. Whom she might or might not choose to marry was none of his concern.

In his chamber, he gently shook Ilian awake from the chair in the corner. Sev dismissed the old fellow for the night with a fond pat on his bent back. It didn't matter how many times he told Ilian not to wait up for him, the old man faithfully did so.

He was tugging his cravat loose when a slight knock at his balcony door made him pause.

Cocking his head, he stared hard at the draperies shielding the glass door, certain he had misheard. Someone could not be knocking out there. He was three stories from the ground—and it was practically midnight.

The tapping came again, this time louder. His every nerve snapped into alert with familiar tension. The same tension he'd lived with for too many years to count. He'd survived both assassins and countless battlefields over the last dozen years only because he'd learned to be alert, constantly vigilant.

He moved to the balcony door carefully, on the balls of his feet—and pulled back the drapes.

There, with her arms crossed and standing in

a belligerent pose, stood Miss Grier Hadley, snow falling gently around her.

With a curse, he yanked the door open.

"What in the hell—"

"I'd like a word with you," she demanded frostily, her lashes blinking with powdery flakes.

He looked her slowly up and down. She wore men's trousers tailored for her. They fit like a glove to her lean limbs. He swallowed a suddenly dry throat, quite certain he had never seen a lady's parts quite so shapely.

Stepping out onto the balcony, he looked down, confirming she had used no ladder to reach his balcony. "How did you get here?"

She waved a hand as if that were a trivial matter. "I simply jumped a few balconies until I reached yours."

"You jumped?" He shook his head. "Which bedchamber is yours?"

She looked to her right. "Three over."

He followed her gaze. At least eight feet separated the multiple balconies attached to each room. He looked down at the snow-covered ground. She was fortunate she did not lie below in a pile of broken limbs. He closed his eyes in a long blink before lifting his face to stare at her again.

"It was easy." She shrugged one shoulder.

"Are you mad?" he barked.

She waved a hand before her lips. "Sssh. Keep your voice down. Do you want to wake the entire house?"

"Why didn't you simply knock on my bed-chamber door?"

She sniffed. "That would be most unseemly. I have a reputation to preserve."

"And this is not improper?"

"I could have been *seen* at the door to your room." She looked annoyed at his suggestion.

His lips quirked. He cast a quick glance to the balconies surrounding them. Arching his brow, he said, "Hate to say it, but your reputation is still in peril, sweetheart. Anyone could look out their balcony and spot you here."

Even in the thin light of the moon, he could see the blush staining her cheeks. "Don't say that," she snapped.

"What? It's true. Anyone could crave a bit of fresh air and see you—"

"Not *that*! Don't call me *sweetheart*," she clarified.

"Ah." He smiled now, forgetting his anger in his enjoyment of seeing her so discomfited. "Well. We're hardly strangers anymore. We've shared intimacies—"

"Intimacies? You make it sound as though

we're . . . as though we've . . ." She stopped and shook her head doggedly. "I think not."

"What would you call kissing on multiple occasions? And in no way would I describe those kisses as chaste." His gaze raked her knowingly, recalling the way she felt against him . . . the way she tasted.

"I would call it a mistake. A brief lapse in judgment. Allow me to disabuse you of the notion that we've been *intimate* in any manner."

His anger returned in a hot surge. "Deny it all you wish. It doesn't change what we did. Or that you want me."

"*I* want *you*?" She propped a hand on her waist.

"Yes," he growled.

She tossed back her head and released a harsh crack of laughter. "Oh, you arrogant pig. You're delusional."

"I speak only the truth. It's in your eyes . . . the way they follow me about whatever room we occupy." The color rode high in her cheeks and he knew he hit a nerve. "Yes, I'm aware of your stares."

"Then you must be staring, too," she accused, jabbing him sharply in the chest with one finger.

He ignored her and the jab of her finger, concentrating on *proving* that she wanted him. "How can

I not stare? I do believe it was you who first kissed me. In a most passionate display, I must say."

Her eyes spit fire at him. She was shaking now, trembling from head to foot, and he didn't doubt she wished to strike him. "What about you, Your *Royal Highness*? When we were locked in that armoire, your actions were far from noble. Are you suggesting that you're merely the helpless victim of my unwanted attentions? Because that's indeed laughable."

He stepped close, his arm stealing around her and pulling her flush against him when she backed up dangerously near the railing. "Oh, I want you. I burn for you."

Had he actually just confessed such a thing to her? He hardly recognized the sound of his voice, or the stark need ripping through him, urging him to take her, possess her.

She gasped at this declaration, and he fixated on those rosy pink lips. She looked up at him dazedly, sagging against him.

His hand tightened around the curve of her waist, delighting in the delicious give of her flesh beneath the pressure. "The only thing stopping me from having you is my restraint."

The slightly mesmerized expression vanished from her face. She was indignant again, her eyes snapping with temper, blinking dusty snowflakes free. "The only thing *stopping* you is *me*! Unhand me. How dare you touch me! You—you disgust me!"

Her insult flew like the slash of a whip and he wondered at her harshness. He felt the sting of her words as keenly as any tear to the flesh—a fact that only infuriated him. When had he come to care what she thought of him? Whether she thought ill of him shouldn't signify.

He shook his head, refusing to believe her. Earlier this evening she'd almost seemed to welcome his attentions. He pulled her tighter against him. "Indeed? If you suddenly so loathe my company, why are you here now?"

She squared her shoulders and lifted her chin, the pose reminiscent of a soldier preparing for battle. "Because I have something to say to you."

"You've said quite a bit already, Miss Hadley. I can't imagine you've left anything out."

"What I need to say will only take a moment."

He looked left and right, assessing the empty balconies. "A moment best not spent here then. Not if you care for your reputation as you claim. We've tarried out here long enough. Come inside."

Her eyes flared wide at the suggestion. She arched back, pushing at his chest with the base of her palms. "I'm not entering your chamber with you." Her voice burned in a low, fevered rush. "If you would simply allow me to speak my piece and release me, I'll be on my way."

"You may be willing to risk your reputation, but I am not." He hauled her resisting figure into his room. She wrenched free and whirled around, moving backward away from him, the hair trickling free of her loose plait with every step she took.

He closed the door with a solid click. Wearing a lazy smile, he crossed his arms over his chest and leaned back against the chilled glass to observe the fetching sight she made.

"Now. Tell me. What makes you risk life, limb, and reputation to speak with me?"

She counted off on one finger. "Firstly, I hardly risked my life. I know you deem me quite *old* and *frail*, but I could hurdle those balconies in my sleep."

"I never said you were old and frail," he interrupted, surveying her again in her deliciously snug trousers. "Quite the contrary."

She tossed her unraveling plait of hair over her shoulder and glared at him. "I know of your plans, and I just wanted you to know that I think you're despicable. Lady Libbie is very unfortunate indeed to fancy herself in love with you."

Frowning, he angled his head, staring at her

and trying to decipher her jumble of words. "I'm afraid you're going to have to explain yourself. What *plans* do you speak of?"

She shot him an exasperated look, propping both hands on her hips. "Come. You needn't play obtuse. I know you intend to elope with Lady Libbie, although why I cannot fathom. I'm sure her father would merrily give his blessing. My guess is that your greedy nature wishes to lay claim to all of Lady Libbie's bridal settlement without delay so that you can return home. I've heard talk that your grandfather is ill."

He pressed two fingers to his temple as if trying to concentrate. "You make no sense. For starters, what led you to believe that I'm eloping with Lady Libbie?"

Her eyes darkened. "Don't toy with me. I overheard her talking with her maid about her plans to—"

"Then she was not talking about *me*. Has that notion not occurred to you?"

She blinked. "You're the only gentleman even paying court to her here. She's scarcely spoken to anyone else. Who could it be if not you?"

"I do not know," he growled, his temper rising now that he realized this was what had gotten her nose out of joint. "I only know it's not me. Pity."

He shrugged. "I came here to woo her. A wasted trip. I'll have to begin anew."

She crossed her arms. "You're very cold-hearted. Do you not even care that the woman you've been courting is plotting to elope with someone else?"

"I care for the delay. Nothing else. I have no emotional attachment to Lady Libbie. I should think you can understand that. Sparks hardly fly through the air between you and the viscount, but word has it that he's going to make an offer."

"Is he?" She blinked in such astonishment that he almost regretted telling her. For some reason the thought of the viscount's hands upon her set his teeth on edge. An untenable reaction. He would have to get accustomed to the notion. If not Tolliver, she would wed someone else.

"Gentlemen talk over cards." Uncrossing his arms, he advanced on her, backing her deeper into the room, hungry to get at the truth of her reason for seeking him out tonight. "And why was it so important that you sneak onto my balcony to confront me with this?"

If possible, that chin went higher. "I couldn't let you leave without telling you what I think of you."

"What *you* think of me eloping with another woman?" he finished.

She nodded once, the motion jerky. He idly

scratched his jaw. "Interesting. And why is that, I wonder?"

She watched him from unblinking eyes as he closed in on her. "I simply wanted to let you know you're incorrigible, a cad . . . flirting so scandalously with me on the eve of your planned elopement. I didn't want you to leave without knowing that I know what you are."

"Ah. A cad. I can see how it would be important to let me know that." He nodded slowly, feeling alive as he hadn't in years. Not since before the war . . . when all he concentrated on was basic survival—his own and that of his people. He was coming to revel in his every dialogue with her. His blood pumped faster.

Her face flushed. "You make me sound . . . foolish."

"I wouldn't say foolish. Jealous would be more correct."

"I'm not jealous." Her eyes followed him like a penned animal. She retreated, gasping when she bumped into the wardrobe.

His smile deepened. She had nowhere to go now. She had to face him—and the truth of what had brought her here. The truth of her desire for him.

"And now that you know I'm not incorrigible? That I did not plan to elope with Lady Libbie."

Her lashes fluttered. "Yes. I was mistaken."

His gaze dropped to the madly thumping pulse on her neck.

"I should go," she whispered weakly.

He lifted one hand, motioning to the empty room around them. "And flee such a perfect opportunity?"

Her gaze sharpened on him. "An opportunity for what?"

He chuckled, dropping his hands on each side of her, effectively caging her in. With a hissed breath, she pressed herself back into the armoire, her head thudding against the rich walnut.

He pressed a soft kiss to the arch of her throat. "An opportunity for this." He kissed higher. "For this." He dragged his lips to her ear and kissed just below the tender lobe. "And this."

She sighed. He barely heard her uttered "No."

He turned his attention to the other side of her throat. The sweet scent of her skin filled his nostrils, heady and intoxicating. "No? How about here then?" He kissed the side of her neck, lightly grazing his teeth along the stretched cord.

Air escaped her in a hiss. Her hands landed on his shoulders, pressing lightly as though she didn't know whether to shove him away or pull him closer.

He pulled back to stare down at her. Dropping his head, their foreheads touched. He tasted her warm breath, sipping and savoring it as he struggled for control, consumed with the need to possess her.

"I want you," he growled fiercely, his hands pushing into the armoire until it creaked beneath the pressure. His throat tightened as he strove to find the words that would persuade her to cast propriety to the wind and fall willingly into his arms . . . into the great four-poster bed mere feet away.

She watched him, her eyes liquid dark, soulful and deep, probing as though she wanted him to say the words that would let her forget herself and surrender to the desire humming between them.

"I burn for you, Grier. I would give us both pleasure," he vowed. "You are the first woman I've wanted this much since I've set foot on this island . . . the first since I've stepped off the battlefield . . ."

Her lips parted in a silent gasp and he took advantage, swooping in, stealing her lips and forgetting himself, forgetting everything in the hot fusion of their mouths.

She opened for the thrust of his tongue and he moaned, kissing harder, sinking his body against her softness.

Her hands came up to tangle in his hair. With a growl, he ran his hand along her trouser-clad hips. He lifted her easily, wrapping her slim limbs around his hips. His cock strained at the front of his trousers. He nestled deeper into her beckoning heat, wanting nothing more than to free himself and drive into her core. He slid his hands to cup each well-rounded cheek, rocking against her.

"You're wicked in these trousers," he muttered against her mouth, nipping and pulling at her bruised bottom lip.

"Wore them all the time back home. No one paid me much heed in them before."

"Either the men were blind, or you were. No red-blooded man could see you in these and not want to reach out and touch you." His hands kneaded her behind, partly for illustration and partly because he could not help himself.

She sighed at his ministrations. "Sevastian."

The sound of his name on her lips undid him. He kissed her deeply, muttering into her mouth, "Call me Sev."

"Sev," she sighed as his hands continued to roam over the delicious curve of her backside.

"It would feel much better if no garments blocked my touch from you. If I could feel all of you."

She stared at him a long moment. Too long. And

he knew she was battling her thoughts, struggling with her inner demons.

"Do you not want this, Grier?" He thrust against her, nestling into the core of her that radiated heat.

She closed her eyes as though in torment. "I can't think when you do that."

Sev sighed. Pulling from a reserve of will he didn't know he possessed, he stepped back. "I'll not coerce you. I'll have you with your mind fully agreeable or not at all."

He ignored the throbbing of his cock that called him a fool. A few more kisses and he'd have her on her back and himself lodged deep between her thighs before she could form a coherent thought. And yet he couldn't do that. That's not how he wanted it.

Not how he wanted *her*.

He wanted the fiery Grier Hadley who'd first tossed her drink on his head. He wanted her begging, naked and writhing against him with an eagerness that echoed his own, craving him as much as he craved her. He wanted her for long hours. Multiple times. Nothing hasty or rushed.

She blinked, looking thoroughly confused. "Y-you want me to go?"

He laughed hoarsely even though he felt decidedly unamused. "I want a woman enthusiastic and willing in my bed. You, unfortunately, aren't coming across as either of those things."

"I—" She gaped rather comically. And yet he found nothing humorous about the situation. He ached for her. Even as he backed away from her he hoped she would call him back, throw herself into his arms, and turn into that passionate creature he wanted so desperately.

He arched a brow, waiting, hoping.

Color rode high in her cheeks. Her mouth snapped shut, folding into a hard line as she gave a jerky nod.

Then she was gone. Fleeing the room quickly, nothing more than a blur. Sev inhaled her lingering scent, woods and winter wind—the only hint left of her. He moved to the balcony, welcoming the cold nip of air washing over him. Hopefully it would douse his ardor. Glancing to his left, he watched as she lithely dropped onto her own balcony, marveling that she would be so bold as to launch herself across balconies. But not bold enough to fall into bed with him.

She lifted her head and met his gaze across the distance. Even in the gloom, he could feel her stare, see the glitter of her eyes in the night.

Yet. The single word floated through his head

like curling smoke, creeping and penetrating deep into his bones. *Yet.* She hadn't fallen into his bed yet.

He smiled slowly, confidence stealing over him. She would. She was too passionate, too brazen to resist her natural impulses. He already knew her well enough to know that. A female who rode at deadly speed for simply the joy of it did not run from desire.

She lingered on her balcony for a moment longer, her slim form little more than shadow staring back at him. Then she vanished inside her bedchamber.

They weren't leaving for days yet. Plenty of time for Miss Hadley to come around and embrace her true nature. Plenty of time for him to persuade her that she wanted him as much as he wanted her.

A slow smile curved his mouth as he moved back inside his room.

Chapter Fifteen

Grier tossed herself onto her bed and wrapped trembling arms around a pillow, squeezing tightly.

That had not gone as planned at all. She jammed her eyes shut in a hard blink. Only now could she be honest. The prince had held a mirror up to her face, forcing her to see the truth within herself. She'd dared to visit his bedchamber because she'd been jealous and hurt. Because she wanted to see him one final time.

Apparently unnecessary. Mortification washed over her in cold waves. And another emotion lurked in the darkest corners of her heart, too. *Relief.*

He was not quite the cad she thought him to be. Lady Libbie was eloping with someone else.

Bloody maid—why must she speak in metaphors? Apparently Lady Libbie's prince was not a true prince.

Grier's cheeks burned over her erroneous assumption. An assumption that had led her to act so rashly and not caused her a small amount of embarrassment. What had she been thinking, confronting him in his private rooms?

Her father's voice echoed in her head. *Ah, Grier, my girl. Your impetuous ways are going to get you into trouble some day.*

Apparently he'd been correct. Her impetuous nature nearly led her into a prince's bed. She buried her face in the pillow and moaned her shame into its soft depths.

Perhaps worst of all was her keen sense of disappointment. She practically found herself wishing he had seduced her. Then she would be in his arms right now, enjoying the delicious way his lips worked over her flesh, instead of alone in her big bed, tormented with longing.

The scary part of it all was she wasn't certain why she had bothered to resist his advances. Everything about him promised pleasure. Why run from it?

She was on the verge of entering matrimony with someone. A staid, predictable fellow who would place her above censure. A loveless union based on convenience and finances and mutual respect. Why not indulge just once?

So what if she surrendered to a brief, discreet liaison with a handsome man who stirred her blood? She was eight and twenty. It was high time she tasted passion. If not now, when?

She would be a faithful wife when the time came. It wasn't in her to renege on vows made before God. But that time wasn't now. Not yet anyway.

Sitting up, she swiped at the tendrils of hair hanging in her face and stared into the relentless dark. Perhaps she needed to make the most of her week here in the country and do more than snare a husband. Perhaps she needed to acquire a lover.

"You retired early last evening." Jack whispered the words close to Grier's ear the following morning as he lowered himself into a seat beside her at the table.

She smiled numbly, swallowing her sip of tea. "I was tired."

His dark gaze drilled into her. There was no mistaking his displeasure. It wasn't the first time she broke away early. And yet beyond his displeasure, she thought she detected something else.

Was that genuine concern in his eyes? "You're not growing ill, are you?" he asked.

She couldn't find her voice for a moment. "No. I'm hale. Thank you."

"It's a dreadful time of year. Everyone is coming down with an ague of some kind. You need to take care of yourself."

Irrationally, a lump formed in her throat. Not since Papa died had anyone cared enough to inquire upon her health. "I'll take care. Thank you."

He gave a single, gruff nod. "Your sister stayed up quite late keeping company with Lord Quibbly."

Grier looked sharply at her sister, unable to disguise her astonishment. The marquis was nudging his seventieth year. Cleo couldn't possibly entertain the notion of marrying him. Could she?

Cleo smiled almost guiltily before looking away and selecting a piece of toast off her plate.

"Lord Quibbly?" Grier queried. Was Cleo truly interested in a doddering, feeble man for a husband?

"Indeed. The marquis is quite the authority on turnips."

"Turnips?"

"Yes," Cleo returned. "He has a fondness for them. I learned that his cook can prepare them several ways. And did you know there are several different species of turnips?"

Persia tittered into her napkin from across the table. "Fascinating!"

Marielle glared at her friend. "It's a subject of great interest to many. Not just Grandfather."

"I'm certain it is." Persia shook with restrained laughter, her glossy brown curls dancing about her shoulders.

Grier studied her half sister in puzzlement. She could not fathom Cleo's desire to align herself with a man old enough to be her grandfather. His own granddaughter, Marielle, was actually one year Cleo's senior. But she did not countenance anyone making a mockery of her, no matter the reason.

At the sight of Grier's glare, Persia ceased her sniggering and returned a glare of her own, evidently not about to be cowed by someone she thought so little of.

Somewhere in the dowager's solarium, a bird released an exotic, trilling call. It was really a lovely setting to break one's fast. Plants of varying colors and sizes shadowed the long table where they sat. Grier could almost imagine some native emerging from the thick press of foliage, his lovely dark skin tattooed with strange symbols.

Not everyone had risen yet. Only half a dozen

sat at the table laden with more food than she had ever eaten in one sitting, especially not so early in the morning. She usually broke her fast with a little porridge drizzled with honey. Possibly a poached egg. An entire roasted hog sat at the center of the table, a server cutting generous slabs that her father consumed as fast as he could chew. He did not make an attractive vision, juice dribbling down his chin as he shoveled ham and thick wedges of baked apples into his mouth.

The prince was nowhere to be seen. She thought it unlikely that he was still abed. After yesterday, she knew he wasn't the stay-abed-all-day sort. More than likely he was out for another ride.

A commotion at the French doors leading into the solarium drew her attention. She winced at the sight of Lady Libbie's red-faced father, having a fairly good idea why he appeared so apoplectic.

He squared off in front of the table, his stout, barrel chest swelling to such a degree she feared one of the buttons of his waistcoat would fly free and strike someone. He reminded her of a bull, ready to charge at the first moving target.

"Have any of you seen my Libbie?"

Everyone exchanged glances, murmuring denials, their expressions avid with curiosity, hounds smelling for blood.

"Where's the prince?" Persia murmured in a singsong voice, clearly under the same misapprehension Grier had labored under the night before. "They seemed cozy the other afternoon."

The earl waved a hand. "I've already spoken to His Highness. He's in the stables, just returning from a ride." He fixed his stare on each of them at the table in slow turn, as if trying to see the truth within, as if one of them hid his daughter away somewhere—or at least possessed the knowledge of her whereabouts. Grier tucked her hands in her lap and struggled for an innocent expression.

A maid approached then, wringing her hands and looking generally fearful. "Her maid is gone, too. I've looked everywhere."

"Hannah, too?" The earl's voice rose shrilly.

"They've run away! Oh dear!" Persia pressed her hands to her cheeks.

"Well, they haven't been abducted," the earl spit out. "Someone has to know something . . . has to have *seen* something!"

Grier's foot tapped uneasily under the table. She was not about to interfere and bring undue notice to herself. Lady Libbie was no child. If she wished to marry someone else, then the decision was hers.

One of the dowager's grooms arrived then,

as if Grier's thoughts had conjured him. He approached hesitantly, lightly clearing his throat. "Um, my lord—"

The earl whirled on him. "What, man? Speak up!" he barked. "Have you news of my Libbie?"

"Well, I've some news, my lord, that might shed light—"

"Out with it."

Everyone at the table leaned forward, heaving a collective breath of anticipation.

"Your groom, John, is missing." At the earl's blank expression, he added, "He didn't sleep in his bed, either."

"John," he echoed, his brow wrinkling in confusion.

Instantly Grier understood, vaguely recalling the handsome young groom. Holding her breath, she waited for the moment of understanding to dawn on the earl. She did not have long to wait.

Color flooded his face anew. "That bloody bastard!"

The viscount lurched to his feet from the table. "Contain yourself, my lord. There are ladies present!"

The earl ignored the viscount. Blustering and cursing, he raced from the solarium, calling for his carriage.

Everyone sat in stunned silence for a moment until Persia suddenly rose in a rustle of lavender skirts. "Well, that was much too exciting for so early an hour as this. I think I'll seek the dowager's calming company . . . see if she's up for a stroll." Her gaze lingered on the viscount for a moment, clearly waiting for him to rise and accompany her.

The viscount looked from her to Grier, clearly weighing what he *should* do with what he wanted to do. As tempting as he found Persia, she clearly did not possess the requisite dowry. With a faintly apologetic smile for Persia, he settled back in his chair, evidently committed to his duty. "Enjoy your stroll, Miss Thrumgoodie," he murmured in strained tones.

Grier stifled a sigh, in that moment wishing he would simply do as he wished to do.

Hurt flickered across Persia's features before she managed to mask it. With a quick inhalation that lifted the charming swell of bosom modestly displayed within the confines of her morning gown, she started from the table with short, quick steps, her eagerness to spread the latest *on dit* apparently returning.

A smile quirked Grier's lips. The girl was no

doubt anxious to be the first to share this latest gossip with the highest lady of rank in residence.

Marielle rose. "I believe I might check in on Grandfather and see about venturing home today. He was looking a bit peaked last night. Too much country air usually gives him the sniffles. I'm afraid country living is not for those of delicate constitutions." Marielle chafed a hand over one plump arm as though to imply she was affected as well. Grier resisted the impulse to roll her eyes. The girl was the picture of bountiful health. "I don't know how the dowager can abide to spend so much time here. Perhaps I can convince her of the wisdom of returning to Town. I so fret for her in this winter clime. It's much warmer in Town."

Grier could no longer fight her smirk. They couldn't stand it. One of London's wealthiest heiresses had run away with her father's groom. A moment wasn't to be wasted sitting on such a juicy tidbit as that. The dowager's house party, it seemed, had come to a swift end.

It was far too important to be one of the first to impart news of the scandal to Society. Grier watched in bemusement as Marielle's plump figure fled the solarium, obviously eager to reach the dowager before Persia shared all the news.

"Well," Cleo announced airily after some moments, "appears we'll be returning to Town earlier than expected."

Jack lifted his head from his plate at this. "Hmm, what's that?" he asked, looking at each of them with blinking dark eyes. "We're leaving early?"

Cleo leaned close and lightly touched his sleeve. "I think the house party is on the verge of dissolving."

He grunted and returned to his meal. "Suppose it doesn't matter where we are so long as you two are out and about in Society."

Bitter indignation ate up her chest and throat. Grier's cheeks burned and prickled. Jack cared only for marrying them off and winning a place among the *ton*. Lately there had been a few times when she'd thought he might actually care for her. She thought fate might have been kind enough to give her a second chance with a new father who might, beneath his gruff exterior, actually love her.

Suddenly feeling the need for some fresh air, she set down her spoon and rose. "Excuse me."

Cleo sent her an encouraging smile.

Grier gave a nod before turning and striding away, her skirts swishing around her ankles. Unaccustomed to the love of a good father, her sister could tolerate Jack far better than she.

She slipped away through the back of the house and took the servants' path to the stables, chafing her hands over her arms as she went, musing that she should perhaps have fetched a cloak. Rather than go back and risk bumping into anyone, she hurried her steps to reach the shelter of the stables.

Once there, she stopped on the threshold, taking comfort in the earthy aromas. The smell of leather, hay, and horseflesh. All familiar. All comfortable. It reminded her of the home she left behind.

Her strides slow and easy, she strolled inside, down the wide lane between several stalls. She felt immediately better. More at peace. A beautiful stallion stuck his head over the door and nickered at her as she passed. She backed up a step to stroke his sable neck. He whinnied in approval and she cooed to him, deepening the stroke of her fingers against his velvety coat.

"Aren't you a handsome boy?" she murmured. "Such a fine lad, hmm?"

"Never thought I'd be jealous of a horse."

Chapter Sixteen

Grier whirled around.

Sev stood before her, his cheeks raw from the cold winter air. His hair was tousled and wind-blown and midnight dark. Her stomach fluttered at the towering sight of him.

She went back to patting the horse's neck, struggling to appear unaffected at his sudden appearance. A definite challenge when she could only think of the night before in his bedchamber.

"Did you enjoy your ride?" she asked in a voice that did not even sound like it belonged to her, so small and breathless.

He advanced on her, looking dangerous and predatory with his piercing eyes and hard jaw.

He didn't answer her, didn't speak. His silence unnerved her more than anything he could have said.

She backed up until the door of the stall stopped her from moving any further. Still, he kept coming.

Her hand tapped at her side nervously, tangling in her skirts. She looked desperately to the right and left. No one. No groom lurked about the many stalls. Not a single soul. They were all alone. For now at least.

Suddenly it was last night again. Only this time she wouldn't run away. This time she would be bold. She would take what she wanted. She would take him.

They leapt at each other, came together in a fierce union of grasping hands and melding lips.

Their mouths met in a furious mating. He fell against her and she slammed back against the stall door. The wood slats knocked from the force. His body flattened against hers, all warm, hard lines covering every inch of her.

She ran her hands through his hair, reveling in the dark silken strands as cold as the wind whipping outside, almost icy against her palms—but that did nothing to chill the heat stirring inside her.

"Grier," he groaned, dragging his mouth down her throat.

She sighed, arching her neck for him. Closing her eyes, she forgot everything. Everything but this. Him. Her.

A sharp male voice cracked over the air and Grier jerked. Someone was approaching.

She beat a small hand against Sev's shoulder, forcing him to stop.

He pulled away from her, chest heaving, staring at her hungrily with his heavy-lidded gaze as the angry voice grew nearer.

Smoothing a trembling hand down her bodice, she stared wide-eyed at him. She shivered at the promise she read there, the promise that this wasn't finished. That they weren't done.

"Dammit, boy, are you mentally deficient? How is it someone absconded with three horses and you heard nothing?"

"I'm sorry, milord. I didn't hear a sound all night."

The earl and a stable boy hurried down the lane between the stables side by side. The earl's man traveled several paces behind, as if he wanted to distance himself from his angry master.

The copper-haired stable lad seemed unaware

that he should proceed with such caution. He sputtered profuse apologies for sleeping through the night and not waking when Lady Libbie and her cohorts snuck three horses from the dowager's stables.

The blustering earl finally reached the end of his control. He turned on the boy and knocked him to the ground.

Grier choked out a small cry as the slight boy flew several feet before landing on his side. His small face crumpled from the pain. He curled himself tight and clutched his arm close to his thin chest.

Grier hurried forward and crouched beside him, gently touching his shoulder. "Are you all right?"

"Leave him be," the earl snarled. "He needs to be schooled on what happens when he falls short on his duties."

Grier lifted her gaze. "You're vile. He's just a boy."

"And you need to mind to your affairs, woman, and guard your tongue when addressing me. You're lucky to even be a guest here."

A low growl emanated from Sev. "Have a care when addressing Miss Hadley."

The boy's face flushed with both pain and embarrassment as he struggled to sit up. He leveled suspiciously wet eyes on his attacker. "You're just angry because your daughter ran away with a groom!"

The earl's eyes bulged. "You insolent little whelp!" He lunged for the boy, his arm pulled back to deliver a backhand slap.

She moved in and shielded the lad. "You'll not harm him again."

The earl wagged a sausagelike finger in her face. "I warned you to—"

Before he could even finish his sentence, Sev stepped in and knocked the earl off his feet with a deft punch to the face. The crack of bone on bone rang out in the stable.

The earl landed with a solid thud on his backside.

Grier gaped, certain she had just not watched Sev strike a gentleman in defense of a servant.

"What'd you do that for?" the earl cried in muffled tones, clutching his afflicted nose where blood trickled thickly between his fingers.

Sev shrugged. "Never been partial to men who bully children and women."

"Well, you can forget ever marrying my daughter!"

Sev chuckled. "Were I even still interested in marrying your daughter, she's presumably on the way to Gretna to marry your groom."

"I'll have it annulled!" he cried.

Sev shrugged again as he moved to take Grier's elbow. "I don't really care what you do—so long as I never see you strike another servant in my presence or speak to Miss Hadley with such disrespect again."

Grier's head reeled. Why should he care how others addressed her?

"Will you be all right, lad?" Sev asked the boy, who stared up at him with adulation.

He nodded his coppery head. "Thank you, milord."

Sev ruffled the lad's hair. "Off with you."

Still astonished over all that had just transpired, Grier watched in bemusement as the boy scampered away on his twig-thin legs.

"Come." Sev grasped her elbow, his touch light but nonetheless searing. She felt the imprint of each finger through the fabric of her gown.

She spared a glance over her shoulder for the earl as Sev led her away. He still lay sprawled on the ground, a hand pressed to his bleeding nose, staring after them in total bewilderment.

"Why'd you do that?" she whispered as they strode from the stables.

"No one should treat another person like that. I don't care who they are, servant or king. No one is so privileged they can simply beat another person when the whim seizes them."

She slid her gaze up at him, studying his fixed, resolute expression. Something loosened inside her chest and a very real panic stole over her as she realized he was nothing she had thought him to be. She *liked* him in that moment. Even admired him.

Once inside the house, she pulled her arm free of him, the desperate need to escape him stronger than ever as a sudden terrible realization seized her.

Her face flashed hot and cold.

She just might be drawn to the prince for more than his delicious good looks and mesmerizing voice. She might in fact be—

The pulse at her neck hammered. "I-I have to go. My sister . . . is waiting."

He released her and crossed his arms over his broad chest, watching her in that probing, intent way of his.

She backed away, wringing her hands anxiously as her slippered feet slid over the slick marbled foyer.

"We made . . . plans," she continued lamely.

Still, he said nothing, simply continued to stare at her with his gold, devouring eyes—seeming to see right through her, past her fabrication to the truth.

With a muttered parting, she lifted her skirts and whirled around. Her slippers pounded up the steps, but she refused to look back at him again.

Chapter Seventeen

$\mathcal{S}$ev watched Grier hurry up the stairs in a flurry of skirts and knew she was fleeing him. His brow furrowed as he watched her depart.

Something had changed.

She had stared at him with almost fear in her eyes. Before there had always been mockery, even scorn when she gazed at him. At least when he wasn't kissing her and her eyes weren't clouded with desire.

But he'd seen none of those things just now.

He'd read only finely-honed panic in the liquid dark of her eyes—as if she had just come face-to-face with a deadly predator that might unleash itself on her any moment. She studied him as though *he* was that something dangerous to her.

And perhaps he was.

He knew only one thing for certain: he would not be leaving England until they settled this thing between them. Until he had Grier Hadley in his bed.

Only then, he rationalized, would he be able to exorcise her from where she had taken up residence inside him—in his very blood. Only then could he follow through and do what he came here to do.

"Ah, cousin. There you are! Been looking all over for you!"

Sev faced Malcolm, pasting a mild smile on his face that reflected none of his inner turmoil. "Have you?"

"Seems the party is coming to an end. The duchess is eager to get back to Town and start spreading the word of Lady Libbie's sudden departure."

Sev rolled his eyes. "Of course. That would be of the most import."

Malcolm chuckled at his sarcasm, then sobered with the sudden realization that Sev had just lost his primary target for a bride. "Oh dear. This does put us back to the beginning of our bride hunt, does it not?"

Sev had realized this instantly, from the moment

the earl questioned him early this morning. For some reason the realization did not trouble him. Not as it should have.

He'd wasted a week pursuing the earl's daughter. Another reason he needed to satisfy this itch with Miss Hadley. Maybe then he could move on—forget Grier and remember what it was he came to England to do.

"Appears everyone is departing tomorrow."

His cousin's words sent a bolt of panic through him. "That soon?" he asked, his voice sharper than he intended.

Tomorrow they would all depart.

Tomorrow he would not have Grier beneath his roof and in such ready access anymore.

"Sev?" Malcolm's reddish eyebrows furrowed. "Something amiss?"

"No." He shook his head. " 'Tis our last night in this fine country air. I shall miss it when we return to Town," he lied.

He slapped the smaller man on the back as resolve swelled through him. "Let's make our last evening count."

Every moment of it.

Grier dragged the brush through her hair until her scalp stung from each crackling pull. Most of the dowager's houseguests had retired early, just after dinner. With a long day of travel ahead of them—several long days, to be precise—they all needed their rest.

Sliding beneath the counterpane, she pulled the heavy covers up to her chin, settling herself deep in the center of the four-poster bed. With a sigh, she turned and punched the pillow beneath her head. She didn't want to leave the dowager's estate, and she knew it had nothing to do with her aversion to Town life.

It had everything to do with *him*.

Her stomach knotted with the realization that she would never be in such close proximity with the prince again. No more sparring words. No more heated glances.

No more stolen kisses.

She sucked in a breath and told herself this was a good thing. Especially considering the relatively new realization that she liked him. Indeed, she was still grappling with that fact. He was more than a handsome face. His aloof veneer was just that. A shield, and behind it breathed a just and magnanimous man with a wicked sense of humor and even more wicked kisses.

Grier stared blindly into the dark, straight and rigid as a slat of wood, her fingers laced tightly over her stomach as her mind mulled through all this.

She hadn't seen him all day. He'd been absent during dinner, a fact that both relieved and disappointed her.

Lowering her hand, she brushed the swell of her stomach. The linen of her nightgown felt soft against her palm. She thought of them together in his bedchamber, in the stables . . . the sinful way their mouths had devoured each other. What would it be like to succumb? To lie with him?

Misery filled her to consider she would never see him again after tomorrow. She would go about hunting for a husband and he would go about searching for his bride. An ache of longing filled her chest that she could not suppress—could not deny.

I'll miss him.

The thought entered her head before she could block it out, and then a question swiftly followed that was equally inappropriate.

Why could he not choose to marry me?

A warmth suffused her at the very idea, at the nights they would have, the leisure they could take to devote to each other. Frowning, she quickly tried to suppress the warmth with a cold dose of reality. He was a prince. Nothing would change that. Typically she was no one who should even cross paths with him. She would not permit herself to fall in love with him. She would not lose such power over herself.

The curtains shifted at her balcony, fluttering with a whisper in the wind. The barest creak sounded as the door swung inward.

She bolted straight up in bed with a gasp, her eyes searching the gloom, widening as a large shape materialized. Her heart hammered wildly. She knew instantly.

He had come.

That he had been so bold as to vault the several balconies to reach her room made her almost giddy.

"Sev?" Her voice fell in a whispery hush on the air as her eyes strained for a better glimpse of his face.

Silence. She shoved back the covers and swung her feet over the side of the bed. Her bare feet dropped down silently. She moved toward the robe she'd draped over her footboard, her gaze straining through the gloom, searching for his shape.

A hard hand shot out and gripped her wrist. "Leave it off. One less item we'll have to remove."

A secret thrill shivered over her skin at his decadent words. There was no mistaking his meaning or what he'd come here to do.

Grier opened her mouth to deliver a ringing setdown, to say what she *should* say, but the words never made it past her lips. His mouth crushed hers and her protest died in her throat.

And really, she was done running. She tangled her hands in his hair, pulling his head closer, deepening their kiss and parrying her tongue with his. He backed her up until she collided with the bed.

He broke the kiss. Her chest rose and fell with each savage breath that shuddered free of her lungs. His eyes glittered at her in the dark, twin spots of gleaming light.

"What are you doing here?" A senseless question, she knew as he gathered her nightgown against her hips.

"I think it's clear what I'm doing." In a single, swift move, he pulled the nightgown over her head. Night air rushed over her and she shivered. "Finishing what we've begun," he breathed against her temple, stirring the fine hairs there. Her heart leapt in her too-tight chest.

She managed a strangled sound, a gurgled affirmation. With every fiber of her being she wanted this. Needed this. It would be all she had of him, of passion.

She would seize it and not regret a moment.

His large hand cupped her bottom and lifted her high against him, snuggling her against his prodding erection. That hand rounded the curve of her bottom, sliding lower, fingers teasing, probing her entrance and ripping a gasp from her throat at the intimate touch.

Then she was falling. His body came down over hers, surrounding her, pinning her to the bed. Instinctively her legs parted wide, allowing him to settle deeper against her. There was no fear. Only desire. Their mouths fused together, a hot, wet melding of lips and tongues, of nips and long, deep drinks from their mouths.

The dam broke at last and she let herself go, reveled in his mouth, his tasting tongue, his hands on her body. Even without marriage, without his love, she could have him, have *this*.

An incredible sense of freedom, of power, seized her, and her hands flew to his trousers. Following her instincts and the deep pull of desire in her pounding blood, she closed her hand around his hard length.

His groan emboldened her. She sighed at the

silken feel of him. A shudder ran through him and vibrated within her as she stroked him— slowly, hesitantly at first, then in long, firm strokes that made him breathe harder. Her own breathing increased, grew into ragged pants.

She rubbed her thumb over the tip of him, delighted at his low groan, at the bead of moisture that rose up to kiss her thumb and coat the head of him.

"What are you doing to me?" He tangled a hand in her hair and dragged her mouth to his for a searing kiss. Meanwhile her hand worked over him, feeling, fondling, caressing, and exploring that part of him which fascinated her and fed her hunger.

Releasing him, she shoved his chest with the flat of her palms. He fell back on the bed. She hovered over him for a moment, wishing she could see the magnificence of his body in the dark chamber. Memory would have to serve.

Hands fumbling in her excitement, she removed his shirt, glad he'd already discarded the rest of his garments.

She traced the ridges of muscles along his stomach, the outline of each rib. Dipping her head, she tasted him, licking her way down his hard chest and tracing the thin line of hair along his navel.

She stopped, perched uncertainly over him.

The rasp of his breath filled the air, encouraging her. "Take me in your mouth."

Clasping him in one hand, she placed a kiss at the tip of him.

"Grier," he croaked in a voice she had never thought to hear from him. Vulnerable. Lost. Totally at her mercy. It thrilled her. Aroused and prompted her as nothing else ever could. Slowly, as if he were the most delectable piece of fruit she had ever sampled, she licked him fully.

His body jerked almost as if in pain.

She released him and turned her face toward him. He sat perched on his elbows, his face tilted toward her in the gloom. "Did I hurt you?"

In response, he clamped down on her arms with his warm hands. Before she could draw a breath she was on her back and he was over her.

The sensation of their naked bodies, all smooth, bare skin sliding sinuously together, left her breathless. Air choked within her throat at the slide of his chest against her breasts. His dark head dipped, his mouth a hot drag down her arching neck.

As his large hand surrounded her breast, her head flew off the pillow, a gurgled cry exploding from her lips. She was undone, utterly ruined for him. As she writhed and panted beneath him, her body afire, her hands clutched the slick flesh of his straining biceps.

Soft pleas spilled from her mouth. For him to make it end . . . *to never stop.*

At the first touch of his mouth to her breast, she bucked beneath him, overcome. She went utterly still, shocked at the sensations rippling through her as he took her nipple deep into his mouth.

Hunger pulled deep in her belly. She threaded her fingers in his hair, squirming beneath him with building frustration, needing, wanting, craving, desperate for something more.

His warm hand trailed between them, delving between her legs, sliding expertly between her quivering thighs.

"I've dreamed of this, Grier. Dreamed of you," he murmured against her breast, his thumb stroking and pressing at a secret hidden spot she never knew existed before. She lurched against him, shuddering in his arms.

He moved his face up to hers. "I can wait no more."

She nodded, speechless, too overcome as spasms racked her body.

And then he was driving into her, so deep, so fully.

She gasped at the intense pressure. It should have hurt; it probably did. He was large and pulsing inside her, but he filled that gnawing, clenching ache in such a way that she didn't care. She felt whole, complete at last.

His mouth slammed over hers as he plunged in and out of her body, mating with her body so fiercely, so thoroughly, she doubted she would ever be the same again.

He took what he needed, pounding into her ruthlessly and she didn't care because she wanted it, too. Needed it.

Needed him.

Her hips rose to meet him and she cried out as he drove harder into her, gripping her hips with digging fingers as if she were a lifeline, the only thing that kept him grounded to earth.

Her heart swelled even as she reminded herself that this wasn't love. Only lust.

Her body splintered from the inside out. He swallowed her ecstatic cry as he drove deep inside her a final time and stilled. She dug her nails deep into his smooth shoulders. His arms quivered, braced on either side of her.

A sad smile curved her mouth. She would always have this.

Long after they each wed someone else. Long

after he sailed for home. This memory, this night, would hold her through the years.

It would be enough. She would make it so.

This was more than lust.

Sev knew it the instant he felt her shudder beneath him, felt her tremble and arch sinuously under him in the throes of her climax.

His own climax followed fast and fierce. He reveled in the sensation of his seed spilling inside her. Even as he knew it was insanity, that he should pull free from her body and spill himself upon the linens. Nothing could tear him from her delectable body, risk or no risk.

Just as he realized this, he accepted the fact that she was not something he could have just once.

For the first time in years, he wanted something for himself. He wanted Grier.

Chapter Eighteen

What's it like? Maldania?" Grier asked much later. Sated as a cat on a sunny day, she curled up on Sev's warm body. Her fingers stroked softly against the smooth expanse of his chest. "Do you miss it?"

"Yes."

She smiled, enjoyed the way his voice rumbled up through his chest and vibrated against her cheek where it rested. "I miss Wales," she announced, her voice whisper-soft. "It's so green there it almost hurts your eyes. And the wind is different. The air smells fresh and new." She released a breathy laugh. "If that makes any sense."

"It does. Maldania is like that. Green hills and

mountains. Forests so deep you can walk through them and believe you're the last person on earth."

"I know that feeling."

His hand brushed through her hair, pulling back when catching in the snarls, and then starting again.

"My brother taught me to fish and hunt in those forests."

"Tell me about your brother."

His chest lifted on an inhalation beneath her. "He was to be king. Not me. I was simply the spare. I should have been the one killed. No one would have missed me."

Her heart clenched at his words. *She* would have missed him. And the notion terrified her. She could have gone through life never knowing Sev. Never knowing this. Never having him. It was torment to consider. "I don't believe that. It's not true. You would have been missed—"

"You're sweet." He kissed her forehead. "But my brother was essential. I was not. He was born to the position, brought up always knowing who and what he was. I only became necessary after his death."

"He was killed during the war?"

"Yes."

"I'm sure everyone is just happy and relieved that they have you."

"Oh yes." His chest tightened beneath her cheek. "To be sure. That's what they tell me— every chance they get."

"They?"

"My grandfather, the consul, people I come across in the streets. They're all so *relieved*. So very relieved that they have their crown prince."

Crown prince. Not Sevastian.

And then Grier understood. In that moment, it all became glaringly clear. She understood his austerity. His lack of levity. His life was not his own. He did not have a right to such emotions. He belonged to Maldania.

She suddenly felt hollow inside with the knowledge that he could never be hers . . . and yes, a secret part of her had begun to long for that. He could belong to no woman because he belonged to Maldania.

She struggled to find something to say. Something heartening. "You have purpose. That must count for something. You can do so many good things for so many people." Even as she said this, she felt only numb inside. He'd have his *purpose* in life. And she would never have him.

"I know." His voice rang grim, but no less determined. "That's why I'm here."

"England, you mean?" Not with her, of course. It would be just silly of her to think he meant with her.

"For my country to even begin recovering I must marry."

An awkward hush fell between them. Everything changed. Their tender intimacy shattered.

Her fingers stilled on his chest. If marriage to a wealthy, respectable woman was his agenda, then what was he doing here with her? *Wasting time.*

She was sure his thoughts echoed her own. Painful but true. She might have the fortune he needed, but she wasn't the queen he sought. She began to pull away.

In one swift move, he flipped her on her back. She gasped as he slid his very muscled thighs between hers.

"What are you doing?" she asked, her voice an eager tremor on the air.

His face stared down at her. Hard. Determined. "I think that would be obvious." The tip of him nudged at her opening. "You were trying to leave."

"And this will keep me here?" She could not even recognize the hoarse croak of her voice.

"You tell me. Will it?" The head of him pushed a fraction inside her before slipping out again.

Tormented, she whimpered, her fingers rising to dig into the smooth flesh of his shoulders. "Please," she begged.

"Please what?"

She breathed heavily beneath him, the tips of her breasts pebble-hard and rubbing his chest in the most arousing way. He propped himself on his elbows and eased slightly inside her again, the tip of him barely inside her. Her head thrashed on the bed, in agony.

"Take me."

Take me.

He wanted to. God, he wanted to have her. Again. And again. And that was just the crux of the matter.

"Grier," he began, determined that tonight would *not* be the last time . . . that this could somehow continue as long as he was in England. The need to have her again burned within him. He refused to examine why. It didn't matter why. It simply . . . *was.*

He'd have this woman again, as often as he could. Every chance. Even if he had to go out of his way to invent those opportunities.

"Hmm." She arched beneath him, moaning. Even in the gloom, he detected the hot need in her gaze.

"I want to see you again. In Town."

Her eyes widened at the suggestion, and he knew he had her attention. "Discounting social gatherings we both might attend, I don't see how."

"It can be arranged. I can arrange it."

She bit her lip. He caught sight of the flash of white teeth. "I don't know."

She pushed at his shoulder, managing to scramble free. "What can come of it?"

He hauled her back and kissed her soundly until they were both panting and clinging to each other.

"This," he growled, sliding his hands beneath her and dragging her thighs apart again. He slid inside her slick heat in one smooth thrust. She arched beneath him, meeting the invasion with a moan of welcome. "And this."

She cried out, dropping back on the bed as he worked over her, taking her in deep, slow strokes, lifting her hips higher until he found the right spot for her to reach climax again. She shrieked when he found it, and he smothered the cry with his lips, drowning the sound as her inner muscles clenched and squeezed his cock, wringing him of his own shuddering release.

They collapsed against each other, clinging and panting. For several moments neither moved, too spent, too overcome.

"I'll leave it to you," she finally said, her voice whisper-soft. "I know we should end it tonight before we're caught and my reputation is truly beyond repair, but my will is weak when it comes to you. So if you wish to meet again—" She stopped, unable to say anymore.

"I do. We shall." He tightened an arm around her waist as if someone threatened to steal her away.

He knew it was foolish to feel so attached to her. Plenty of women had shared his bed before and he'd never felt this . . . this desire, this deep attachment, this *need*. Especially after sex.

Sex was fun. A physical release. Usually after he'd had a woman in his bed, after the chase ended, his interest ended, too.

Something told him it would never be that way with Grier. He would never tire of her.

Her soft sigh brushed his cheek. "Should you go now?"

"No. I'll stay until you fall asleep." Until it

wasn't so hard to tear himself away from her. Regrettably, that moment never came and he wondered if it ever would.

An hour before dawn he slipped away, leaving Grier lost to her dreams.

She had a lover.

The thought reverberated through her head countless times as she sat in the carriage beside Cleo. Jack slept across from her, snoring loudly, but she was glad for it. Glad she did not have to hear reminders that she must renew her search for a husband upon their return to Town. She bit her lip until the pain lanced sharply along her nerves. She welcomed the sensation, preferring it over the unease knotting her stomach at the prospect of finding a husband—of letting another man into her bed, her body. Swallowing the sudden surge of bile rising in her throat, she turned her face to the tightly drawn curtains as if something of interest could be seen there.

They made a caravan of sorts, the dowager's houseguests all departing at once for London. Occasionally she would part the velvet curtains to glimpse outside, acting as though she merely studied the countryside, but she actually searched for Sev atop his stallion. Several of the gentlemen rode alongside the carriages. Grier longed to ride outside among them. Another reason to loathe the constraints of Society.

"Close the curtain. Letting in a draft." Jack opened his eyes long enough to complain before turning on the squabs and settling back into his nap.

Grier dropped the curtain and resettled back against the squabs. Her mind drifted to the evening ahead when they would stop at the inn. Her heart raced to consider that she would see Sev again then.

She had no expectation that they would manage to steal a moment alone . . . but just to see him again . . . to feast her gaze on him made her belly flip and her heart ache in the most alarming way. This really was getting out of hand. How was she to let another gentleman pay her court when she could only think of the Crown Prince of Maldania in her bed, doing the most sinful, improper things to her? She had to put a stop to this at once. Such thinking would lead her nowhere but heartache.

She'd caught a glimpse of him this morning before ascending the carriage but it had been reminder enough. One look into his gold eyes and her face caught fire as memories of the night before—mere hours ago—consumed her.

Color had heated her face at the sight of him. How could she function in his presence without drawing suspicion? Cleo especially would be certain to notice.

Last night she had been weak to agree to an affair. Could she find the strength today to tell him she'd been wrong? Senseless and lost to passion. Her thoughts spinning, she sighed.

"Tired?" Cleo spoke from beside her.

Grier nodded. "Yes. A bit."

Cleo parted the curtain on her side of the carriage. "We should be at the inn soon. It's dusk now."

Grier nodded mutely, a thick lump rising in her throat that she shouldn't feel.

More encounters with Sev and the more attached she would become until it was impossible to disengage herself without breaking her heart.

She rested her head back against the seat. They'd be there soon—and she'd find the strength to tell the prince that she'd been wrong. That they could not continue their affair. Their one night together had been just that—one night.

The dowager's house party occupied every table in the inn. While their evening fare was being fetched, Grier stood before the giant fireplace, thawing herself by holding her bare hands out to the welcoming heat.

The dowager herself sat in a hardback chair, complaining of her sore muscles and the long days left until they reached London. "I'm too old to keep making this journey. It's a misery."

"No one said you had to return to Town, Grandmother," the duke intoned from where he stood beside her chair, one hand behind his back, the other propped upon the top of her chair. He looked bored and disdainful all at once. Had she ever thought him and the prince alike?

"And miss all the excitement when it's learned that the scandal of the year took place beneath my very roof? Indeed not." She huffed mightily and took the cup of chocolate her maid fetched from the serving girl. She sent her grandson a glare as though he had lost all sense. He rolled his eyes.

The serving girl moved along with the tray of steaming cups, stopping before Grier to offer her one. Grier took the proffered cup, glad to wrap her chilled fingers around the warm ceramic. She carefully sipped the rich, steaming liquid. Her gaze drifted, finding Sev where he stood at the second fireplace several yards away. His cousin hovered beside him, as always.

Sev's gaze collided with hers almost as though he felt her stare. Finding herself under his scrutiny, she sucked down too much drink and scalded her tongue. She hissed at the burn.

People moved about the room. Conversation rumbled on the air, but she could focus on nothing save Sev.

She read the hunger in his gaze, felt its echo inside her, and wondered how on earth she was going to tell him they needed to end this thing between them.

"Grier!"

At the sudden sound of her name, she jerked as if caught committing an offense. She snapped her gaze around the room, searching for the source.

And that was when she saw him.

Her mug slipped from her fingers, cracking into jagged pieces on the stone floor. Others exclaimed around her, but she could say nothing, could offer no explanation. She could only stare at the man bearing down on her with long strides. Her heart hammered, her mind reeling with a single question.

What was Trevis doing here?

Chapter Nineteen

"Grier, my dear girl! I can't properly express my relief to find you at last!"

She stared up at the boy she'd known all her life. He was a man now—the very one she had thought she would wake up with in her twilight years. It was with some bemusement that she studied him with fresh eyes and felt . . . nothing.

He seemed smaller than she remembered. His eyes were rather beady, his gaze slitted with a cagey look to them. The color? A bland shade of blue. His hair? An equally bland brown. Strange how none of it made an impression on her now.

He seized her hand with no care for their audience. "I've been looking for you."

Horrified, she shook her head and attempted to

tug her hand free. She had to look. Her gaze slid to Sev. He no longer watched her. His stare fixed with deadly intent on Trevis. She shivered at the ruthless glitter in his gold eyes. She'd never seen him look such a way, and she felt convinced she had an image of him in war, the battle lust bright in his gaze.

Trevis's voice intruded, pulling her attention. "I've searched everywhere for you."

She shook her head. "Why?"

At this question, he glanced around them. Grier managed to free her hand and bury it in her skirts.

"Miss Hadley?" the dowager demanded from where she sat, perking to life at the sudden drama unfolding. "Who is this—this person?"

"Your Grace." Grier waved a hand toward Trevis, seeing no way around the introduction. "This is Mr. Powell. We were . . . neighbors in Wales." She sent Trevis a warning glance that urged him not to announce himself as her former employer.

At that moment Jack arrived, his gaze immediately landing on Trevis hovering near her. Sharp suspicion flared in her father's eyes. "Grier, what is the meaning of this?"

Jack swept a measuring gaze over Trevis, doubtlessly noting his fine cloak and Hessians. Grier sensed his barely checked aggression. The fact that Trevis was a gentleman was likely the only thing stilling Jack from leaping upon him.

"Mr. Hadley." Trevis dipped his head, greeting her father with the confidence of a man accustomed to getting his way. *Not always. He couldn't get me.* "A pleasure, sir. I've heard a great deal about you." *He had?* Liar. "So glad to finally make your acquaintance. I hope you do not mind me tracking you down like this. I called upon you in Town and they told me how I might find you."

"My staff told you where I went?" He frowned slightly. "Seems my people aren't as loyal as I thought."

Trevis cleared his throat awkwardly. For the first time, unease flickered over his face. His hand slipped back on her arm as if seeking to reclaim his confidence.

Grier shook her arm free from his grip, beyond irritated. "What are you doing here?" She did not bother to hide her annoyance. Or bewilderment.

He turned his attention back to her and gave her a slow, deep smile, followed with a quick, smug wink.

Grier blinked, her nerves bristling with agitation. She remembered that smile and that wink, remembered how they had affected her before. And how they failed to affect her now.

She shook her head once, wondering what had ever possessed her to think so highly of Trevis.

Instead of answering her question, he turned back to her father, "Mr. Hadley, might we have a word in private?" He slid Grier a knowing look as he said this—and again that infernal wink. She frowned, utterly baffled. Why was he here? Why would he want to speak with Jack?

For a moment Jack looked as though he might demand an explanation right there and then, but then he glanced around at their captivated audience. "I suppose so," he said gruffly. "I'm sure we can find someplace private to talk."

Jack motioned a servant forward and spoke to her in low tones. Grier could only stare at Trevis, grappling with the collision of past and present before her very eyes.

Suddenly Jack and Trevis were moving. Not about to let them depart the room without her, she lifted her skirts to follow.

Jack hesitated, gauging her with a look. She lifted her chin and gave him a very determined stare, conveying that he would *not* be conversing *about* her with Trevis while she was not present. She would know what was afoot.

Jack motioned for her to precede him and she fell in line behind the maid leading them to the small back parlor. It took every ounce of will not to look behind her for a glimpse of Sev.

Was he still watching her? Watching Trevis with that killing gaze? She imagined he was. Thanks to Trevis's mysterious arrival, every member of their party watched her. She shivered. Attention she did not want or need.

Arriving in the cozy parlor, the maid left them alone, closing the door and closeting the three of them in.

Crossing her arms, Grier faced Trevis. "What are you doing here?"

"I'm here for you, of course."

She dropped her arms and looked at him in utter incredulity. "What for?"

Trevis looked uncertain. "Grier," he said softly, sounding pathetically hurt. "I thought you would be glad to see me, my love."

She cringed. "Don't call me that."

He pouted as though her words wounded him.

"What makes you think I would want to see you? I left home. Did my resignation not convey that I wanted nothing more to do with you?"

"Will someone tell me what this is all about?" Jack blustered. "I've a fine bowl of venison stew growing cold as we stand here."

"Jack, this is Trevis Powell. You may recall that

when your man located me, I was working on his estate as his game master."

"Oh. Powell. That's right." Jack grunted, thoroughly unimpressed as he looked Trevis over. "Thought the name was familiar."

Trevis snapped his heels together, standing tall and erect as though he faced a firing squad. "Yes, Mr. Hadley. I quickly realized my mistake in letting your daughter go. I should never have let her leave my life."

"You didn't *let* me do anything." Her hands opened and shut into fists at her sides. "I *chose* to leave because I had no wish to remain on as your mistress. You do recall that, do you not, Trevis? You refused to marry me, but wished to take our relationship to a more intimate level."

Faint color stained his swarthy cheeks. His eyes darted nervously at her father. "That was wretched of me, I confess. My apologies."

Jack snorted. "You've gall calling upon me after you propositioned my daughter. I should put a bullet through you."

Trevis visibly swallowed.

Grier rolled her eyes at what sounded like actual fatherly protectiveness . . . and for Trevis doing nothing more than what Jack did to her own mother. Still . . . the notion did curl warmly around her heart.

Trevis held out his hands in supplication. "I've come to make amends."

Grier crossed arms once again. "Is that so? And how do you intend to do that?"

"By marrying you, of course."

Grier dropped her arms. "Marry me?"

Jack laughed roughly, shaking his head side-to-side. "Too late on that score, lad. Grier's destined for bigger fish than you."

Trevis's features reddened. "I'm considered quite the catch back home."

"Aye, back *home*. You're in a different pond now."

Trevis slid angry eyes from her father to Grier. "This is up to you, Grier. We don't need his approval."

Jack sobered instantly, all laughter fleeing his voice as he said, "Actually you do, you little bastard. If you think you'll get one coin of mine, you're mistaken."

Trevis blinked in such an astonished way that Grier instantly understood. It all made perfect sense. Somehow, someway, he'd learned of her sudden turn of fortune. He was here for one reason and one reason only.

Grier was an heiress now and worth his time. That's what brought him sniffing about now.

"So. How'd you find out?"

Trevis stared at her for a long moment, not understanding. Or feigning to not understand.

She asked again, her voice a snapping bite on the air. "Come now, the truth. How'd you find out?"

He pulled back his shoulder and stared at her coolly, the lovesick swain gone. "The Reverend and Mrs. Hollings returned from their trip to Town. It seems they saw you at the opera."

Grier smiled mirthlessly, nodding as she recalled bumping into the couple. Especially memorable had been their sagging mouths when they'd seen her in her fine silks. "Ah, the lovely Hollingses. Carried tales of me, did they? Let everyone know the bastard of Carynwedd found herself a fortune. I should have guessed." It was actually difficult to say who gossiped more—the reverend or his wife.

"She's too smart for the likes of you, lad. Best return home," Jack advised. "You'll not snare yourself an heiress here."

Trevis flushed. "Grier," he began. "What about everything we've shared?"

"You know . . . it's all a bit foggy."

"That's not true," he denied, his chest swelling. Clearly he did not believe any woman could forget him.

Grier glared at Trevis. "You're unbelievable. Did you truly think I would toss my arms around you with gratitude?"

He shrugged. "You wanted me then—"

"That was then, Trevis. This is now." Grier moved toward the parlor door. Pulling it open, she turned to face the boy she'd spent the better part of her life pining after—and felt nothing. "Good-bye, Trevis. Sorry you made the journey for nothing."

Trevis's face grew splotchy. "This is your last chance. I shan't ask again, Grier."

She cocked her head and smiled sweetly at him. "I truly hope not."

With his face burning brighter, he stormed past her and out the small parlor.

Once he was gone, her shoulders slumped and the smile slipped from her face. Suddenly she felt very wearied.

"You all right?" Jack asked gruffly.

She stared at him, surprised that he should even care to ask, that he still stood here and had not rushed back to finish his stew.

Grier nodded. "I'll be fine. Just need a few moments."

Jack tugged on his cuffs as if suddenly uncomfortable. "I expect you can do a lot better than him, Grier. Fortune or no fortune."

Grier looked at him sharply, quite certain he had not meant to compliment her. "Thank you."

"Forget about him. You'll find yourself a better man."

"I know, I know." She sighed, the weariness back. "Someone titled."

"Well, yes. But perhaps someone who can appreciate you, too . . . and not be so bloody obvious about the fact that he's after your dowry. You've a lot to recommend you besides my fortune."

Grier blinked, unsure what to make of the fact that Jack Hadley was actually being kind to her . . . as a true father would be.

"Yes," she agreed, a smile twitching her lips. "He could at least possess intelligence enough to disguise the fact that he only wants your money."

With another nod and tug on his waistcoat, Jack cleared his throat. "I'm going to return to my dinner."

"Enjoy," she murmured. As Jack passed through the door, she added. "And . . . thank you."

He looked over his shoulder, the uncomfortable expression once again on his face. "For what?"

"Acting like a father."

A flicker of emotion cracked his gruff exterior. "Th-that's what I am. Like it or not, I'm your father."

She smiled at him, surprised at how easy it was to do. "I like it."

He shifted on his feet, clearly uncomfortable with what amounted to her praise. "Don't tarry. You need to eat."

She nodded. "I'll be along soon."

With a nod of his own, he turned from the room.

She watched him walk from sight before moving back into the parlor and dropping onto an overstuffed chair, convinced she could fall asleep and spend the night right there.

"Grier."

Opening her eyes, her heart skipped to life to see Sev crossing the threshold. She shot upright. "Sev."

He stopped before her chair. Squatting down before her, he took her chilled hand into his own. "Are you all right?"

She gave a wavery smile, her heart softening at the concern in his voice. "Fine." She looked down at his large hand clasped in her own. "Fine now any rate." She released a pent-up breath. Just how true that was frightened her. In a mere moment his presence could put all her troubles to rest.

"Who was that man?"

She waved a hand dismissively, hoping he would not force the topic of Trevis. "No one."

"Clearly not no one."

"His name is Trevis Powell."

"Who is he to you?"

A muscle rippled the skin of his jaw and that dark look came back into his eyes. "He touched you with much familiarity," he added in a thick voice.

"He's no one to me," she insisted. "Let us just leave it at that."

"How do you come to know him? What was he doing here? He was looking for you specifically."

"After my father passed on, I stayed on as his gamekeeper. He came here to convince me to go back with him."

Sev's lion eyes narrowed. "And why would he want you to do that?"

"Because he thought I would want to," she hedged, looking down at her lap where their fingers clung to each other. Sev's fingers tightened the slightest amount around hers, clearly dissatisfied with her vague response.

"Grier," he prompted.

She sighed and continued, relenting to the embarrassing truth. "He learned that I'm an heiress now. He wants my money—or rather Jack's. The same as every other man that pays me the slightest heed." She snorted. "Well, except you. To the rest I'm simply a fat banknote."

"He proposed to you then?"

She nodded. "Only he's lacking the required title to meet Jack's criteria . . . oh, and there's the fact that I can't stomach the sight of him. That, too. Those factors make it hard to accept an offer of marriage from such a man."

"I sense bitterness in you. Why do you dislike him so much? Did he do . . . something to you?"

She inhaled a bracing breath. "He promised to marry me for years."

His fingers almost hurt where they wrapped around hers. "Are you in love with him?"

"No! God, no! He's a wretch. I was just inexperienced. It took me a while to realize what he truly was. When I did I left Wales. I couldn't stay on."

"What happened?"

"For years he kept me dangling on a hook with the promise of marriage." She winced, thinking how foolish she'd been to ever believe him. To ever even *want* him. "Finally he admitted he could never marry me. He confessed to my face that I was beneath him and that he must marry someone respectable. Someone with a dowry." She laughed lightly. "But he didn't want me to be totally disappointed. He kindly offered to keep me on as his game master, so long as I agreed to be his mistress. A role he thought me aptly suited for." She lifted one shoulder. "And that's when I decided I would leave Wales. Jack's summons came not a moment too soon."

Sev growled beneath his breath. "Bastard."

She looked him steadily in the face. "And why would you say that? He's not so unlike you. You've offered me nothing but a place in your bed." Even as she uttered the words, she regretted them, knew them to be untrue. He was nothing like Trevis. He possessed responsibilities too great to let himself take her for a wife. She knew he cared for her, that he would consider her for a wife if he could.

Sev blinked, his hand loosening around hers. "If that's how you see me, why are you even talking to me? Why even let me touch you?"

Because I love you. The realization stunned her, knocked the wind loose from her chest and filled her with raw panic. It only confirmed in her mind what she had to do. She blinked, fighting back the burn in her eyes. She couldn't break down and weep now. She had to end this before they became any more entangled. Before it became impossible to walk away.

"Good question," she replied through numb lips. As much as it hurt to say the words, they needed to be said. "This can't continue. We can't."

Every moment with him pushed her closer to ruin. To say nothing of the danger to her heart. As much as severing with him hurt, if she delayed any longer she might not be able to extricate herself at all. She'd be lost to him. And she didn't want to make this any harder for him either. He had a duty to perform. It impacted thousands of people, an entire country. She couldn't be so selfish as to put her own desires first.

As if burned from the touch of her, he dropped his hand completely from hers and rose to his full looming height. Her gaze drifted up to his face, drinking in the sight of him as if it were her last. And essentially it was. The next time she saw him, there would be nothing between them.

He stared down at her so impassively, the old prince, austere and unfeeling again.

She licked her lips. "Good-bye, Sevastian."

He didn't move for the longest moment. She held her breath, willing him to leave. *Willing him to stay.*

Finally, without a word, he turned on his heels and departed the room with solid steps.

She released the breath she had been holding and remained in her chair, as still as stone for several moments, the ticking clock on the mantel timing the seconds it took her heart to break.

A sob broke from her lips and she collapsed, dropping her head into her shuddering lap. It didn't take long at all.

Chapter Twenty

Sev strode toward the front door of the inn, ignoring his cousin calling to him from a table to let him know their dinner waited.

He welcomed the hard bite of winter on his cheeks as he stepped out into the windswept yard, relishing any discomfort the cold brought, hoping it helped mask the uncomfortable knotting in his gut. Perhaps anyone who looked at him would fail to notice that he'd been struck a blow.

She'd ended it. Their affair.

Them.

He burrowed deeper within his jacket, realizing he should have grabbed his long coat but not about to go back for it. He was in no mood for people. He was especially in no mood to face her again.

His jaw clenched so hard his teeth ached. She'd walked away from him when they were only just starting to enjoy each other. They were just . . . beginning. What, precisely, he couldn't say, but something more than an illicit, sordid affair. For the first time in his life, he'd felt himself with another person. Himself. Sevastian. Not the crown prince, or war hero. He'd felt like he could be his true self with her.

And with a word, she'd killed that.

His hands opened and shut at his sides at the memory of her silken skin. He hadn't done half the things he wished to do to her yet. He hadn't heard half the things he wanted to hear from her lips yet . . .

This last thought jarred him. Since when did he long to hear a woman *talk* . . . to spill her soul to him?

His hands unclenched. They weren't finished. He'd had affairs aplenty before and walked away with no regrets, with no painful knotting in his stomach. But this—Grier. They weren't done. She was sorely mistaken if she thought she'd seen the last of him.

At that moment a man emerged from the stables tugging on his gloves and adjusting his hat upon his head. A groom led a horse before him.

A low growl rose from the back of his throat as he recognized the man from Grier's past. The man she thought to compare him to. They were nothing alike. Sev would never be fool enough to let her go. Not if he truly wanted her. And he did.

She said she didn't love the man, but Sev wondered if that was true. Was that why his arrival today hurt her so much? Was that why she ended their affair?

Had seeing Powell reminded her that she cared for him? More than whatever feelings she harbored for Sev?

She turned down his proposal, a voice reminded in the back of his mind. *She couldn't still want him.*

At the thought of that proposal, that this man hoped to claim Grier for his wife, Sev's vision clouded with a rage he'd never felt before. Not even in the heat of battle, when his blood pumped so hard all thought fled and he only acted.

He strode quick, hard strides across the yard. Without a word, he grabbed Trevis Powell's shoulder and whirled him around.

Powell didn't have time to speak before Sev planted his fist in his face with a satisfying crunch.

The man staggered, but didn't fall. He glared at

Sev over the hand he held to his afflicted cheek. "What the bloody hell was that for?"

"For thinking you could come back here and claim her after you threw her away."

The bewilderment gradually cleared from his eyes. "Ah, got to you, too, did she? There's certainly something about her, isn't there? She has a way about her. I should know. I tried for years to get beneath her skirts. I think it's that lovely mouth. Makes a man imagine the places he'd like her to put it."

Sev growled and took a menacing step toward him.

Powell held up a hand to ward him off while his other hand fingered his tender cheek. "No need for violence, chap. She's just a bit of common trash."

"Bastard!" With a roar, Sev charged him like a bull and knocked him to the ground. They rolled, throwing punches and striking each other wherever their fists could connect. He felt nothing, registered no pain. Each crack of bone on bone fueled his fury, egging him further.

Sev gained the advantage and pinned Powell to the cold ground, striking him again and again.

"Sev! Sev! Stop!"

Malcolm was there, pulling on him with two grooms, grunting as they tried to haul him off the bloodied man.

Sev blinked and looked around. A crowd had gathered. The dowager's houseguests gawked at him with sagging mouths, their breaths smoky puffs on the cold night air. He cared for none of them. His gaze sought only one.

He found her, standing just inside the threshold, for once looking pale as milk. Her face was leached of all color beneath her sun-browned skin. He freckles stood out in stark relief, and something almost painful knifed near his heart.

She looked from him to Powell writhing on the ground. When her gaze found him again, her eyes gleamed bright with disapproval.

He didn't flinch, didn't show the slightest sign of regret for his actions. He'd beat the bastard to a pulp again for speaking of her so crudely . . . for hurting her.

She hugged herself but he somehow doubted it was the cold that made her embrace herself so tightly. Her sister stood beside her, gripping her arm in a gesture of support. *As if he'd done something wrong.*

He stared at Grier, wiping the blood from his

lip with the back of his hand, indifferent to who watched him and what they thought of the Crown Prince of Maldania tussling in the dirt outside an inn like a common peasant.

Malcolm growled close to his ear, "Have you gone mad? People are watching!"

"Let them watch." He took a step, intent on reaching her, when she turned with a sudden jerk and went back inside, dismissing him.

And then he recalled with bitter clarity that she wanted nothing more to do with him. He stopped and glanced around at the crowd of avid spectators and took a bracing breath. For now. He'd let her go for now. He'd let her think they were finished. He wouldn't risk her reputation by chasing after her—as every fiber of his being urged him to do.

They weren't even close to being finished. She'd know that soon enough.

Grier fled inside to the small parlor where she'd attended Trevis earlier. She stood at the window and stared out at the snow, seeing and unseeing at the same time.

Trevis was even now being assisted to a bed somewhere inside the inn. *Because of Sevastian. Because of her.*

When she woke this morning she could not have imagined such an incredible scenario.

Holy hellfire. She closed her eyes in a tight blink and tried to summon a speck of guilt for that fact, but she could only marvel upon why Sevastian would do such a thing.

She could guess at the ugly things Trevis had said about her if Sev confronted him, and she knew enough about Sev to know that honor drove him to protect those harmed, be it with words or a raised fist.

Even though she'd ended their affair, Sev would feel honor-bound to defend her. *Affair.* It seemed silly to even call it that. Did one night constitute an affair? And yet at the same time it seemed wholly inadequate, too.

"Grier?" Cleo hesitantly called her name from the threshold.

Grier turned to face her.

"Are you all right? What happened?"

Even she didn't know how to answer that. She inhaled a steadying breath, her fingers lightly thrumming against her lips. "Nothing. We're going home, Cleo. Back to London."

Cleo nodded, looking at Grier as if she feared she might have lost her mind. "I know that."

"We're going back to Town." She ceased playing with her mouth and dropped her hand. "And I'm going to find a husband. No more hanging about ferns."

Cleo arched a jet black brow. "Indeed?"

"Yes." She was done dragging her feet. The quicker she wed someone else, the sooner she could forget about Sevastian.

Chapter Twenty-one

want to hear everything. How was the dowager's house party?" Grier's half sister Marguerite leaned close and whispered over the lilting notes of the soprano who sang at the front of the room, "Do you have any prospects? Any handsome men sweep you off your feet?"

Grier ignored the sudden pinch in her chest and slid her gaze from the Italian opera singer the dowager had acquired for the evening to her half sister. "The viscount has made himself amenable."

Marguerite looked over at the gentleman sitting one row behind them in the dowager's ballroom. Several rows of chairs lined the ballroom, occupied by gentlemen and ladies all listening raptly to the soprano performing on a small dais at the head of the room. The singer's generous bosom swelled from her gown. Grier feared that she might spill free with her next note.

Smiling, Marguerite whispered, "I'm sure the viscount has been more than amenable. His imposing grandmamma would see to that, I imagine."

Grier nodded, her stomach cramping a bit because her single marriage prospect was due to one intimidating old lady. Far from romantic.

At that thought, her gaze swept the room, searching for the familiar dark hair of her prince. A weakness to be certain, that she should still search for him after she ended their affair, but in the last week since her return to Town she found herself searching for him everywhere she went.

She took a bracing breath. Sooner or later they would bump into each other, and she must be strong when that moment arrived. As stalwart as she'd been at the inn, severing their relationship with nary a tear. At least in his presence.

"Are you looking for someone?" Marguerite asked.

"No." Grier forced a bright smile. "Thank you for accompanying me tonight. We've had so little opportunity to visit."

"I'm thrilled you invited me. With Ash out of

town on business, I'm happy for the distraction. I'm only sorry Cleo isn't feeling well."

"She's been spending a good deal of time with Lord Quibbly."

"Lord Quibbly? That ancient old man who practically accosted us when we arrived, demanding to know where Cleo was?"

"The same." Grier readjusted herself on the hard-backed chair and sighed, not understanding why Cleo encouraged the old man's suit. "I think she wanted a reprieve from his attentions."

"That I can understand."

Marguerite shuddered, and Grier couldn't help teasing, "Not everyone can be married to an Adonis."

Marguerite smiled pertly and whispered back, "True. There is no one his match."

Grier snorted. "Braggart."

"Although that gentleman who just entered the room with his gaze fixated on you would be a close second."

Grier's gaze jerked to land on Sevastian, standing tall and handsome in his black jacket. Only he wasn't alone.

Other than his ever-present cousin, a pair of ladies accompanied them. One was older—the mother, Grier guessed from her resemblance to the young, fair-haired woman that Sev gallantly led into a seat.

Grier's eyes burned. He wasted no time moving on.

"Grier, are you all right?"

Grier nodded, staring her aching eyes hard at the back of Sev's head two rows before her. So much for remaining stalwart. Her hands shook in her lap.

The room broke into applause as the soprano's final note faded to an end.

Shaking, she rose to her feet. "Excuse me, Marguerite. I need some air."

"Would you like me to come with—"

"No. I'll be but a moment." If she should succumb to tears, she didn't want her sister to witness her display of weakness. They were only just beginning to know each other. Grier would rather Marguerite not know that she had fallen in love with a man so above her station that she was guaranteed nothing but heartache.

She glimpsed her father as she fled, standing near the back with other gentlemen less inclined to appreciate the evening's musical performance. She ignored his scowl as she fled. Ignored meeting anyone's eyes directly, most specifically a dark-haired, gold-eyed prince she'd shut out from her life. She blinked burning eyes, her steps eating up the parquet floor as she hurried from the ballroom. She wondered if she could beg off for the night and go home—tell everyone she was ill with whatever allegedly ailed Cleo.

"Grier!"

A small squeak escaped her at the sight of Sev striding toward her.

Whirling back around, she increased her pace, hoping he would get the hint that she didn't want to see him . . . especially with her eyes burning and tears that threatened to fall at any moment.

He said her name louder, a barked command. A quick glance revealed he was running now, his face set in hard, determined lines.

Lifting her skirts, she gave in to a full run, not caring how absurd she was being, running from him like he was a crazed murderer.

Rounding a corner, she seized the latch on a door, fumbling with it, hoping to dive inside and hide.

Just as she got the door opened, he was there. Every hard imposing inch of him pressed at her back. Instantly she was enveloped in him. He was no longer a memory, but a live, real, flesh and blood man pressed hotly against her.

Her heart spiked against her throat. Panic warred with the inexplicable fury in her heart.

She whipped around, brought her palm crashing against his face with a loud crack.

He grabbed her wrist before she could strike him again and pushed her back into the room. Darkness engulfed them, thick and pervasive as a cocoon.

They wrestled, he trying to grab one of her flailing hands desperate to hit him, punish him again—to hurt him for all the pain in her heart.

Sobs choked her throat. He hauled her against him, her arms trapped between their bodies.

He grasped her face with his one free hand, forcing her still, immobilizing her. His mouth claimed hers in a fierce stamp of his desire. Heat seared her at the contact and she was helpless to resist. She kissed him back with equal fervor, their lips brutal and thorough, teeth clanging in their feverish need for each other.

The throbbing darkness enhanced everything. Her skin sizzled where he touched. He eased up, freeing her hands. It was as though they read each other's minds. Her fingers flew to his trousers, freed him as he dove beneath her skirts.

Fabric ripped. Her drawers, she supposed—didn't care.

The barest hint of air caressed that exposed part of her before he was there, plunging himself deep.

She arched, crying out beneath him as he worked himself over her. Their bodies made savage sounds as they came together again and again in a fierce coupling.

His hands gripped her bottom, lifting her up for his penetration. She went willingly, moved with his every motion, reveling, exulting, exploding into a million particles.

The air itself seemed to shudder around her as she convulsed, trembling in his arms. And still, it was not over. He flipped her so that she rode him. After a moment's awkwardness, she found her rhythm, encouraged by his deep, guttural sounds of satisfaction.

He cupped her breasts through her dress, abraded the nipples through the sheer muslin until she moaned and rode him harder, finding that spot and hitting it as hard as she could manage.

"Mine," he whispered so softly she wondered if she had heard him correctly through all their sounds and noises.

Ripples of sensation burst through her again, spreading from the core of her to each and every nerve ending. With an exultant shout, she collapsed. Draped over him, it was some moments before she could even move.

His light touch at the back of her head spiked her to awareness.

She lurched upright and scrambled off him, rearranging her skirts over her. "What have we done? In the midst of the dowager's musicale, no less? You've gone mad and you've dragged me with you!"

"It was bound to happen." His disembodied voice stroked the air, infuriatingly even. "It will happen again if we try to ignore each other."

She rose unsteadily to her feet. "What do you recommend? We schedule regular trysts?" She thought of the fair-haired lady waiting for him in the dowager's ballroom and her anger returned. "That might impede your courtship."

She thought she caught the gleam of his lion's eyes in the dark. "You're jealous."

"Why would I be jealous?" she snapped. "I broke it off with you. It's you who needs to stop hounding me."

Her hands quickly assessed her hair. There was hardly a strand properly in place. *Holy hellfire.* One look at her and anyone would surmise she had been engaging in relations of an illicit nature.

"How could I have been so stupid?" She furiously attacked her hair, readjusting the pins without a hope.

"Grier." Suddenly his warm hand was on her arm. "We can't go on ignoring each other. I'm going to keep hounding you, as you put it."

"Don't touch me." Her voice quivered as she tried to pull free.

The last time he touched her they ended up rutting on the floor like a pair of wild animals. Her face burned and she arched away.

Instead of releasing her, he took her by both arms and held her close as though trying to comfort her. Or calm her. Perhaps both.

And that was how they were discovered, locked in each other's arms, her hair tumbling wildly around her, the smell of their desire ripe on the air.

Light bathed them as the door to the room opened wide.

Chapter Twenty-two

Grier!"

She couldn't quite identify the emotion that hummed through her father's voice. He was shocked to be sure, but there was an excited tremor there as well. She closed her eyes in a tight blink, well imagining his thoughts—if his daughter was caught in a compromising position, it might as well be with a prince.

Marguerite stood beside Jack as well, looking perfectly apologetic as she looked between Sev and Grier. "I-I'm sorry, Grier. I feared you were ill."

"Your Highness, there can be no excuse for this display!"

"I've none to give." Sev nodded.

"Jack," Grier pleaded, "would you keep your voice down. There's no need to alert the house—"

"What's this?" a new voice inquired.

Grier sighed as the viscount stepped into view.

"Miss Hadley," he murmured, his tone reflecting his surprise as he looked from her to Sev.

"Maksimi," Jack growled, doing a poor imitation of an outraged papa. His eyes gleamed with glee. "I demand you do the honorable thing by my daughter."

"Don't be absurd. Nothing untoward occurred," Grier lied, glad they had not come upon them five minutes sooner.

Everyone swept their gazes over her disheveled self. She fought not to fidget beneath their dubious appraisal of her.

Jack snorted.

The viscount arched an eyebrow in disbelief. "Indeed."

Sev took a menacing step. "Have a care."

Jack shook a fist. "I demand the honorable thing be done—"

"And it shall," Sev snapped.

Grier swung her gaze to him. "No. You cannot—"

"It's done," Sev declared flatly. "I've compromised you and we will marry."

Grier gaped, thinking back to the first night they met and his proclamation that he would never marry her—even if caught together in a compromising situation.

"You can't mean that," she whispered.

"Of course I do."

She shook her head, stunned, feeling as though she'd been struck a blow.

Sev coolly addressed her father. "Mr. Hadley, I'll call on you tomorrow with my formal offer and we can discuss the arrangements."

Jack looked almost as stunned as Grier felt. For all his demands, she doubted he really thought he'd get his way on the matter. At least not so easily.

Sev faced her, his face all hard lines, again the stoic resolve of a marble statue. Fleetingly she marveled that this must have been what he looked like on the dawn of a battle. Was that how he viewed agreeing to marry her? An unpleasant yet necessary task?

His eyes revealed nothing, staring through her as if he didn't see her at all. "We'll speak to-morrow."

She shook her head. "Sev . . . no. You don't have to—"

"I do," he bit out. "We both do." With a curt nod, he turned and left her alone.

The viscount looked her over, his eyes bitterly cold before he, too, turned and left. In minutes everyone would know she'd been caught in a compromising situation with the Crown Prince of Maldania.

Marguerite hurried to her side. "Come, we'll find a room to repair your hair."

"I just want to go home," Grier murmured, stunned, shaken, and unwilling to face anyone else. She wanted to crawl into her bed and pull the coverlet over her head.

Her sister laced her fingers with Grier's. "Certainly, come."

At the threshold, Jack clapped her on the back so hard it jarred her teeth. "You did good, girl. You did good."

Mortifying heat washed her face. She had to stop herself from striking him. Did he think she planned this?

He looked at her face and frowned. His brow knit in concern. "What's wrong? You're not ill, are you?"

She shook her head. "No."

"Then why aren't you pleased? You should be.

Grier, you'll one day be a queen. Just think of it."

He didn't understand. Only she did.

She knew Sev already regretted it, and his regret would grow, fester into bitterness until he hated the sight of her.

Sev walked a hard line into the library of his rented townhouse, his booted heels clicking over the marble as he made his way for the tray of brandy. After tonight, he could use a drink. Something to steady his nerves.

Not that he regretted his decision. Not that he ever would. He merely needed time to consider how he was going to present his new bride to his grandfather without sending the old man into a seizure that robbed him of his last breath.

Sev's top lip curled into a grimace. The old man was stronger than that. He'd outlived two sons, a wife and multiple grandchildren. Dropping into a plush wingback chair, he stared at the smoldering logs in the fireplace, feeling moody and pensive.

For several moments he didn't move, simply stared at the sparking embers, waiting for guilt to attack him. Or regret for failing to do the one thing expected of him.

Only it didn't come.

So his wife-to-be didn't possess the most stellar of pedigrees. He knew he should care, but at that moment he was having trouble mustering much anger at himself for the situation.

Grier was smart and beautiful and strong—everything he wanted in the wife who would stand beside him and lead Maldania into the future.

In the distance, a door slammed.

Moments later the door to the study banged open. "What have you done?" Malcolm demanded in tones so shrill they resembled a woman's.

Sev winced. He didn't need to ask Malcolm to explain himself. He understood perfectly.

"I had to find out from some old hag that my own cousin just offered marriage to Miss Grier Hadley after being caught in a state of dishabille with her."

"Nothing as dramatic as that, I assure you. We were both dressed."

An expression of vast relief crossed Malcolm's features. "So you didn't propose?"

"Oh, I proposed."

Malcolm marched to stand before Sev, his hands propped belligerently upon his hips as he glared down at him. "Why would you do such a thing?"

"I'm honor-bound to offer marriage."

"Rubbish. She's gotten into your blood. That is all. You've wanted her from the first minute you clapped eyes on her." Malcolm shook his head vehemently. "You're not thinking. You'll soon tire of her. The last thing you shall want is to then find yourself shackled to her."

"That won't happen."

"Listen to yourself! You sound like you're in love with the chit!"

Sev opened his mouth to deny the charge, but instead closed it with a snap.

He . . . shrugged. For some reason he had no wish to deny the allegation. He angled his head, scratching his jaw thoughtfully. Perhaps there was a kernel of truth to it.

He'd known when he followed Grier into that room he played with fire. He knew what would happen when he followed her . . . that he would have to touch her. Taste her.

He'd missed her abominably. She'd haunted his every waking moment—hell, even his dreams. He'd found courting other women, abiding their inane chatter, intolerable.

Even more intolerable was the notion that she was being courted. By the viscount or some other man. That some other man could be putting a hand on her . . . that a man other than he could kiss her, take her to his bed. He couldn't stomach the notion.

"What will your grandfather say?"

A muscle near his eye ticked and he rubbed at the bothersome area, hoping to be rid of the sensation. "He'll be happy I've married," he replied vaguely.

"To someone as common as the Hadley girl? A chit as long in the tooth as she is?" Malcolm snorted. "I think not."

His jaw clenched. "He'll get over it. Once Grier's delivered him his first grandchild, he'll be satisfied."

Malcolm's faced flushed red and he stamped a foot. "He won't! He won't be happy. He won't!"

Sev frowned at his cousin's strange words and stranger behavior. *He won't be happy.* Sev was unsure if he was stating this as fact . . . or as a wish. Either way, Sev was in no mood for such theatrics.

Sev rose to his feet. "This isn't up for discussion, cousin."

"You're making a mistake." Malcolm's eyes glittered brightly.

"I think not. Even so, it's my mistake to make. My life." He held his cousin's gaze for a long moment. "I'll hear no more on the subject, Malcolm. I'm going to bed."

Turning, he felt his cousin's stare drilling into his back as he left the room. Taking the stairs to his room, he wondered at Malcolm's strange behavior . . . wondered if he really knew him at all. Or if he even wanted to.

Chapter Twenty-three

$\mathcal{S}$ev called upon Grier promptly the following morning. Cleo rushed into her bedchamber to alert her of the fact. She danced lightly on her slippered feet, her deep brown ringlets bouncing over her shoulders. "He's in the library with Jack. Do you want me to listen at the door?"

Grier smiled—the first time since last night—imagining Cleo eavesdropping. "No. I imagine they're discussing the settlement and other matters."

She walked toward the window and gazed down at the gardens below, unable to hold her sister's stare in that moment, reluctant to let her see all her misgivings so plainly writ upon her face.

She was marrying Sevastian. She would have him . . . the man for whom her heart beat these last weeks. It was exciting and terrifying. She hadn't been able to catch her breath since last night.

"I'm happy for you, Grier. You're going to be so happy."

Grier turned slowly to face the sister she'd only recently come to know . . . and realized there was so much of her she still didn't know. For starters, why she wished to entertain the courtship of a much older man.

"You think so?" she asked, eyeing Cleo's fresh young face and loathing the notion of her shackled to the ancient marquis.

Cleo nodded, her brown waves bouncing over her shoulder. "Yes. You've won a prince! You're going to be a queen, Grier. Think of it!"

Her stomach heaved. She pressed a hand to her lurching belly. "I'd rather not."

"You'll be a marvelous queen. Think of the insights you will have. All the good you can do."

She angled her head, considering that for the first time, and suddenly not feeling so . . . scared anymore.

"I hadn't thought of that before."

Cleo nodded encouragingly. "You can be a

voice for the people. Someone real, not some royal so elevated and removed from the common man's existence. You'll be one of them, and they're going to adore you!"

Grier dropped her hand from her stomach, suddenly a little more optimistic. She could do something . . . make a difference. *Yes.* "I shall miss you. You must visit. And Marguerite. Even Jack."

"As if you can keep me away. And you know Jack will be there." Cleo gave her hand a squeeze. "You've found your fairy tale, Grier. You're going to be so very happy."

Would she? So much of that seemed wrapped up in whether Sev would be happy with her as his queen. It still seemed an impossibility. Her momentary optimism fled.

Would Sev wake one day hating her, regretting his impulsive decision to wed her? A knock sounded at the door before a maid entered. "Your presence is desired in the study, Miss Grier."

Her stomach plummeted to her feet. She nodded jerkily.

"Have a good time!" Cleo called cheerfully as she departed the room.

Grier sent her a bewildered look over her shoulder. Did she think she was going for a jaunt in the park?

Shaking her head, she descended the stairs, carefully masking her face, for when she first met Sev's gaze. Would she already see the chill of regret there? Would it begin now?

Upon entering the library, she saw that it was only Sev. Her father was nowhere in sight as she expected.

Sev stood at the window overlooking the street. She hovered on the threshold, the only sounds those of the clacking of hooves and the creaking of wheels from outside.

She must have made a sound that alerted him to her presence. He turned, arms still locked behind him. He looked so stern and forbidding that she blurted the first thought that crossed her mind.

"We don't have to do this."

He said nothing. Merely gazed at her with an implacable expression on his face.

She moistened her lips and continued, "I won't hold you to it. I'll tell everyone I refused your offer. No one will think less of you."

He moved, walking steadily toward her. Her breath hitched as he closed the distance between them.

Then . . . he walked straight past her.

She swung around, heart hammering. She

watched in bewilderment, her eyes wide and aching in her face.

Was he leaving? Was this it then? She'd given him the out he desired?

He stepped from the room, arms extending until he clasped the latch on each door and shut them soundly, closing them in from prying eyes.

"What are you doing?" She squeezed her hands together in front of her.

He turned to face her, his gold eyes glinting. "Giving a newly affianced couple a few moments of privacy."

"Sev." She shook her head. "What are we doing? This is madness. Let's stop this before it goes any further."

"There's no going back now, Grier."

"How can you possibly marry me, Sev?" She shook her head and sliced a hand through the air. "Your country needs a proper queen. Not some girl who was a game master in a past life."

"I decide what's proper, do I not? I'll be king someday. No one's authority supersedes mine. What is it you're so afraid of? Who, precisely, do you think will object to you?"

"Your grandfather—"

"My grandfather shall have nothing to say once

we hand him his first great-grandchild. He'll be too busy weeping joyful tears."

Heat flushed her face and she looked down at her hands, secretly delighted at the mere thought of having a child. *Sev's child.* Hardening her heart, she looked back up to stare him in the eyes. "And what if that doesn't happen? You yourself proclaimed me old. What if I can't—"

"And I believe you proclaimed me a jackass," he cut in. "I rather think you were correct."

She choked on laughter even as her eyes burned with tears.

He strode forward and took her hand. With a tug, he lowered her onto a settee next to him. "It's too late to go back now, so stop talking about it."

"But you didn't want this—"

He pressed a finger to her lips. "I want you. More than any other woman I've crossed paths with in my search for a bride."

She swallowed down the sudden lump in her throat and snatched his finger from her lips. "But I'm not what your grandfather sent you here to—"

"He can't object to your fortune."

"But he *can* object to *me*."

Sev smiled then, his lips a crooked grin that made her belly twist. "No matter how much you try, you're not going to talk me out of this."

She sighed in exasperation.

"Trust me," Sev coaxed. "Will you?"

And she wanted to. Desperately.

I want you. His words almost convinced her. Except she'd heard them before. And she knew a man's desires changed with the wind.

If he'd said *love* . . .

If she even thought he might love her some-day . . .

Shaking her head, she told herself to stop being fanciful. She hadn't expected a love match before. She only wanted it now because she wanted a guarantee that he would not one day stare at her with embarrassment and regret. She only wanted it because when that day arrived it would break her heart. A heart that was fully and hopelessly bound to him.

For a fleeting moment she considered baring her heart and professing her love to him. But she wasn't that courageous. Or foolish. One of the two. She wasn't sure which.

Instead she pasted a smile on her face. "Yes. I trust you," she murmured, wondering if she wasn't perhaps making the worst mistake of her life. If she shouldn't perhaps pack up her things and flee to Wales.

Sev stared at her in such a way that she wondered if he read her mind, if he guessed her thoughts. His next words confirmed this.

"Run from me, Grier Hadley, and I'll follow. I'll track you down and find you."

A small shiver scraped her spine.

"I don't need to run away." She squared her shoulders and lifted her chin defiantly. "I'm an independent female. I make my own choices. If I don't want you, I simply won't have you. No one can force me to marry you."

His mouth twitched and he scooted closer. His warm breath fanned her neck, sending the most delicious tremors rippling through her.

"If we're relying on you *wanting* me, then I won't need to force you to marry me."

Grier choked on a breath. "Arrogant, aren't you?"

He looked at her, his gaze rather grim. "We're both here right now because we can't help ourselves when it comes to each other."

That much was true.

He continued, "I'm not going to even pretend that I'm doing this against my will . . . that I'm led by honor."

She gazed at him unblinkingly, his face so close that their breaths mingled. Hope blossomed in her chest at the possibility that perhaps, just maybe, this wasn't a colossal mistake. That she

could find her storybook ending with a storybook prince.

Before Sev's lips touched hers, the door to the
library opened. "Ah, just as I expected."

Jack rocked on his heels, looking far too pleased
with himself as he surveyed them. "Best keep an
eye on you two until the nuptials take place."

Grier's cheeks burned.

Sev rose to his feet. "As discussed, I'll see the
banns posted posthaste."

"Very good." Jack practically rubbed his hands
in glee.

Sev looked back down at Grier. "I'll call on you
tomorrow and we'll discuss travel arrangements.
We'll be wed in Maldania where my grandfather
can attend."

Her stomach plummeted at this announcement. To leave her country, the sisters she had just
met, would be hard. If only she felt more confi-
dent about their match, if it were based on mutual
affection, if Sev loved her even a little bit . . . she
would suffer no doubts.

"Yes." Jack nodded in agreement. "Just as we
discussed. A royal wedding in the infamous St.
Ignatius Cathedral." He looked at Grier meaning-
fully. "I'm told it's even older than St. Paul's. A
grand event, to be certain."

Grier's stomach twisted so violently she feared she would be ill. *A royal wedding*. She should have expected no less.

Only it was easy to forget, here in her father's library with Sev sitting so close to her, whispering in that low, seductive voice of his, that they were from two different worlds. People with nothing in common between them but desire.

Desire was fleeting. She knew that from her own father. He'd taken her mother, used her, and then tossed her aside. She inhaled deeply, staving off the burn in her eyes with several hard blinks.

Sev bowed over her hand, his fingers warm around her chilled ones. "Until tomorrow."

Grier watched him depart, wondering how she could feel such love and despair at the same time.

Chapter Twenty-four

$\mathcal{G}$rier clasped the piece of parchment close to her chest, the words printed there whispering through her head. *I long to see you without the presence of others. Meet me outside the back of the house as soon as you can get away. I wait with a carriage.*

"Thank you," she murmured to the servant who delivered the missive, a small tremor of delight rippling through her. The girl—Marie, Grier thought her name was—ducked her head almost shyly before slipping from the room.

Grier looked down at the letter again, and a secret smile lifted the corners of her mouth. Over the last three days, she and Sev scarcely had a moment alone. Her father insisted they be seen about Town as much as possible, presenting themselves as the happily affianced couple. But always they were surrounded by others. Grier told herself it wouldn't be like this after they married . . . that they would have ample opportunity to be alone together then.

But three days in his constant company and never a word in private, not a touch, not a stolen kiss . . . Her doubts had resurfaced to take hold, and she worried with the whirl of wedding and travel arrangements if a little regret had not entered his head.

She'd entered a state of breathless agitation. If he had the slightest remorse for his hasty offer of marriage, she hoped he would call a halt to this madly racing train at once. Tomorrow they left for Maldania. The next step toward their real life together. A life that could be hell for both of them if Sev was already regretting their union.

The letter crinkled against her fingers, reviving her with hope that Sev wasn't afflicted with regret.

"What do you have there?" Cleo asked, looking up from her novel, her finger marking her spot in the book.

"Nothing."

"Nothing! Nothing made you smile?"

Grier's smile only deepened.

Cleo rolled her eyes. "A love letter from Sevastian, perhaps?"

"Something like that . . ." she hedged, rising from the sofa. "If you'll excuse me." *Sevastian waited.*

Cleo waggled her fingers in the air. "Run along, reread your letter in privacy where I don't have to hear your lovesick sighs."

Grier hurried from the drawing room, stopping only to fetch a cloak. Her heart raced at Sevastian's romantic gesture . . . it gave her hope that what he felt for her was deep and true . . . strong enough to withstand his grandfather's disappointment. *Strong enough to last.*

She earned a few speculative glances as she passed servants on the stairs, but she didn't let it deter her. She stepped outside the back servants' entrance and burrowed into her cloak, scanning the narrow alley where deliveries were usually made.

A carriage idled alongside the wrought-iron gate, the driver blowing into his hands.

She skipped down the steps and quickly made her way along the path, mindful not to let the iron gate clang too loudly behind her. She gave a quick glance around to be certain that no one lurked about. No servant stood outside. She was all alone in the gray afternoon . . . only a few yards separating her from Sev.

Her feet flew faster, her heart beating like an anxious drum in her chest. Until this moment she didn't realize how desperately she needed to see him . . . needed soothing that everything was going to be all right.

At the carriage door, she hesitated, expecting Sev to reveal himself . . . open the door and greet her, assist her inside with him, perhaps pull her into his arms for one of those kisses that melted her from the inside out. She'd missed his kisses.

"Sevastian?" she called, looking to the left and right, wondering if she could be mistaken, if this wasn't his carriage at all and she'd made some kind of mistake.

A long moment passed until the door finally opened.

And yet it wasn't Sev's face that emerged behind the door.

His cousin stared down at her with a welcoming smile—a smile that did not reach his eyes. Her heart stuttered in her chest before resuming its beating. Something lurked in those eyes. Something that made her feel decidedly unsafe. The same as when she confronted a wildcat hunting in the mountains back home. He had that same cagey look in his eyes as an animal cornered.

Only he wasn't the one cornered.

"Ah, Miss Hadley." He leaned out of the carriage. "Thank you for coming so quickly."

"Where's Sevastian?" She looked over his shoulder into the dim confines of the carriage even though she didn't really expect to see him there.

"He sent me to fetch you."

She felt her brow furrow. "But the letter . . ."

"The missive was indeed from him." He nodded jovially, his red hair bright even in the murky air. "He asked that I convey it to you and then fetch you for him."

Grier frowned and angled her head, mulling.

If Sev longed to see her as his letter claimed, why would he have sent his cousin in his stead? It just didn't sound like Sev. In fact none of this felt quite like something Sev would do.

Malcolm stretched out a hand to her from inside the carriage. "Come. You don't want to keep Sev waiting."

She shook her head slowly side to side and

hedged back a step, now quite convinced something was amiss. The tiny hairs on her nape tingled in an alarming manner.

Malcolm sighed as if beleaguered and dropped down from the carriage. "Come, Miss Hadley." His tone cut like the whip of a schoolmaster's rod and she blinked, her skin shivering with growing alarm. "I haven't all day to linger here." He reached for her arm and she jerked it clear of his grasping hand.

"No, thank you," she said sharply. "I just remembered I have several things to do today. I'll wait to see Sevastian at the theater tonight." Reluctant to turn her back on him, she inched away again.

She didn't make it another step before Malcolm lunged for her and grabbed her arm.

She cried out and shoved at his chest with her free hand. "What are you doing?"

He ignored her and clamped down on her other arm, hauling her toward the open door of the carriage. She dragged her heels, but her soft-soled slippers slid like butter over the ground.

"Stop!" she cried, certain Sev was not behind any of this, but her mind didn't have time to process why any of this was happening . . . why Malcolm would treat her in this rough manner.

"Stop fighting me," he panted, locking his arms around her and hauling her off her feet, squeezing her ribs to the point of agony.

And with those words, she knew she absolutely had to fight. He meant her harm. With her very last breath, she could not stop fighting him!

Spots danced before her eyes and the edges of her vision blurred. Realizing how close she inched toward swooning, she bucked against him in one fierce surge of strength.

He cursed. His arms loosened and she broke free for a fraction of a moment before he snatched her by the back of the head, digging his fingers deep into her hair. He spun her around and slapped her soundly in the face.

Her head snapped back. She bit the inside of her cheek, and the copper tang of blood filled her mouth, running over her teeth in a warm, metallic flood.

Stunned from the blow, Grier fell limp, the struggle temporarily gone from her.

Malcolm swung her up in his arms like a limp doll and secured her inside the carriage. She was dimly aware of the door closing and his weight dropping down beside her.

The carriage started to move, swaying her on the squabs, and she panicked, a fist wringing her heart. Seized with the need to act, she jumped upright, fighting the surge of dizziness.

She flung her body at the door, grappling for the latch, her hair a wild tangle around her.

"Oh no you don't!" Malcolm's hand grabbed her by the back of the neck and shoved her forward, crashing her head into the carriage door with crushing force.

Her body crumpled, pain vibrating in her skull.

She toppled back onto the carriage floor as though every bone in her body had suddenly dissolved, was nothing more than liquid.

Unable to move, helpless in her own skin, she gazed up at the carriage ceiling as darkness crept over her in a descending fog from which she could never escape. *Sev.* Her lips moved numbly around his name.

Malcolm's face filled her hazy vision.

She lifted a hand in a weak attempt to strike him, to claw at his shadowy face, but she never made contact. Her hand fell limply at her side, dead weight.

And then there was nothing.

Evening light trickled through the damask drapes as Sev faced his future father-in-law in his well-appointed library.

"What do you mean you can't find her?" he demanded. "She's not a glove to be lost."

"She's not here," Jack repeated, waving his hands. "She took no carriage. All the mounts are accounted for in the stables. She's gone."

Cleo cleared her throat from where she sat in shadow near the window. She was elegantly attired in a grand gown fringed with satiny pink rosettes, ostensibly ready for their evening at the theater. It only served to remind him of the evening he would not be sharing with Grier.

He stared pointedly at Cleo. "Did you want to say something? Do you know where Grier is?"

"I didn't want to say anything sooner, but as you're here now . . . clearly something has gone amiss."

"You know something of Grier's whereabouts?" Jack snapped. "We've been looking for her for hours now and you haven't uttered a word."

Cleo ignored Jack, training her gaze on Sev. "She received a letter this afternoon . . . from *you*. I assumed you were together all this time."

His heart stuttered in his chest before it picked up speed and began racing. "I didn't send her any note."

"She rushed from the room as soon as it was

delivered. She didn't say, but I suspected that the two of you planned to rendezvous."

"Who delivered it?" His gaze yanked to Jack. "Assemble all the servants at once."

With a quick nod, Jack marched from the room, bellowing for his butler.

In moments, Sev stood on the bottom steps of the grand staircase, overlooking two dozen liveried servants. Their upturned faces watched him warily. A few whispered among themselves— until Cleo quickly pointed out the girl who had delivered the note to Grier that morning, and a hush fell as all eyes swung to her.

"There she is. Marie." At Cleo's announcement, the whispering began anew.

Sev stepped down one more step and addressed her in an even voice, trying to hide his anxiousness lest she become even more agitated. "Marie, did you deliver a note today to Miss Grier?"

She muttered something softly beneath her breath, her wide eyes fearful. Sev cocked his head in an effort to better hear her and resisted the urge to storm across the foyer and grab her by the arms and give her the shake his tightly stretched nerves urged him to do. He'd have nothing out of her if she was too frightened to speak.

"Speak up, girl. Answer him!" Jack growled, making her jump.

Sev flicked him an annoyed look and moved into the mass of servants to stand before the cowering maid. Ducking his head, he connected with her fearful gaze. Using a gentle voice, he asked, "Who gave you the note to give to Miss Hadley?"

"He was out back. Just a driver. He asked me to deliver the letter for his master. I didn't see him though . . . the gentleman was waiting inside the carriage."

Sev swept his gaze over everyone in the foyer. "Did no one see Miss Hadley outside?"

"I saw her through an upstairs window," a maid volunteered. "She was behind the house, talking to a gentleman."

"Who?" Sev demanded.

The servant shook her capped head. "I've never seen him before and I would have remembered for certain."

"Why?" Sev pressed, desperate for some clue, something, anything that would lead him to Grier. "Why would you have remembered him?"

"Well, it was his hair. It was a really bright red—almost hurt my eyes to look upon it."

Red hair. So bright it could hurt one's eyes. He

knew one such man. Or rather, he didn't know him. Not in the least. Not if he would abduct Grier.

"Malcolm," he breathed. A myriad of feelings flooded him. *Betrayal. Confusion.* Why would Malcolm steal Grier away? Simply because he didn't wish Sev to marry her? He couldn't wrap his head around it.

Even as he failed to understand why, the reality of the situation pressed down on him.

She was gone.

Malcolm took her . . . could harm her . . .

Impotent rage burned through him. His hands curled into fists at his sides until he wanted to break something. Namely his cousin.

"Your cousin?" Cleo angled her head "What would he want with Grier?"

"To keep us from marrying, I suspect. He wasn't keen on our match . . . unfortunately now I realize just how much."

Jack blustered, various shades of red and purple churning over his face. "If he harms one hair on her head—"

"She will come to no harm," Sev swiftly cut in, his voice an icy wind, even as he knew nothing anymore. Not the ground he stood upon, not the gnawing fear inside him.

He never suspected Malcolm would do such a thing. Why should he care so much whom Sev married? It didn't affect him.

"Where did he take her?" Cleo echoed his own thoughts, looking at him with expectation bright in her eyes. As though he should know.

Sev shook his head, despising that he didn't. That this terrible thing had somehow come to pass and he hadn't seen it coming.

"You don't know?" Jack bellowed.

"No. He didn't exactly inform me of his plan to abduct my fiancée." He dragged a hand through his hair. "Look," he said in a calm voice that reflected none of his turmoil. "He doesn't know I know that he took her."

As much as he wanted to do something, scour the vastness of London and the world beyond— that would be senseless. He hadn't a clue where to begin searching.

"So? What does that help?" Jack snapped.

"He'll return. With nothing to fear, Malcolm shall return. Either here or to his mother's residence."

"So we wait?" Cleo shook her head, looking as frustrated as he felt.

"We haven't another choice." As much as he

loathed the idea of doing nothing and sitting around while Malcolm did God knew what to Grier, he saw no other solution.

He'd wait.

And be ready for Malcolm when he returned.

True fear flickered across Cleo's young face. "While we wait your cousin could be doing anything—"

"We'll wait out his return," Sev cut in, not wanting to discuss the wretched scenarios already playing out in his thoughts—all the possible horrors that Grier could be suffering at his cousin's hands.

"I don't think Malcolm will harm her," he said, even though he knew no such thing but felt the need to placate Grier's sister.

"He abducted her. I'm certain you didn't think he would do that, either!" Hot color splashed Cleo's cheeks.

"No. I confess, I did not," he replied uneasily, admitting that he did not know his cousin at all.

"What if he kills her," Jack grimly inserted with no care for anyone's feelings. "While we *wait*, as you suggest, what if your cousin decides to kill my daughter?"

A tremor ran through Sev as he was forced to meet the possibility. As he was forced to recognize that a piece of himself would die, too. That nothing would matter to him in the event of Grier's death—not his life, not his future.

Nothing would ever matter again.

Instead of answering, he turned and motioned to five strapping-looking grooms watching them as if they were street performers putting on a grand show. "You five there." He snapped off directions to his Aunt Nesha's rooms in Seven Dials. "Wait there in case my cousin returns. Watch the street for him. I want him *and* the driver that conveys him. Do not let the driver leave, do you understand? If my cousin proves unwillingly to talk, good coin should break the driver's silence. Come, I'll put you all in a carriage."

"And where are you going to be?"

"At my townhouse. I suspect he'll return there. Better lodgings and finer fare. I'll be in wait for him and his driver. One way or another, I'll have him. And Grier's whereabouts."

"Don't think things will go light for you if something befalls my daughter, Maksimi. You'll not find another bride so easily when everyone hears you're responsible for killing the last one."

"Father," Cleo whispered harshly, her wide eyes horrified at his blunt words. "He didn't intend for any of this to happen."

"But it did happen. All because of him."

Sev stopped in his tracks but didn't turn around. Rage coursed through him, hot and acrid as the fear he battled inside himself for Grier.

Jack Hadley was completely correct. Sev was at fault here. He should have seen, should have somehow known his cousin was as rotten as his sire.

But Jack was wrong to think Sev would ever try to replace Grier. Grier was more to him than a bridal settlement. She could not be replaced.

Perhaps Grier thought the same thing that Jack did. His stomach churned uncomfortably at the notion. Perhaps she didn't know what he was just discovering standing in the middle of Jack Hadley's foyer with gawking servants all around him.

He was in love with Grier Hadley.

He'd fallen totally and irrevocably in love with the most unseemly female of his acquaintance.

For no other reason had he offered her marriage. For no other reason would it break him if something happened to her. If he lost her from his life, he would be lost as well.

Chapter Twenty-five

When Grier woke she wasn't certain she was not in fact still sleeping. Trapped in darkness, she considered that maybe she dreamed, caught in some state between sleep and waking, the air as deep and pulsing as a night in the thickest woods.

She shivered as the cold penetrated her consciousness. The icy wet saturated her bones and she knew this was no dream.

Memory flooded her. She saw Malcolm's face, remembered his cruel hands, the sting of his slap on her face.

Blinking, she peered into the penetrating dark. It seemed lighter to her left. She listened hard, trying to glean something about her surroundings. Nothing. The silence was deafening. That ruled out Town. Even in her room at night the sounds of life in the city prevailed, a living, breathing thing all around her. Wherever she was the air was still, dormant.

Wincing at the throbbing pain in her head, she pushed up with her hands. Grit and dirt scraped her palms. The floorboards creaked beneath the pressure.

Footsteps suddenly sounded. She froze, considering dropping back down and feigning sleep, but the door slammed open. Light flooded the small room. It was too late. Malcolm stood on the threshold, gazing down at her.

"You're awake. I began to wonder if maybe I'd hit you too hard."

Grier rose to a sitting position. "Why are you doing this?

"Because you can't marry Sev," he snapped, stepping deeper into the room.

"Why not?" Her gaze moved beyond him, calculating her chances of making it past him.

"No one can. At least not until our grandfather is dead."

Grier pushed herself unsteadily to her feet. "I don't understand."

"Did Sev not tell you about me? That I'm the black sheep of the family? Or at least my father was. My grandfather banished my father, humiliated and shamed my parents—me." He gestured wildly and paced the room. "That old bastard wants the satisfaction of seeing Sev married before he dies? He would like to go to his final rest knowing the Maksimi line is secured? Well, he shall not have such peace. I've waited years to make that old man suffer. I'll make bloody hell certain of that."

Grier moistened her lips, quite convinced she was in the hands of a madman. He would thwart Sev's matrimonial goals for the sake of *disappointing* their grandfather. No. She doubted he'd stop there. He was too obsessed with devastating the king. She wouldn't put it past him to try and destroy Sev. He was simply warming up with her. She doubted he would ever let Sev return to Maldania alive.

"But weren't you encouraging Sev to court Lady Libbie?"

"Of course. Because I knew it would go nowhere." The light from the main room cast one side of his face into relief while the other side stayed hidden in shadow. "I'd heard rumors. Servants talk. I knew she was sneaking about with her father's groom. I didn't anticipate she would run away with him quite so soon, however."

Grier shook her head and then stopped at the sudden lancing pain.

Malcolm continued, his voice taking on an accusatory whine. "You weren't even to be considered."

She lifted her chin and squared her shoulders, glad that the motion didn't make her feel instantly ill. "What do you intend to do with me then?" she demanded. "Hide me away until your grandfather finally expires?"

Malcolm crossed his arms, the motion as petulant as a child. "I hadn't quite thought as far as that. I was simply determined to keep you from sailing for Maldania."

Grier nodded and edged closer to the door. The fact that he hadn't yet decided what to do with her didn't bode well. She didn't intend to stick around waiting for him to make up his mind.

Although he hadn't said it, it was there, a dark shadow lurking in the back of her mind. *He could simply kill her to be rid of her.*

No one would ever know the truth. Her disappearance would forever be a mystery. She would simply have vanished.

Sev would never know. Not what happened to her. Not that she loved him. Her stomach lurched sickly.

She watched Malcolm, her chest tightening almost painfully. She shoved tangled strands of hair from her face and took a bracing breath.

He paced the room, tugging at the ends of his hair as if he might tug free a solution from that mad mind of his. Every once in a while he'd shoot her a measuring glance, seemingly unaware that she had been moving at a cautious, crawling pace toward the door, her fingers twitching at her sides as her nerves snapped and trembled throughout her.

"I can't believe Sev actually decided to marry you! This shouldn't have happened." He sliced the murky air angrily with one hand. "He's the bloody crown prince and he should damn well act like it!"

She couldn't help rolling her eyes as she inched closer yet toward the door leading into the well-lit room from which he'd emerged.

"You've bewitched him! Snared him in your woman's web . . . just like that whore who tempted my father so many years ago and then cried rape after he took what she offered!" His eyes glittered with a frightening faraway light and Grier swallowed against the sudden bitter taste in her throat. "I should take you myself . . . see what the great allure of you is."

She stiffened, her pulse spiking into a feverish rhythm against the flesh of her throat. Her every muscle tensed, bracing for an attack.

Without looking at her he continued, as if he had not just voiced that he *might* like to assault her. "If I didn't fear that you would weave a spell on me, I would." His lips twisted into a snarling grin. "I should like to take something that is Sevastian's . . . arrogant bastard. He doesn't know what it's like to suffer, to have everything taken away. . . ."

Grier refrained from pointing out that Sev had spent the last ten years fighting a war in which he lost his own brother, countless friends and comrades. Malcolm was past the point of reason. He was deteriorating—making less and less sense as he paced back and forth in the small room, his boots scuffing the grimy wood planks.

Again, her gaze darted to the lighted room beyond. She didn't know what waited outside the meager dwelling he'd taken her to, but she knew her odds were better out there than here with him.

As Malcolm dove into another diatribe on all the injustices delivered to him and his family, she sucked in a deep breath and bolted for the door.

Adrenaline rushed her veins at his shout. She cleared the door into the main room and skirted a small table, her gaze locking on the single door. Her hand grasped the latch. She yanked the door open in one clean pull and burst outdoors.

She didn't waste a moment to acclimate herself. Malcolm's curses burned her ears. He sounded close, terrifyingly close, but she refused to waste a second to look behind her.

Dark night surrounded her. The cold winter wind cut through her clothes, but she didn't let it affect her—didn't let it stop her from diving into the woods pressing all around the small cottage she had just escaped.

The loamy odor of wild earth filled her nose. Clearly he'd taken her somewhere outside the city.

With a fortifying reminder that the forest never scared her, she plunged headlong into the teeth of it.

He followed, crashing through trees and brush behind her like an angry boar. He was faster than she would have expected.

Or perhaps her injuries slowed her—that or her

heavy skirts. Her thin-soled slippers couldn't gain much traction on the slushy ground. Whatever the case, she couldn't lose him as she raced into deep woods, her legs pumping hard and furiously beneath her cumbersome garments. Her muscles burned, but she didn't stop. Her wet hem dragged across the frozen ground and she grasped a fistful of skirt, trying to lift the fabric high as she zigzagged wildly through trees.

He shouted her name, the sound echoing on the frigid air, sending the birds above squawking and flying from their night nests.

Ugly sobs tore at her throat, but still she ran on, a certain, stark knowledge pressing its full weight on her.

He'd kill her if he caught her.

He was past reason at this point and enraged as he tried to run her to ground like a hound after the hare.

Panted breaths crashed from her lips. Tears trailed cold wet paths down her cheeks. Branches tore at her exposed face, snagging her clothing. Her chest hurt, but she pushed on, blindly running through the moon-soaked night. Still, there wasn't enough light. Not nearly enough. Not enough to see any great distance ahead of her.

Suddenly the trees and undergrowth thinned out on every side of her. But by the time she realized this it was too late. She couldn't stop in time.

She jerked to a halt, just as the ground beneath her feet ended. Her arms flailed wildly, fighting for balance. The tips of her slippers toed the rocky edge. Rocks hissed and slid loose.

She yelped, hovering, wobbling precariously on the precipice. Arms sawing at the air, she struggled to fling herself back away from the drop.

All to no avail. She toppled forward, her scream a horrible unearthly sound on the night.

Icy air rushed past her as she careened down the side of the steep incline with no hope of stopping. Not until she reached bottom.

Wind tore at her body. Her hands dragged against the craggy wall, ripped to bloody shreds as she fought for purchase, a handhold, anything to stop her descent.

The floor of the earth loomed somewhere below, waiting to greet her. To break her with cold, relentless force.

Sev. She'd never see him again. Never tell him how she really felt . . . that she wanted to marry him. Only him. And not because she'd decided she *needed* to marry. Not because of security or because she craved respectability. Not because marriage was that *thing* every woman should do.

She loved him and he would never know it. She would be gone. Forever lost, forgotten at the base of some ravine.

With a desperate cry, she fought harder, her nails splitting as she clawed. Bits of rocks and grass flew around her as she plummeted, but nothing more. She couldn't save herself.

Malcolm had gotten his wish after all.

Chapter Twenty-six

The hand on the mantel clock chimed the hour as a carriage clattered to a stop in front of Sev's townhouse. Sev held his breath, waiting at the window to see who stepped down. The instant Malcolm emerged from the carriage, Sev signaled the grooms hiding behind the hedges and along the side of his townhouse.

They barreled forward and hauled the driver from his perch first, per Sev's orders. He wanted to make sure the driver didn't escape into the night in case Malcolm proved uncooperative.

Sev rushed from the drawing room, Jack Hadley and Cleo fast on his heels. They converged all at once in the foyer.

Malcolm thrashed in his captor's hands.

"Unhand me at once! What's this about?" His eyes alighted on Sev. "Cousin! What the devil is going on? Tell these ruffians to release me!"

Sev walked a sharp line toward him. The closer he approached, the more alarmed Malcolm appeared, his eyes widening at whatever he read in Sev's face.

"Where is she?" Sev spat.

"Wh-what are you talking about? Who?"

Sev's hands flexed at his sides. Savage fury hummed through him. "I will ask you only one more time. Where is Grier?"

Malcolm started to shake his head, and then he stopped, paused, cocking his head to the side in a considering manner. As if relenting to the truth, he sneered, "Somewhere you'll never find her."

Sev lunged for him, an animallike growl erupting from his throat as he ripped Malcolm free from the grooms who held him captive.

They crashed to the parquet floor with bone-jarring force. Sev straddled him, striking him again and again until he couldn't feel his hands anymore, until his knuckles were slick with blood—until several grooms stepped in and pulled him off.

"Where is she?" he shouted, rage and desperation riding hot in his chest, tightening his lungs so that every breath felt raw and anguished. As anguished as he felt inside.

Malcolm laughed maniacally, staggering to his feet. He pressed a hand to his profusely bleeding nose. "Good luck finding her."

Sev lunged free and grabbed for him, ready to rip him apart.

Malcolm dodged and dove out the door.

Sev followed, chasing him down the path.

Malcolm looked over his shoulder, laughing wildly. "Guess you'll have to start all over again looking for a bride! I'm sure that will prove no small feat considering the last one—"

The rest of his words were lost, twisting into a scream that shattered the cold night as he stepped into the path of an oncoming carriage.

Malcolm went down, crumpling beneath razor-sharp hooves and spinning wheels. The horses screeched as they plowed over him.

The carriage slowed several yards away, but Sev's gaze rested on the still, broken body in the middle of the street. Sev reached the middle of the street first. Others soon joined him, morbid fascination drawing them like moths to the flame.

As he gazed down at the dull, unseeing eyes

of his cousin, he felt nothing. No sorrow for the bastard who stole Grier from him . . . and quite possibly murdered her. Nothing.

A shudder racked him. With a gulp of icy air, he swung back toward his house. Countless people poured from the townhouses lining up and down the street to examine the spectacle of a dead body.

Then he remembered the coachman. He rushed back inside, unwilling to accept that Grier was gone, lost from him and this world. Vaulting up the steps to his townhouse, he shoved his way through the crowd of servants, relieved to see the driver still restrained—that he had not managed to slip away in the chaos.

Grabbing him by the front of his frock coat, Sev shoved his face close. "Where is she? Where did you take them?" He gave him a good shake. "If you've a wish to breathe another breath, you'll take me there at once."

The driver nodded fiercely, waving his hands helplessly between them. "Aye. I don't want no trouble. We went to a cottage, an ol' hunting box just outside Town. I'll show you."

Sev nodded, his heart tight and aching in his chest. He refused to believe she was gone. That he could have lost her. He'd have to see her with his own eyes . . . touch her lifeless body with his hands before he let her go.

And even then . . . he might never be able to do that.

The cold woke her, a bitter shroud that she could not escape. It clung like the worst of dreams. Shivering, Grier parted heavy eyelids to peer out at a predawn gray. Even though it wasn't the brightest of light, she squinted against it. Stabbing sharp pain hit her everywhere. No part of her body was free of it.

Her last sight had been of murky night . . . and she'd been careening toward her death.

At that reminder, she sat up. Every nerve in her body screamed in protest and she fell back down, her cheek scraping the rough ground. She hissed at the newfound sting of pain, but supposed she should be glad for it.

Glad that she lived, that she felt anything at all.

Panting heavily, she scanned her surroundings. A frigid mist curled on the air like smoke. She could see nothing. Just the small stretch of ground she huddled upon and endless gray sky all around her.

Rolling onto her back on the hard ground, she

looked up, her gaze following the endless stretch of rocky wall to her right.

She slid down that?

It was a miracle she survived.

Lying there for several moments, she listened to the howling wind and the birds chirping in the distance. The clouds' underbellies looked swollen, threatening with rain or snow.

Gathering her strength, she breathed in and out before finally lifting herself up again, bit by slow bit. Every muscle strained in agony as she shifted herself into a sitting position. A hissing breath escaped between her teeth.

She assessed herself, checking for injuries. When she wiggled her right ankle, she winced and bit her lip against the sudden lancing agony that shot up her calf. She doubted she could stand without help.

Using blood-crusted hands, she dragged her body to the point where the ground appeared to break off and vanish.

She looked down. And down.

Far below a tiny stream trickled between banks dotted with snow and grass the color of withered straw. She'd never survive the fall. Nor could she climb down. Or up. Despair threatened to engulf her, but she shoved it away.

Even faced with such a grim scenario, she looked around as if expecting to find another solution. Something. Anything to help escape this nightmare. This wasn't her fate. She would not die like this.

The wind increased, battering her where she huddled upon the ledge. If not for the precarious shelf of earth, she would have fallen to her death.

She pushed tangled strands of hair from her face and shook her head slowly, staving off the hot tide of panic that threatened to devour her.

You're not meant to die. Not now. Not like this.

And yet she shook with fear despite her brave thoughts. Cupping her hands around her mouth, she shouted, "Hello! Can anyone help me?"

Nothing.

The birds fell silent at her voice. She shouted again and again, until her words grew hoarse and her tongue felt thick and dry in her mouth.

The wind seemed to whip even more fiercely. Its lonely howl intensified her fright that no one was going to find her. That she was going to waste away on this small shelf of ground jutting from the side of a crag.

She choked on a sob and blinked back burning tears. Years later her bones would be found with no clue as to who she was.

Pulling herself into a tight ball inside her tattered cloak, she held herself tightly, vowing to hang on, to not let despair claim her even when rescue loomed as distant and elusive as the stars.

"Grier!" Sev shouted her name yet again as he tromped through the woods surrounding the small hunting box the driver led him to. It had been empty, of course, the door wide open as if its last occupants had left in a hurry.

He wasn't the only one shouting for her. The sound of her name echoed through the trees, winding through dark, gnarled branches and floating on the curling wind. Over three dozen servants, his and Jack's combined, spread out through the thick woods.

His long strides ate up the ground, his gaze straining, taking in every shrub, every twig for some sign of her—the slightest evidence that she'd passed through the area. If Grier was out here, he'd find her.

Cleo tromped over the ground next to him, panting hard but keeping up with admirable effort. She wore a simple wool gown and heavy boots. Her voice rang out hoarsely as she called for her sister.

"Look! Here!" Jack shouted not far away from them.

Sev ran ahead and inspected the bit of fabric Jack plucked from a thorny bush.

Cleo arrived at his side and took the material to examine it. "That looks like a piece of Grier's cloak."

A hound on the scent, Sev pushed on, practically running through the trees, calling for Grier. He stopped abruptly when he came to where the ground suddenly ended. His heart froze in his chest as he toed the broken edge of ground.

Others soon arrived behind him. Like him, they scanned right and left. Only open air stretched before them. There was no going forward at this point. It was either back or . . . down.

"Oh, Grier," Cleo whispered.

Jack cursed.

Sev immediately saw her in his mind, her freckles standing out in stark relief against her frightened face as she ran through the night, Malcolm in pursuit. She couldn't have seen five feet in front of her in the darkness. She wouldn't have had time to stop . . .

Tossing back his head, he shouted up at the sky, startling birds from the silent trees. No one made a sound around him.

Cleo placed a hand on his shoulder and he shuddered, fighting the violent impulse to shake her off, to toss himself off the cliff, too—so that he would feel none of this pain. None of this tearing grief.

"Hello!"

He stilled, cocking his head to the side at the faint sound.

It came again, distinct . . . and familiar, vibrating with a terror similar to the one that had moments ago seized hold of him so completely. "Hello! Help! Help me!"

He dropped to his knees and peered over the edge of earth, digging his hands into the rough soil. "Grier! Are you down there!"

"Sev! Sev!" His name sounded garbled, tangled up in her sobs. "I'm down here! On a ledge!"

A good forty yards down, he caught sight of her, bedraggled but alive on a small shelf of earth jutting from the side of the crag. His stomach twisted at her precarious position. The ledge could give out and crumble at any time, tumbling her to her death.

"Don't move! Not even an inch! Do you understand me?"

He didn't wait for her answer before turning and shouting to the gathered crowd of servants for a rope. Several men turned and ran back into the woods toward the lodge.

Time stretched interminably as he waited for their return.

"Grier! Are you injured?" he bellowed down.

"I hurt my ankle! I can't stand."

He nodded grimly. An ankle would heal. He just had to get her on solid ground and then he could keep her warm and safe and forever in his arms.

The men returned with a rope. Sev made short work knotting it about his waist as securely as he could.

"Your Highness, perhaps I should go?" a groom proposed.

Sev shook his head severely. "I'm going." He would not trust Grier's fate to anyone else.

The groom nodded. "Yes, Your Highness."

Sev took position at the edge of the cliff.

Bracing his booted feet apart, he gripped the rope tightly as they lowered him down, perfectly agreeable to the notion of risking his life if it meant saving Grier.

Chapter Twenty-seven

Grier watched as Sev descended toward her, her breath frozen in her chest until he dropped down and landed solidly, safely beside her.

She released a strangled cry as he pulled her into his arms, holding her tightly. The tears flowed then. Sobs racked her frame as his strong arms held her up, so firm and reassuring.

"I thought no one would ever find me."

His hand buried in the snarls of her hair. "I wouldn't have stopped until I found you. Come. Let's get you out of here." He pulled back to look at her face, his hand warm and caressing on her cheek. "Can you ride my back?"

She nodded.

His gaze searched her face. "Truly? Are you too weak? You'll need to hold on tightly."

She smiled tremulously. "I can hang on. Just get us out of here."

With deft fingers, Sev quickly checked that his rope was still fastened securely about him. Satisfied, he squatted so that she could straddle his back.

"We're ready," he shouted up, and then they were ascending. Sev's legs worked, his booted feet moving along the rocky wall, helping leverage them as they were hauled upward by several pairs of hands.

Grier clutched closely to him, mindful that she not choke him with her clinging arms. It seemed like forever before they cleared the top, but in reality it could only have been a few minutes.

She and Sev collapsed together in a tangled pile. He breathed heavily beside her, his hand reaching for hers, fingers lacing with her own.

"Grier!" Cleo dropped down beside her, pressing her much warmer hand to Grier's grimy face. "Oh dear, you're cold as ice."

As if that was the only reminder Sev needed that she had spent the night injured and exposed to the harsh elements, he jumped to his feet and swept her up in his arms.

She rested her cheek against the warm solidness of his chest as he marched them through the same woods she had raced through last night, a real-life devil in pursuit of her, intent on stopping her from marrying Sev—even if it meant ending her life.

She moistened her parched lips. "Your cousin—"

"He's dead."

She lifted her head and studied the hard set of his profile. "Did you—"

"He ran in front of a carriage. I doubt he suffered." A muscle flexed along his jaw. "Not as he should have. Not as I would have had him suffer." His fiery gaze locked with hers then. "For what he's done to you . . . what he wanted to do, he deserved far worse than a swift end."

Shaken at the intensity of his expression, she lowered her head back to his chest, let the rocking motion of his strides lull her into deep relaxation.

Content, secure that she was free from danger and safe in Sev's arms, she surrendered to the pulling drag of sleep.

A warm glow of light greeted Grier as her eyes fluttered open. She jerked at first, immediately back on that outcropping of rock, still hovering there, trapped on the cusp of death.

Swallowing back a whimper, she scanned her surroundings. The tension ebbed from her body as she realized she was safely tucked in her own bed, the soft sheets pulled to her chest. Warm and safe.

A familiar dark-haired head rested beside her on the bed, buried facedown in his arms.

She lightly touched the silky strands, running her fingers through the luxurious thickness.

Sev lifted his head, muttering her name as he sat upright in his chair beside her bed. Blinking, he dragged a hand over his face. "You're awake."

"And it appears you're not. Why don't you find a bed?"

"I did." His glittering gold eyes held hers. "Yours is sufficient."

"Sevastian." She stroked his cheek. "You must be exhausted."

He seized her hand, trapped it against his face. "It's nothing compared to what I've endured when I thought I lost you. Grier, I can't ever live through that again."

She moistened her lips, remembering her time trapped on that ledge. Even before that. She remembered when she'd awakened on the floor of that lodge and confronted the harsh reality that Malcolm would never let her return to Sev. She'd been filled with regret for not telling Sev how she felt about him—that he'd come to mean everything to her. But she could do that now.

"Sev," she began, clearing the dry scratchiness from her voice, but he didn't let her continue.

"As soon as you're rested and fully mended, we'll leave for Maldania—"

"Sevastian." She said his name sharply, determined to bare her heart to him, to expose herself as she once vowed never to do. Fear would no longer hold her back.

He looked at her, stared curiously at her face.

She could only stare back at him, conveying with her eyes the words that hung on the tip of her tongue.

A slow smile curved his mouth. "I love you, Grier." His smile deepened. "Is that what you're trying to say?"

Her breath locked in her chest. She released a gust of breath and with it the word, "No."

His smile slipped.

"I was going to say . . ." She propped herself up on her elbows. "I love you . . . *Sevastian*."

His smile returned. "Amusing imp, aren't you?" He leaned down, brushing his mouth over hers once, twice, and then a third time. This final kiss lingered, slower and deeper, almost as though he couldn't help himself. She was panting, clinging to his shoulders with clenched fingers when he finally pulled away.

"So you love me?" His mouth quirked into a smug smile.

She smiled, giddy inside. "Hmm-mm. And you love me?"

"I do." His expression turned sly. "Enough to know your actual birthday."

"You're still harping on that!" She half laughed, half snorted. "Nice try. You're going to have to do better than that. It might take years of loving me to get that out."

His mouth lowered to hers again. "Years of loving you sounds simple enough. I can content myself that I shall have it out of you one day."

Grier slipped her arms around his neck, ecstatic to think of those long years ahead. Of them sharing it all together. It was more than she ever hoped for . . . more than she dared dream.

Epilogue

Eight months later . . .

Sunlight filtered through the mullioned windows lining the lavish bedchamber. Grier crossed her arms and stared at the beams of light enviously. "When can I get out of bed? This is absurd, you know."

"Not until the physician declares it safe," her husband announced beside her where he reclined upon the bed. Unlike her he was dressed for the day and had already enjoyed a morning ride. She could smell the crisp autumn air on him.

She punched the bed between them in a display of pique. "Holy hellfire—I'm having a baby. Women do it every day. I'm not dying."

He set down his paper and gave her his full attention. "Be that as it may, you're not just *any* woman. Not to Grandfather and especially not to me."

"Don't tell me you agree with all this cosseting. Truly. I'm fine. A little nauseated in the mornings. Nothing more. I'm fit and hale. The physician will say whatever your grandfather wants him to say. He's terrified of the old goat."

Sev's lips twitched. "Most people are."

She lifted her chin. "I'm not." At least not anymore. As apprehensive as she'd been upon first arriving at the palace, she quickly realized the king was more bark than bite. He was not about to tell the grandson he so obviously loved that he'd disappointed him or made a mistake in marrying her. Although the king looked at her through narrowed eyes at first, he'd held his tongue. And even that had changed in recent months as he observed Grier and Sev together. His narrow-eyed gaze had vanished altogether when she announced that she was increasing. Now she could do no wrong. Newfound life danced in his eyes.

"Your lack of fear is a fact which impresses him endlessly. Oh, and the fact that you've so quickly managed to find yourself with child."

This time Grier grinned. She stroked Sev's

arm. "I cannot take credit for that alone. You see, I happen to be married to this very virile man who bothers me to no end with his insatiable appetites."

He chuckled. "And you've been unwilling, have you?"

Sev kissed her until they both grew heated and anxious, writhing against each other, she in her nightgown, he in his jacket and trousers. She slid her hands beneath his jacket, palming his firm chest through his shirt. "I know the perfect cure for me."

"Do you now?" he asked huskily against her mouth.

She cupped his hardness beneath his breeches. "You can call it an early present, too."

"Present," he murmured against her throat. "For what?"

"Oh, for tomorrow."

He pulled back to gaze at her with a strange expression on his face. "What's tomorrow?

She smiled coyly. "I suppose I can tell you." She slid a hand over his hard belly, loving how the taut muscles rippled beneath her fingers. "Tomorrow's my birthday. And now you know that you've married an older woman."

A wide smile stretched his lips. "Not quite."

She cocked her head.

He continued, "You see . . . tomorrow's my birthday, too."

She stilled. "You jest."

He laughed and the sound vibrated through her. "This is rich! We have the same birthday."

"We're the same age?" She shook her head, marveling.

Chuckling, he kissed her again, nibbling at her bottom lip. "Which begs the question . . ."

"Hmm?" she murmured, then gasped with pleasure as his hand found her sensitive breast.

"What time of day were you born?"

She didn't answer. Instead she pushed him back on the bed and straddled him. Lowering her head, she whispered against his lips, "You'll have to work very hard to earn that information."

And he did.

Brilliant and ambitious dressmaker Marcelline Noirot is London's rising star, and she's determined to gain the patronage of the most talked about lady of the ton: *the Duke of Clevedon's intended bride. To get to her, though, Marcelline must win over Clevedon, whose standards are as high as his morals are . . . not. The prize seems worth the risk—but this time Marcelline's met her match. Clevedon can design a seduction as irresistible as her dresses; and what begins as a flicker of desire soon ignites into a delicious inferno . . . and a blazing scandal.*

The instant the interval began—and before the other audience members had risen from their seats—Clevedon entered Mademoiselle Fontenay's opera box with the Comte d'Orefeur.

The first thing he saw was the rear view of the brunette: smooth shoulders and back exposed a fraction of an inch beyond what most Parisian women dared, and the skin, pure cream. Disorderly dark curls dangled enticingly against the nape of her neck.

He looked at her neck and forgot about Clara and Madame St. Pierre and every other woman in the world.

A lifetime seemed to pass before he was standing in front of her, looking down into brilliant dark eyes, where laughter glinted . . . looking down at the ripe curve of her mouth, laughter, again, lurking at its corners. Then she moved a little, and it was only a little—the slightest shift of her shoulders—but she did it in the way of a lover turning in bed, or so his body believed, his groin tightening.

The light caught her hair and gilded her skin and danced in those laughing eyes. His gaze drifted lower, to the silken swell of her breasts . . . the sleek curve to her waist . . .

He was vaguely aware of the people about him talking, but he couldn't concentrate on anyone else. Her voice was low, a contralto shaded with a slight huskiness.

Her name, he learned, was Noirot.

Fitting.

Having done the pretty by Mademoiselle Fontenay, he turned to the woman who'd disrupted the opera house. Heart racing, he bent over her gloved hand.

"Madame Noirot," he said. *"Enchanté."* He

touched his lips to the soft kid. A light but exotic scent swam into his nostrils. Jasmine?

He lifted his head and met a gaze as deep as midnight. For a long, pulsing moment, their gazes held.

Then she waved her fan at the empty seat nearby. "It's uncomfortable to converse with my head tipped back, Your Grace," she said.

"Forgive me." He sat. "How rude of me to loom over you in that way. But the view from above was . . ."

He trailed off as it belatedly dawned on him: She'd spoken in English, in the accents of his own class, no less. He'd answered automatically, taught from childhood to show his conversational partner the courtesy of responding in the latter's language.

"But this is diabolical," he said. "I should have wagered anything that you were French." French, and a commoner. She had to be. He'd heard her speak to Orefeur in flawless Parisian French, superior to Clevedon's, certainly. The accent was refined, but her friend—forty if she was a day—was an actress. Ladies of the upper ranks did not consort with actresses. He'd assumed she was an actress or courtesan.

Yet if he closed his eyes, he'd swear he conversed at present with an English aristocrat.

"You'd wager *anything*?" she said. Her dark gaze lifted to his head and slid down slowly, leaving a heat trail in its wake, and coming to rest at his neck cloth. "That pretty pin, for instance?"

The scent and the voice and the body were slowing his brain. "A wager?" he said blankly.

"Or we could discuss the merits of the present Figaro, or debate whether Rosina ought properly to be a contralto or a mezzo-soprano," she said. "But I think you were not paying attention to the opera." She plied her fan slowly. "Why should I think that, I wonder?"

He collected his wits. "What I don't understand," he said, "is how anyone could pay attention to the opera when you were in the place."

"They're French," she said. "They take art seriously."

"And you're not French?"

She smiled. "That's the question, it seems."

"French," he said. "You're a brilliant mimic, but you're French."

"You're so sure," she said.

"I'm merely a thickheaded Englishman, I know," he said. "But even I can tell French and English women apart. One might dress an Englishwoman in French fashion from head to toe and she'll still look English. You . . ."

He trailed off, letting his gaze skim over her. Only consider her hair. It was as stylish as the precise coifs of other Frenchwomen . . . yet, no, not the same. Hers was more . . . something. It was as though she'd flung out of bed and thrown herself together in a hurry. Yet she wasn't disheveled. She was . . . different.

"You're French, through and through," he said. "If I'm wrong, the stickpin is yours."

"And if you're right?" she said.

He thought quickly. "If I'm right, you'll do me the honor of riding with me in the Bois de Boulogne tomorrow," he said.

"That's all?" she said, in French this time.

"It's a great deal to me."

She rose abruptly in a rustle of silk. Surprised—*again*—he was slow coming to his feet.

"I need air," she said. "It grows warm in here."

He opened the door to the corridor and she swept past him. He followed her out, his pulse racing.

Marcelline had seen him countless times, from as little as a few yards away. She'd observed a handsome, expensively elegant English aristocrat.

At close quarters . . .

She was still reeling.

The body first. She'd surreptitiously studied that while he made polite chitchat with Sylvie. The splendid physique was not, as she'd assumed, created or even assisted by fine tailoring, though the tailoring was exquisite. His broad shoulders were not padded, and his tapering torso wasn't cinched in by anything but muscle.

Muscle everywhere—the arms, the long legs. And no tailor could create the lithe power emanating from that tall frame.

It's hot in here, was her first coherent thought.

Then he was standing in front of her, bending over her hand, and the place grew hotter still.

She was aware of his hair, black curls gleaming like silk and artfully tousled.

He lifted his head.

She saw a mouth that should have been a woman's, so full and sensuous it was. But it was pure male, purely carnal.

An instant later she was looking up into eyes of a rare color—a green like jade—while a low masculine voice caressed her ear and seemed to be caressing parts of her not publicly visible.

Good grief.

She walked quickly as they left the box, thinking quickly, too, as she went. She was aware of the clusters of opera goers in the corridor making way for her. That amused her, even while she pondered the unexpected problem walking alongside.

She'd known the Duke of Clevedon was a handful.

She'd vastly underestimated.

Still, she was a Noirot, and the risks only excited her.

She came to rest at last in a quieter part of the corridor, near a window. For a time, she gazed out of the window. It showed her only her own reflection: a magnificently dressed, alluring woman, a walking advertisement for what would one day—soon, with a little help from him—be London's foremost dressmaking establishment. Once they had the Duchess of Clevedon, royal patronage was sure to follow: the moon and the stars, almost within her grasp.

"I hope you're not unwell, madame," he said in his English-accented French.

"No, but it occurs to me that I've been absurd," she said. "What a ridiculous wager it is!"

He smiled. "You're not backing down? Is riding with me in the Bois de Boulogne so dreadful a fate?"

It was a boyish smile, and he spoke with a

self-deprecating charm that must have slain the morals of hundreds of women.

She said, "As I see it, either way I win. No matter how I look at it, this wager is silly. Only think, when I tell you whether you are right or wrong, how will you know I'm telling the truth?"

"Did you think I'd demand your passport?" he said.

"Were you planning to take my word for it?" she said.

"Of course."

"That may be gallant or it may be naïve," she said. "I can't decide which."

"You won't lie to me," he said.

Had her sisters been present, they would have fallen down laughing.

"That's an exceptionally fine diamond," she said. "If you think a woman wouldn't lie to have it, you are catastrophically innocent."

The arresting green gaze searched her face. In English he said, "I was wrong, completely wrong. I see it now. You're English."

She smiled. "What gave me away? The plain speaking?"

"More or less," he said. "If you were French, we should be debating what truth is. They can't let anything alone. They must always put it under the microscope of philosophy. It's rather endearing, but they're so predictable in that regard. Everything must be anatomized and sorted. Rules. They need rules. They make so many."

"That wouldn't be a wise speech, were I a Frenchwoman," she said.

"But you're not. We've settled it."

"Have we?"

He nodded.

"You wagered in haste," she said. "Are you always so rash?"

"Sometimes, yes," he said. "But you had me at a disadvantage. You're like no one I've ever met before."

"Yet in some ways I am," she said. "My parents were English."

"And a little French?" he said. Humor danced in his green eyes, and her cold, calculating heart gave a little skip in response.

Damn but he was good.

"A very little," she said. "One purely French great-grandfather. But he and his sons fancied Englishwomen."

"One great-grandfather is too little to count," he said. "I'm stuck all over with French names, but I'm hopelessly English—and typically slow—except to jump to wrong conclusions. Ah, well.

Farewell, my little pin." He brought his hands up to remove it.

He wore gloves, but she knew they didn't hide calluses or broken nails. His hands would be typical of his class: smooth and neatly manicured. They were larger than was fashionable, though, the fingers long and graceful.

Well, not so graceful at the moment. His valet had placed the pin firmly and precisely among the folds of his neck cloth, and he was struggling with it.

Or seeming to.

"You'd better let me," she said. "You can't see what you're doing."

She moved his hands away, hers lightly brushing his. Glove against glove, that was all. Yet she felt the shock of contact as though skin had touched skin, and the sensation traveled the length of her body.

She was acutely aware of the broad chest under the expensive layers of neck cloth and waistcoat and shirt. All the same, her hands neither faltered nor trembled. She'd had years of practice. Years of holding cards steady while her heart pounded. Years of bluffing, never letting so much as a flicker of an eye, a twitch of a facial muscle, betray her.

The pin came free, winking in the light. She regarded the snowy linen she'd wrinkled.

"How naked it looks," she said. "Your neck cloth."

"What is this?" he said. "Remorse?"

"Never," she said, and that was pristine truth. "But the empty place offends my aesthetic sensibilities."

"In that case, I shall hasten to my hotel and have my valet replace it."

"You're strangely eager to please," she said.

"There's nothing strange about it."

"Be calm, Your Grace," she said. "I have an exquisite solution."

She took a pin from her bodice and set his in its place. She set her pin into the neck cloth. Hers was nothing so magnificent as his, merely a smallish pearl. But it was a pretty one, of a fine luster. Softly it glowed in its snug place among the folds of his linen.

She was aware of his gaze, so intent, and of the utter stillness with which he waited.

She lightly smoothed the surrounding fabric, then stepped back and eyed her work critically. "That will do very well," she said.

"Will it?" He was looking at her, not the pearl.

"Let the window be your looking glass," she said.

He was still watching her.

"The glass, Your Grace. You might at least admire my handiwork."

"I do," he said. "Very much."

But he turned away, wearing the faintest smile, and studied himself in the glass.

"I see," he said. "Your eye is as good as my valet's—and that's a compliment I don't give lightly."

"My eye ought to be good," she said. "I am the greatest modiste in all the world."